Silverbirch Summer

Fred Sokol

Anatevka Press

ISBN: 979-8985910605

Silverbirch Summer is a work of fiction. Names, characters, places and incidents are the product of the author's imagination or are used fictitiously and are not to be construed as real. Any resemblance to actual events, locations, organizations or persons, living or dead, is entirely coincidental.

Anatevka Press

88 Westmoreland Avenue

Longmeadow, MA 01106

Contents

Praise for the Storytelling of Fred Sokol

Lively Dialogue – The author of Mendel and Morris lovingly portrays the friendship of two elderly men as they travel from the shuffleboard courts of Springfield, Massachusetts to Florida and back again. The friendship of these unique characters comes alive through their lively and authentic dialogue with one another as well as with the women who befriend them. These two guys grew on me as their journey progressed, and as they themselves grew in humane wisdom. For a window into a vital life that defies the bland stereotypes of "the golden years," I recommend this book.

A Great Read – Not only are the characters a hoot; so are many of the predicaments they get themselves into. But this book also takes a serious look at the opportunities and limitations of old age, which may slow us down even as it opens new doors and renews our appetite for living. Sokol has a real talent for writing realistic yet distinctive dialogue. By the end I had grown to love the characters and wanted the story to continue. Readers of all ages will enjoy Mendel and Morris.

Growing Younger with Age – Fred Sokol's sparkling new novel had me hooked on the first page, where he launches us straightway into the hilarious and no-holds-barred dialogue between two men friends who are well beyond middle age. With humor worthy of Woody Allen and a poignant tale of friendship that could have come from Mitch Albom... it is like a fresh breeze to see an author's imaginative powers focused on the metaphorical goblins and trolls that face us everyday humans as we grow into old age.

They're back! – The two hilarious characters featured in Fred Sokol's 2011 debut novel, "Mendel and Morris," have returned... As in "Mendel and Morris," Sokol's main storytelling vehicle is the hilarious dialogue, primarily between the smaller and grumpier Mendel and the oversized and impulsive Morris. Like a vaudeville comedy team, their bickering and insulting does much of the storytelling, while it also provides them with safe camouflage for the obvious love they have for each other. - *Kevin McVeigh*

Also by Fred Sokol

Fiction

Mendel and Morris

Destiny

Plays

The Forever Boys
The Lewis Sisters

Non Fiction

Muses in Arcadia: Cultural Life in the Berkshires
(co-author)

Dedication

SILVERBIRCH SUMMER IS DEDICATED to my life partner for the past half century or so, Betsy Pirtle Sokol. Thanks for the first fifty and looking forward to many more.

Silverbirch Summer

Fred Sokol

Chapter One

Home

April LIED ABOUT HER age to get the job, to get herself to the Catskills, by claiming she would be nineteen at the start of the summer of '65. After all, there was nothing left for her on the Island, the mythologized Long Island, the picket fence dream in the middling Nassau County home her parents had fashioned while they wondered if they would ever get out of the Bronx. Previously, these two were hopelessly separated by an ocean as the Second World War threatened eradication.

She never even thought of it as an island. April was certain it was connected, county to county, town to town, and borough to borough. All roads and train tracks led to the city. Why couldn't they just have stayed put? Had they never moved from the West 12th Street walk-up, she would have been a late-afternoon beatnik or an early-morning hippie—or she might have created her own lifestyle category: something involving yoga and bluegrass. She knew that while people practiced yoga thousands of years back, it didn't really start in the U.S.

until 1960-something, when the form practiced in India took on life in big cities like New York. Bluegrass, too, caught people's attention or ears when she was a little girl during the 50s, and it began to flourish several years later. It was an innovative essay assignment by the only teacher at her high school worth a few shakes of salt that spurred this well of information. She had a crush on him, this Jonathan Hudson.

He was skinny and tall and had a head like Ichabod Crane, and if you got to know him, he sometimes allowed you to call him by his first name. He asked his students, when they were juniors and not fully terrified by the pressure of upcoming college applications, to write about art forms that were sometimes foreign to them. He asked them to connect artistic dots. For April, these were genius questions and she fully fell in love with his intellect. She felt like he was asking what she thought because he knew she understood and appreciated this kind of deep thinking. The others in her class thought he was nice enough yet weird, even bizarre. How could they? Yoga and bluegrass. She lay in bed one night and thought of Johnny Hudson and whether he wore a solid color T-shirt and matching boxers. At first, that was all.

The next day, she found out where he lived, which was in an adjacent town, and she rode her bike to his house after dinner one night and waited. When no one came out of the house, she went around the block, then into the neighborhood, but always ventured back. Her parents made it clear, when she mumbled where she was going, that she shouldn't be there by herself. She, at eighteen, didn't particularly care for the advice.

She lingered and then, without incident, biked home. April dreamt blissfully, so gratified was she for the time to check out his place and imagine his life. Probably, on the inside, Jonathan Hudson had photos of Jack Kerouac and maybe someone like Mahatma Gandhi. She was certain he had a room, like a greenhouse, filled with lush, flowering plants. Surely, he had a girlfriend, and maybe even a wife. On the way back into her house after dropping her bike in the garage, she bumped into the side screen door, proof that she was swooning. April went to her room, turned on radio oldies, and wondered what it would be like to have his hand around her waist.

He couldn't be more than thirty-six and was probably younger. Men might have wives ten or fifteen years younger, April knew, though not the reverse. Jonathan could be a musician and a dancer, or both. When she had mentioned yoga and blue-grass, he was genuinely responsive. Hudson was so much smarter than anyone else, so why was he stuck in this clammy, backward school? She would smuggle a get-out-of-jail card to him so that he could escape.

Except April wasn't ready to be anyone's girl-friend, let alone wife. Boys circled around her, and she didn't know why. She thought it might have something to do with her saxophone playing. The only girl on tenor in the jazz band, she enjoyed that status but not the attention her heaving chest drew as she took in a breath and then exhaled with a rush. It was totally embarrassing—so much so that she thought seriously about quitting the instrument. Except that she adored the sound great sax players made and thought she just might be able to produce something sweet every so often. Mr. Reed (no one could believe a band teacher could be so named) called the music pungent, which she sort of liked. Maybe he was not actually staring at her breasts. Then again, he was a man. What was she supposed to do?

Mr. Hudson, on the other hand, looked right into her eyes and sometimes, she thought, through them. April wanted to engage him intellectually, but she wasn't sure of his interests. She remembered once, when he had talked about the blues, his eyes had kind of glazed over and he had said, "A few years back, I was asked to a summer conference. And I thought, sure, I like talking about literature. When I got there, they asked if I could run a blues workshop. Loved that."

April's parents, who could hover at times, were smother-with-love types who wanted the best for their only daughter. They urged her to marry a professional, a man who happened to be Jewish.

"It's just what we do," was her mother Lil's non-explanation.

"I understand your point," April's father Bert said when she questioned the logic, "but your mom's right. We might all expire."

Well, maybe. But April currently contemplated neither her demise nor an abyss. Instead, what was on her mind was the senior prom. Bert and Lil did not sense her fascination with her teacher, and neither did Jonathan Hudson himself. The dance, though, was an event for winners; only losers were absent—whether by choice or simply because of lack of invitation. She had to go. He might be chaperoning. On the one hand, that would create immediate emotional complexity for her. On the other hand, she could secretly stare at him over her date's shoulder—whoever that may be. Conclusion: She needed to get someone to take her.

There could be problems created by actually attending a prom. If you went, expectations were abundant. April wanted to be thought of as capable, appealing, even sexy—but not easy. Loose girls were identified and pursued—that would be the worst.

She needed to be there with someone halfway good-looking yet never a threat to her. He had to be known but not by everyone. And sweetly respectful but not in a wimpy way. She had to find someone, and her answer slept a hundred feet away: Richie. The two of them had met within weeks of their parents' having fled the big city in 1953. April and Richie were close at first, then awkwardly distant; now, in their late teens, their relationship was tightening up once again. Richie spoke to April before anyone else, including his parents. He was unusually slow to fully get the R sound, he first called her Apie and she loved it except you could never say that you loved it because that meant something else to a boy. Like third base—and she didn't want that, especially with Richie. Even brushing up against him when they danced would be awkward, and totally embarrassing.

Chapter Two

Date with Richie

APRIL REALIZED THAT SHE and Richie had touched one another many times. He actually was cupping her butt that time she climbed the birch tree standing tall between their houses. She blushed deep red when the tree sagged a bit from the weight of her body—and never did spring upward to reach toward the sky again. A bent birch sounded sexy and dirty to her. That was when they were both eleven. He was stronger, but she was definitely skinnier. And then they did the gymnastics class together after school, even though only the four parents were in favor of this. She had to wear a leotard. Her physical development was late yet dramatic. Richie wore a white T-shirt that showed off how much of him there was.

Now, though, she noticed that he wasn't really fat at all. In fact, unless he let his shirt hike up, he looked okay. If he forgot, sure, a small bit of flesh poked out but not over—like it used to. Not that she wanted it against her. She knew how to hug sideways and pretty much minimize skin on skin.

Behind it all, she told herself, that was really what she was after. No, not with Richie but with someone else. Hudson came to mind.

A first date could happen only with April's initiative. It was still too much to imagine him at the prom but, well, gotta start somewhere. After all, they were now young teens. Richie was far from the life center of any block let alone a major party. He was, however, her friend. He had even lied for her—like the time she was asked, after school, to join Mercy (Mercy was an even weirder name than April) at her house, which was directly on the water that led to the beach. April told Richie she wanted to go and his response was, "I got it, no problem. I'll lay a whopper on your folks." He told them she was on a nature field trip. It was actually true that their science teacher had a special interest in botany and took people to a field to search for mushrooms. Lilly and Bert bought it without a shrug or glance.

April, always a tomboy, and Richie, imbued with distinctive hand/eye coordination, began tossing tennis balls back and forth when they were six. Mostly, though, free throw shooting and games of PIG took precedence. Thus, April figured, a walk to the school and maybe a round of HORSE would give her an opportunity to ease into conversation. She went next door and threw a pebble at his window, and he was almost instantly out the side door to meet her. They quickly moved to the street.

"You rang?" Richie asked.

"HORSE," said April.

"What, not PIG?" he asked.

"Special reason," she replied, realizing they were speaking in fragments.

"Oh, cupcakes at the end?"

Ever since they were little, April and Richie shared a love of cupcakes. He was vanilla and she strawberry. By now, chocolate donuts ruled. They agreed that Entenmann's were the best by far.

April smiled. She made a circle with her thumb and forefinger: donuts.

She was aware that when they strolled past neighbors' houses, people took note. They were teenagers with hormones both raging and roaming. The squinting observers could fantasize as they wished; April was amused. They were kid buddies—not a couple or an item or boyfriend and girlfriend.

She knocked the ball from Richie's grasp and dribbled to her side as he said, "Clean steal, but I'm still way ahead on the stat sheet."

They split the street, each walking on the edge of the sidewalk on either side, and began to pass the basketball: bounce or chest or overhead and even, when necessary, above car roofs. This had been the routine since they became strong enough to snap the ball back and forth. April began to whistle "Sweet Georgia Brown," the theme song of the Harlem Globetrotters. She watched them yearly on TV and had seen them once in person. Her father was a whistler, and April seemed to have inherited the knack.

Though living in New York Knicks territory, April latched onto the Boston Celtics and, especially, Bob Cousy. She watched him for years on Channel 7 during many Sunday games as he would pass behind his back and maybe zip the ball in, with perfection, to Bill Russell, and she imagined herself doing the same. Ever since The Cooz had retired a few years earlier, she didn't know who to watch, what to do. Rules for women and girls were still antiquated, but April practiced by herself and imagined a game with more freedom. She had her mother, adept with sewing and creating, devise and design a jersey with a #14 written in magic marker on the back. The issue with the shirt was that April had grown since getting it, but she still liked to wear it when she shot hoops and, upon occasion, elsewhere. She knew men fixed upon her shape and, to be truthful, April was beginning to feel more comfortable with her curves. She realized she needed to get used to her new body.

April was sorry she didn't tell her mom to make the jersey extra-large. It had fit great a couple of years ago, but she was a bit more womanly now. When she tucked it in, she was still sticking out all over the place. She actually liked the new contours, at least for the most part, but not for basketball. Even with Richie. After all, he was still a boy. She couldn't believe they used to run down the street together and hold hands to cross major roads on the way to Carvel.

Richie could catch and shoot a basketball, but he knew that April was by far the more naturally athletic of the two. He was a little bigger but not necessarily stronger. The real problem, he now realized, was that she was curvy and he didn't know what to do about that. He couldn't touch her, not April. She would take it the wrong way. The truth was that he wanted to collide with her, at the very least. But he would be mortified if she knew.

On the way to the schoolyard, April thought maybe it would be a good idea for her and Richie to not just go to the movies as ever but with maybe romance in mind? Her idea was to try this some time before talking about the prom. She imagined them sitting next to each other in a dark theater. She knew what his hand felt like. That touch was not surprising. As they walked, she saw that his feet were much bigger than hers. He might end up at six feet four. Wouldn't that be strange? She wasn't getting any longer, and he was. She dribbled the ball off her foot and into nearby bushes.

"What are you thinking about, Apie?" Richie asked.

"Maybe nothing," she said.

"Liar. You never lose your dribble unless your mind wanders."

April tugged on the stretched-out shirt so that, momentarily, it met her shorts. Instantly, though, a line of flesh played peekaboo with Richie. Her stomach was relatively smooth, but she felt humiliated. She sucked in her midsection, then lost her breath and coughed.

"You okay?" asked Richie.

"Sure."

"Good. Let's jog the rest of the way."

"Wanna race?"

"Nah, just get warmed up for shooting."

They used to race often, and that was fine with April as long as she won. But now, she thought his long strides might compensate for her foot speed and that he was likely to beat her. Besides, she had to deal with increasingly bouncy boobs. She felt that all eyes were focused on her chest as she loped by neighborhood houses; the harder she ran, the more they hurt. So why push it? "Just let's go slow, Richie."

"Easy," he said.

April's competitive nature soon took over. She sprinted ahead, stopped, pivoted, and stuck her tongue out at Richie. Laughing hard, he caught up, gently patted her lower back, and fell in step beside her.

April could feel his hand resting an inch or two away from her backside. She felt conflicted: Being touched by Richie in that exact region might be a bit much. To be truthful, however, she wanted someone to massage her down there. Richie? The nerdy kid next door whom she thought of like a brother? She intentionally bumped into him, causing both of them to lose their balance and fall over one another.

"Hey, what are you doing?" Richie asked, laughing.

"Clumsy in my old age," said April, blushing as she sat beneath him. "Right now, I'm just trying to get up. Did you get hurt?"

"No. You?"

"I learned how to fall in a gym class, believe it or not."

This was not exactly what April had imagined, nor was Richie the man of her dreams. That would be Jonathan Hudson, with his herky-jerky carriage, tousled dark hair, and stray forelock that was intent on covering his left eye. He was the man she wondered about, the unattainable ideal it would be fun to chase. Now, though, Richie was part of a photo she was creating in her mind, edging his way in—and she couldn't eradicate him. The quandary was that she was not trying to do so.

They scrambled upward, each regaining their balance as if nothing had happened, as if April wasn't practically straddling him from the pavement. No bruises, no harm, no memory. That's what she told herself.

Richie was aware that April was pretty—enticing, actually, even when she wasn't trying to be. Conflicting emotions were tough to sort out. He knew her so well, maybe too well. On the other hand, there was no need to break the ice with April. They had been in one another's houses forever. He understood her, and he had always kind of liked her, even if she was the girl who skinned her knees playing hoops with him or sliding into second base during a makeshift baseball game at the school field. *Drop that thought*, he told himself regarding the notion of her toppling into him or vice versa. *Crude. Get rid of that image.*

They walked side by side, in rhythm, the rest of the way to the school basketball court. April dribbled for a block, then bounced the ball to Richie and said, "It's all yours. Take us to the hoop, ha."

They arrived and, much to their pleasure, found a half court unoccupied. April grabbed the ball and immediately drove to the left side of the basket for a layup.

"HORSE. That's the first shot," she said, pulled the Cousy downward, and tossed Richie the ball.

He duplicated her move, and they were off. Tied, soon, at HORS to HORS, Richie grabbed onto the support pole for the hoop, extended his right arm, and shot. The ball hit both sides of the rim before dropping through.

April immediately took the basketball, placed her hand on the pole, and tossed the ball upward. It went through the hoop without touching any net. "Top that," she said.

"I don't have to," replied Richie. "I already made that shot, Apie."

He went to the out of bounds line and threw the ball, two-handed, at the basket. It missed, and he stomped his foot.

April, as she shot from the foul line, called out, "Banker!"

Richie, trying to duplicate the make, saw the ball smack hard against the wooden backboard and spin away. He had lost the game. Still, he was quick to point out, "Twelve to ten, me, in this set we began yesterday."

April smiled. Just as she was about to pat him on the back, he turned, and so her hand tapped the middle of his stomach instead. No jiggle. She was surprised. Boys, as opposed to girls her age, played defense with their hands. So, when she was at the park and in a game with boys, that's what she did. She was used to reaching out for Richie when he drove to the basket and steadying herself with his belly. But the belly just wasn't there anymore. No more sponge.

"You been working out?" she asked.

"Some. Just fewer cookies, I suppose, really."

"Nice," April said, and she meant it. Still, this was perplexing. She was playing basketball, just as ever, with the offbeat but cute kid living next door, and somehow he wasn't an ugly duckling any longer. Why hadn't she noticed earlier? Moreover, what now? "Trick shots?" she asked.

"You mean my shot which I thought would be a game winner was a circus toss?"

"I should have called you on that but didn't. Let's keep it going, yes?"

Richie responded with a yawn that opened his mouth wider than April could have imagined. He took the ball, shouting "game winner!!" and attempted, with no luck, to spin it off his index finger, then fired toward the hoop—and hit the underside of the backboard. "Back to my usual," he said.

"Listen, do you want to go to the movies?" asked April.

"Now?" Richie said.

"Not exactly. I can't go looking like this," she replied.

"You look okay to me," he said.

"Thank you?"

"Remember, we have that big essay for Hudson that is due tomorrow," said Richie.

"Uh huh, but what a great topic, don't you think?"

"The vanishing hero in America? I don't even know what Bones means."

"Bones?"

"What? That pretty much describes the guy if you ever size him up," said Richie.

Which is exactly what April did when she was in Hudson's class, in the hallway, at home—it was happening more often than she would ever admit. She could visualize him instantly—except right now, with Richie standing beside her, sweating slightly. She found that she did not mind the heat coming off his body. April couldn't understand just what was going on. "How about tomorrow night? It's the weekend."

"What?" asked Richie.

"The movies."

"Yeah, sure, okay. That'll be fun," he said.

April had been to the movies with Richie many times before, but not like this. She stood in front of the mirror and considered the image before her. Reasonable, decent, unexceptional, passable features including her nose, hair, and body. She had heard that boys didn't like skinny, and that was no longer her. April thought often about her upper body. She did not have huge breasts, but they surely did exist. April could not decide whether she wanted to hide them within a looser blouse or draw attention to them. After all, it was Richie. April had let it slip to one person at school that the two of them were going to the movies. Within hours, someone was wondering why it took so long and someone else was obviously jealous. She didn't really reply and wondered why she let out the word that maybe this little date with Richie might be different or more important to her.

April was trying to figure out whether she wanted him to feel her up. There were clear positives: He wasn't so bad-looking anymore, and his body was actually appealing. And she knew he wouldn't hurt her. She would be comfortable telling him when to stop. There were negatives, too. Like everyone would know about it the next day, even if nothing was said. Somehow, the grapevine had eyes and ears.

April didn't know if Riche found her attractive. He never let on, but she was guessing yes. It better be yes. Maybe she should make it easy for him to get to her bra, even find one that was flimsy or, even better, easy to unhook. That would be good for him.

What was she thinking, encouraging this guy to fondle her? Sure, she had been out once with another boy and allowed him to do some exploring when she was fully clothed. And yes, she wanted to get in some investigation of her own. But her folks kept up the talk about what happened if she became pregnant. She was about to go to college and looking forward to it. She wasn't anywhere near being ready to have a child; she could not even imagine it.

Back to her look, though. Should she decide to cover up, there would be no obvious skin or cleavage. Baggy, however, would be hideous. Her insides were making statements. There was no way to suppress those feelings, even if she didn't fully understand them.

She studied her reflection in the looking glass—a concept she did understand since she had been going through versions of the Alice in Wonderland series, well, ever since they were first read to her. The girl staring back at her seemed curious and sparky or sparkly. A boy her age should be interested in her, but a man who was in his thirties? Never. With a few freckles and hints of dimples on either side of her mouth, she looked like a kid, not a woman—and certainly not a siren. She had been trying recently to conceal the curves of her body, to the point where she had convinced even herself that they did not exist. But now, drinking in her form, she had to admit that her physique of valleys and, well, the opposite just might catch the attention of a boy—if she had the courage to honor her shape.

After due consideration, she picked out a cushiony bra that plunged just a bit. What went with that? She had a V-neck T-shirt that was perfectly appropriate for a movie with Richie. After all, was she trying to impress him?

That was the wrong word, but she did want him to pay attention to her. Well, he always had, but only as a friend. And it was only right that she should see him as a guy, not as a little boy looking for someone to run up and down the street with and around the corner to the park. She had to be more than a ball-playing buddy. She was almost a woman, at least on the outside. Emotionally, that was different. The sexual part was confusing. Lil had given her the talk, and Bert always told her, "You've got a good head on your shoulders, April. Use it." The implication was that she should focus her mind to ward off single-minded adventurous boys and that would be enough.

She had her underwear and top now and was moving along to pants. Some good jeans, black ones, would go well with the sneakily scooping shirt. Or, was she asking for it, for his hand and even more? For boys, dressing was not nearly as complicated. Any old pair of jeans, even bad ones, were acceptable. Hers had to be just so. Not dungarees meant for climbing a tree but almost pressed pants. If they were baggy, she might as well be a boy. Too tight and she risked leading him on. Richie. It was getting to be a non-choice. She was a senior in high school, off to college in four months. She might as well get used to boys being close. As an only daughter, she didn't get the advantage of having a big brother around.

She still had an hour to get ready before Richie picked her up. She could really walk over since he lived just across the driveway separating their two houses, but he told her he was getting his parents' new car, a 1965 Plymouth, to take her out. She wondered if he was honest with his parents or spun some elaborate story to get dibs on that vehicle. She also wondered whether she was obliged to slide near him on the front bench seat so that he could stretch his right arm around her. She didn't want to falsely encourage him, but she also wouldn't mind feeling his arm across her shoulders—at least, not too much.

April finished getting dressed and closed her bedroom door for a full assessment through the long mirror attached to the back of the door. She saw, immediately, that the shirt had to go. It was definitely lame—like someone's hand-me-down. If she was going to do this, she might as well open the throttle a bit more. She had read that wearing something a size too small could make you look bigger. So, April took out one of her older tops—a tight, dark blue blouse that buttoned up. When she put it on, she instantly recoiled. It practically outlined her bra and shined a spotlight on her breasts. *Great*, she thought. *Might as well wear nothing*. Then again, it clung to her body, and she figured this was a new Richie who probably would have a great time checking it out.

There was this other concern, one she had never faced before: The blouse made her look fat. According to the height and weight chart, she was fine, okay. Still, just as with the Cousy jersey, this top wouldn't quite pull down to her waistband. April wanted to be perfect. She had noticed that girls who were at the end of college were not skinny. Her legs, at least from knees down, seemed thinner than ever. April realized that she was hyperconscious of her body and, well, many bodies. She didn't know if this was unusual; it wasn't something she often discussed. She had brought it up once with her mom, who assured April, "You are a dream catch." April found this response evasive and tame.

"So," she said aloud to the back of her door, "mirror, mirror, how can I possibly be fat and skinny at the same time?" This must be the worst of all possible combinations. Well, the truth is that she had been heading—or, more appropriately, growing—in this direction for the past year. She would notice, smooth down her shirt, and forget it. It was stupid of her to be upset about this right now, she decided. After all, it was only a movie with Richie, not her muse, Jonathan Hudson. But if all went well, the movie might lead to the prom, which would help her get used to dating and going out and acting like she was experienced.

Lost in thought, she heard neither the doorbell nor the first knock on her door. The second series of raps caught her attention.

"What?" April yelled out.

"He's here, downstairs, waiting for you," said her mother.

"That's impossible. It's not six o'clock yet," answered April without opening the door.

"He's early, Apie. Richie lives next to us."

"Oh, he always surprises me by being early."

"Exactly. What should I say?"

"Five minutes and I'll be down. Thanks, Mom."

This gave April time to wash her face and pull back her hair, which she liked. April often wore a ponytail. When she let her hair fly and flow, boys were impressed. She could tell. April didn't have time to try anything more than the ponytail. Besides, she wasn't that clever when it came to hair. In the midst of slinging a sweater around her shoulders and tying the sleeves across her chest, all the better to hide imperfections, April heard Richie and her mother conversing. She slammed the door behind her and hopped, then ran, down the stairs.

"Hi, I'm ready at last," she said.

"Wow, what did you do? You look amazing, April."

April waved her mother away, and Lil caught the signal. "You two have fun," Lil said, moving off toward the kitchen. "I mean, enjoy the movie."

"Not much, really," said April, in answer to Richie's question, "but I at least thought about changes."

"No, I mean, you look like April but not exactly like the April I've known for a dozen years. Your features are the same, but it's different."

"We're on a date, Richie." She recovered quickly enough to look at him and saw that Richie had taken the time to put himself together. He was wearing a white button-down, short-sleeve shirt with black Levi's and, just like her, had a sweater around his shoulders; his was a tennis type—white with a red and blue border shaped like a V on its neck. "You don't look the same either," she said.

"I shaved. Again. I never do that. Once is enough, but I just felt like doing it. Only one cut." He pointed beneath his chin. "It's always a tough spot for me. Either I don't reach it and there's stubble or I nick it and it bleeds."

She didn't spend much time thinking of men's cosmetics and rituals.

"I don't like electric razors," he continued. "Not close enough. Still feels like fine sandpaper after you're done."

"Oh, I get it," said April. "Ready to go?"

Richie nodded, walked to the front door, and held it open for April.

"Thanks," she said, with a hint of surprise in her voice.

Richie hadn't brought his parents' 1965 Plymouth after all. They walked to the blue car, and when Richie opened the door for her, April just stared. The only time she had been in it was soon after Richie purchased this oldie and it was just short of junk material. Now, though, someone had sewn fabric of blue sky, clouds, and sun above the seating areas. The upholstery was new, and even the windows gleamed.

"How?" was all April could say.

"I've been working on this car for a while," Richie answered. "It was pretty bad, too embarrassing to bring to school, so I decided to fix it up myself—at least, as much as I could since I'm no mechanic. And, yes, I told you I was bringing the new car, but it was taken. So, we have this one."

April decided not to sit next to the window and not to sidle up too closely to Richie. She didn't want to lead him on, but she didn't want to be in Siberia either. April was glad to be in Richie's car and not his parents', about to begin what she considered a safe excursion with someone who would always be her friend. Yes, a boy who was her friend.

He drove carefully. Each of them had taken Driver Ed in school and received a license within the past year. They passed by houses April had seen since she was little and, knowing that she was off to college soon, she looked at them in a different light. Sure, she would come home for summer jobs and visits upon visits, but she wouldn't be a full-timer on the Island any longer. Some of the homes were truly tiny, with little more than three bedrooms and only one of those full-sized. Her house at least had a second floor, and she adored the dormer windows. On her side of the street, no two houses were the same color: it was okay to have variations of blue but not royal upon royal. Richie seemed to understand that this tour was a treat for her. She moved two or three inches along the bench seat in his direction, and she thought she saw the corners of his lips turn upward ever so slightly. That was sweet. When he reached across with his arm, April didn't know what to do. It looked as if he was searching for something in front of her; clearly, he wasn't trying to get anywhere behind her. She looked over at Richie and smiled. He was still driving one-handed and was preoccupied, fortunately, with navigating and the road.

"Richie?" she asked.

"What?"

"Is there something you want?"

"No, why?" he responded.

"It looks like you're waving or something."

"Stretching," he said.

"Oh, now I see," said April. She edged closer to him so that he could place his arm around her shoulder or neck if he wanted to. For now, that would be it, she thought. April smelled something she liked, perhaps the Old Spice aftershave. She realized she already loved this day, this occasion.

"April, do you really want to go to the movies?" Richie asked.

She was thrown off by the question. "Well, yes. That's what we agreed, right?"

He nodded. "Yeah, it's just that . . ."

"What?" she asked.

"We're the kids living next door to each other."

"I know," April said.

"Being this way, doing this, can we possibly mess up our kid friendship?" he asked.

"A movie ruins twelve or thirteen years? Us, girl and boy hanging out, is pretty cool." She figured that was enough to say.

They grew silent as Richie drove through town. Taking back roads, they arrived at the local movie house within fifteen minutes. They each got out of the car and agreed that going to Playhouse was a good idea. April loved the small, offbeat features before the main show. Sometimes, the manager came out to introduce the movie. It was so homespun. There was even a live sprinkler system, complete with spouts, hung from the ceiling and above all patrons. It felt like a cocoon to Richie and similarly comforting to April. That was all before today. Now, each was apprehensive—for different reasons. April was sure Richie was about to make a move on her. Richie was so nervous he began to sweat all over.

"You know anything about this movie?" she asked.

"It's called "Act I."

"Yeah, I know the title. Mr. Hudson mentioned it," April said. "He talks a lot about this guy Jason Robards who plays maybe a man named Kaufman? He was a writer and paired with another one named Moss Hart. All I can remember."

"You think Hudson's pretty fantastic, don't you?"

"He's more interesting than a lot of our teachers, Richie."

"For a person who looks like he's a collection of sticks glued together, he sometimes breaks out of that dull and boring routine all of the others use," Richie conceded. "He doesn't seem to care what anyone thinks of his opinions. I'll say that much."

April was heartened that Richie gave Hudson the benefit of the doubt. There was a note of something in his voice, though, that worried her. Was it possible that he knew of her crush on Mr. Hudson? Was Richie jealous?

"What I love about this movie theater is that it has what none of the others have. It doesn't just show movies trying to get us going—like horror and soupy romance."

"What else is there?" he asked.

"Just more of the movies that stay in the city usually. He brings them here—black-and-white ones sometimes, and movies about real people: the documentaries, the art films . . ."

"What is it about you and Hudson?" asked Richie.

"Nothing other than a teacher who can challenge me," April replied. And then she cuddled up to Richie.

Richie shocked them both when he said, "Thanks, April. I might have broken my arm trying."

They both laughed and briefly held onto one another.

April missed much of "Act I." She felt securely at home within Richie's grasp. That could be a problem. She, if only to herself, considered Hudson to be her love interest. But she reminded herself that was ridiculous. He surely must have a girlfriend, if not a wife and maybe even children. Who cared, however, since a love affair with this English teacher was pure fantasy?

As the movie ended, Richie gently pulled April to him. She said, "Well, I can see why Hudson thinks this Robards is a good actor." April knew she had to say something, and she hoped a conversation about the movie would be safe.

They walked out of the Playhouse to his car. Richie took her hand, and she quickly grasped his.

They reached the old vehicle, and this time she slid next to Richie until they were touching. He drove off, and she was aware that she did not know where they were going. Neither spoke for a time.

"My dad mentioned Jason Robards a few times when I was just becoming aware of acting a little. He looks so different now. I get it a little," said Richie, finally.

April could not resist an almost magnetic pull to him.

"Why was it that you became interested in school plays?"

"I started in eighth grade, do you remember, because they needed someone and my teacher pushed me."

"You mean that woman who was only here for half the year and vanished and we don't know why?"

"Yes, Miss Silverman. I only knew that she was Jewish because both my parents impressed me with that information. They were doing a remake of *Oklahoma!* and needed a replacement for Jud Fry when a kid couldn't do it. I knew his part from listening to the LP in our house. But who wanted to do that when you could play basketball instead?"

April said, "We still shot around and all."

"I would never have stopped that, April, but the main thing was it meant I could spend time with you. Now I can tell you never even knew that much."

April actually thought about what to do next. Time slowed to a crawl, and there was no question that she wanted to keep this, whatever this was, going. But she wasn't sure how to act. She remembered one time, a few years back, when she and Richie had actually talked, indirectly, about what ifs. Little did she know how he felt.

"Remember when I asked you how to act with boys, Richie?"

"Yes."

"Yes and . . ." said April.

". . . And I was already doing some acting. It wasn't that hard for me to pretend. I knew what was going on."

She laughed. "You mean that advice about cereal was made up?"

"You mean when I told you that if you talked about Frosted Flakes, a boy could get distracted? That that was, well, a lie?"

"That is a strong word but, yeah, something like that. You told me to be careful, Richie."

"You were my best friend, April. A few years ago, I sort of wanted to protect you."

April didn't quite know what to think. Sure, it was flattering to have the boy next door looking out for her. At the same time, she was developing then and she not-so-secretly wanted boys to notice that she was a girl. She couldn't really talk to anyone about this—surely not her parents, and she didn't have any siblings. Richie didn't have brothers or sisters either. Here they were: two not-so-only children who took to each other almost immediately and then held onto one another above all others.

Richie continued, "You were my sister, April, except that we pretty much were always like/like instead of love/hate. You know?"

"I feel the same, and I thank you for looking out for me, Richie." She moved even closer to him, leaning against his side.

He pulled the car to the curb, and she realized she was ready. She wanted to kiss him.

"Hey, Ap, want to get a sundae?" he asked.

"Well, I guess," said April, not knowing what to think. Before she knew what she was doing, she reached across her body, clutched him to her, and kissed him. When he responded with his lips and then his hands, April knew it was right.

The next morning, April began to mark off the days on her bedroom wall calendar till prom. April wouldn't allow herself to project further in the future than that.

She and Richie could not stay away from one another. They walked to and from school together. They went to Donut Diner for snacks and ate late breakfasts there on weekends. Although they were not officially a couple, friends could guess what was going on. Perhaps their parents did, too.

April was dizzy and intoxicated and confused. Most often, she thought, *Why not?* A tinier part of her asked, *Why him, why now, and where is this heading?*

Chapter Three

Prom

APRIL WAS ESPECIALLY AMAZED to be going to the Copacabana for her prom. She mostly knew about it because her favorite baseball players on her favorite team, the Yankees, had had a brawl there back in 1957. That was when she was 10 and knew nothing about drinking, and she heard her parents arguing about who was in the right. Nothing Mickey Mantle did, she thought, could be bad.

Now, she decided to ask her dad, Bert, at breakfast one day what he knew. After all, her father was well versed in Yankees lore. He had seen Babe Ruth and Lou Gehrig and Joe DiMaggio and everyone else, including Mickey, play.

"Dad, our prom is at the Copa. What do you know about the Yankees' thing there?"

Bert rolled his eyes and smoothed out his mustache before responding.

"It was like this, Apie. Billy Martin had a birthday, and he brought the gang there: Mickey, Whitey, Yogi, and Hank Bauer, too. Sammy Davis, Jr. was headlining, and some lunkheads starting calling him . . . started up with him because Sammy's so dark."

"And who clocked the guy because he had brown skin?" she asked. "Just a nut?"

"They say some bowler, and then Bauer ran after the guy and broke his jaw with an uppercut. Something like that. Who knows what the truth was? But that's why they traded away Billy."

"Bobby Richardson's better," she said.

"He likes God, and Billy Martin liked booze," said Bert.

"Did you ever go to the Copa?" April asked. "You know who Dean Martin is?"

"Yes. We saw him there." Bert hesitated. "It was special, and he was terrific—even sang to your mother."

"What?"

"Everybody loves somebody sometime," he sang.

"Was he drunk on television?" she asked.

"Tough to tell," her father replied. "He always seemed drunk, but it might be part of his schtick, his act."

"You and Mom are lucky, but I would have been more thrilled to meet Billy Martin than Dean."

"Close one, April. On a given day, me, too. But Dean was in form, and it was great." He paused. "You told me you're going to the prom."

"Yes, Dad. With Richie."

"I have to admit, I'm not that surprised about the Richie part."

"Why not?"

"We tend to get closer to the people we know really well," said Bert.

"Huh?"

"Like when people have office romances and everyone's shocked. Why not? I'm surprised it doesn't happen every day," he said.

As he was talking, April had successive thoughts: Her father worked in an office; he must have had an affair.

"You have an office, Dad. I mean it's a different kind, in a school, but it's still an office."

Bert looked down as if he were searching for an answer within his bowl of Frosted Flakes. Even if he beat it out of the school building every afternoon, Bert did enjoy having a small spot of his own. In his office, Bert kept one tall plant someone had given him, pictures of the family, and two of Lil's still life paintings. No, he didn't smoke cigars in there or keep a library of sketchy magazines, but he could, if he wished, hide out in his office during those rare quiet moments of the day. As the school psychologist, he never knew who or what was next.

Bert realized that April's statement implied a question. He should have dismissed her inquisitiveness with a shrug, but he got caught up. The truth was, he had been tempted—and he had not absolutely resisted. He thanked whatever god there was that she was a junior colleague and not a student. It had happened just a few years ago. The school had hired Cynthia to work specifically with ninth-grade girls, those making the transition from junior high. In her early thirties, Cynthia looked like she might be eighteen. On top of that, she had revealed in her application that, in college, she had been approached inappropriately by a faculty member. All things considered, it was reasonable to believe she might be able to help girls who were coming of age, physically and otherwise.

It worked. She opened her door to freshmen, was there all the time—well past the final school bell—and seemed to enjoy her job. Boys liked her, too, and why not? She tried to dress down but, given her shape, any camouflage was ineffective. The football quarterback, on a dare, asked her out. She advised him that she didn't go out with students. Bert, though, on the other side of fifty, was safe. She thought he was adorable, in a teddy bear way, what with the goatee, the wavy hair, even if it was thinning, and the ever-present smile.

As he helped her acclimate to her new job, they shared coffee from the vending machine each morning. He brought cream and, a short while later, she began to add biscuits to the morning treat. He heard something of her story—the upbringing in northern Jersey, times at Boston University, a failed experiment as a graduate student before this, her first full-time job. One morning, when the machine was mysteriously out of coffee, Bert invited her to his office. She was wearing a sky blue dress that zipped up the back.

He noticed that the zipper wasn't fully fastened and asked if she wanted him to close it.

"Sure, if you want to," she said. "I wouldn't risk getting written up—not for this."

He stepped behind her, thinking a quick zip would suffice. But when Bert tugged, the zipper split, revealing her lace, pink bra. He moved a few paces backward and profusely apologized.

"Not the first time," she said.

Bert checked any response.

"Just work it gently, you know," Cynthia said.

He silently tried to connect the two sides of the broken zipper, but it would not cooperate.

"I'll get some pins from my closet and we can close it up, makeshift, for the moment," he said.

"You're kind," she said, and he was caught off guard by the remark. "Why do you have pins in your office?"

"It's an auxiliary storage place for theater supplies—costumes and such."

She was still standing, and Bert realized Cynthia was a good two inches taller than he was. He walked behind her, pins between his teeth as he'd seen at the tailor shop.

"Not much room," he said.

"It's tight?" she asked. "I need to lose a few pounds."

"I don't think so," said Bert. He immediately wished he hadn't made the comment.

"I was ten pounds lighter when I did the pageants," Cynthia added. "They don't like even hints of bulges."

Bert managed to get four pins across the garment. "This will work, maybe, for first period. But it can't hold for the day," he said. "What do you mean by pageants?"

"I was in New Jersey. Back then, I went by Cindy. Some people called me Sin D, as in a bad deed."

Bert wanted to know something of her past, but this? "You hardly strike me as evil, Cynthia."

"You would be surprised," she said, which was the most surprising response he could imagine.

With that, she turned and stared directly at him, freezing Bert in place. He backed up a step; she did not move forward but, instead, gazed through him. That unnerved him.

"We only have a few minutes till the bell rings. Can you make it through until your break with a dress like that?" he asked.

"I'm used to people staring at me," said Cynthia.

Bert knew he had to get out of there. "I have a 9:00," he said. Without thinking, he added, "Let's do lunch and see how my fastening job held up."

"Deal," Cynthia said and extended her hand.

Bert felt the charge flow though him as he took her hand in both of his. He did his best to convince himself this was nothing out of the ordinary.

Cynthia brushed up against him before turning to leave the office. As she did so, Bert saw the gleaming silver pins and hoped she could avoid a tiny scratch on her skin.

"Noon," she said, and he thought the smile she flashed him over her shoulder was a coy one.

Bert had a few morning appointments: a kid needed credits through summer school to keep on track but was looking for a way out; an eager father wanted to talk about colleges, even if his son would not enroll for a couple more years; another complaint that the biology teacher was lecherous. Not what Bert wished to hear.

He saw Cynthia by the buffet line as he entered the cafeteria, and she was wearing a black sweater over the same dress

"Well?" Bert asked.

"Mostly okay, but one came loose," she replied. "One of the girls in the class noticed and, without saying anything, brought me the sweater. She told me, right after class, to keep it. She and I are, I guess, pretty much the same size."

"It did work out, though, for the most part?"

"As long as I hunch over a little bit. But I'm used to doing that. If I don't, I always have a problem."

"I don't understand."

"If I get fully straight, I can pop a button if my dress has buttons on the front."

Bert had to admit he liked imagining this.

"Should I try it? Show you what it would look like if this dress had buttons?" Cynthia asked, smiling.

Bert, while picturing Lil's appalled reaction if only she knew, slowly nodded his head up and down. He led Cynthia away from the buffet and down a hallway.

Cynthia shook free her long, golden hair. She stopped walking and turned directly toward Bert, who could not avert his eyes as she stood tall and her breasts pressed forward. He inched backward and then pushed his remaining hair back. "Okay," said Bert.

"Dad!" April called and snapped her fingers in front of his eyes.

Bert recovered quickly, dismissed the image of Cynthia moving against him, and said, "Not always. People with offices next to one another sometimes become enemies, not best of friends."

"I know that, Dad. But I go to movies. They can also end up being lovers."

"Since when do you know about that?"

"I'm eighteen, Dad, not seven."

"Of course you are. I'm sorry, April."

"I'll always be your little girl. Don't worry, Dad."

Bert wanted to discuss something familiar even if redundant and asked, "You still going to the prom with Richie?"

"I guess," she said without a hint of emotion.

"Why so excited?"

"It's not exactly a revolutionary stretch to be seen with Richie."

"Uh huh. Well, he's changing, you know. He's becoming a man."

"You think so?"

"Yes, I do," said Bert.

"Me, too," April said, and her smile was authentic.

April was beaming all afternoon before the big evening. Lil had taken her to buy a dress, and she'd chosen silver and sequins. April had looked through magazines till she found the dress she wanted. She didn't want to break the bank, but Bert and Lil had told her that money wasn't a consideration, that she would only have one senior prom. "Get something, sweetie, you will always remember," was the way her father had put it. April imagined Richie would love it, and she saw herself dancing with him. She did wish to be touched, but she didn't want to come on as too seductive. Just now, she placed the dress flat on her bed and examined the wires that supported the cups at the bust line. This, she thought, would be comfortable enough. April tugged at the neck area and the garment, stitched together with precision, did not respond. The midsection was snug, and she was glad.

April was both excited and concerned about the drinking part. She never did have much interest in alcohol, but rumor had it that it flowed smoothly and in great quantities at proms. She thought Richie was a pretty light drinker, and she didn't want to embarrass him by having even one glass too many. Besides, it was the Copa; it had a reputation and all.

He was picking her up at 6:00, so she had four hours to prepare. She had never been to a night-club in the city, and she hadn't gone to the junior prom. This was it. Unable to get Richie's face out of her mind, she tried to switch to Jonathan Hudson's before admitting that, at least for this evening, it wasn't the best idea. On the other hand, the situation with Richie was getting complicated. She held the dress up to her, assessed the match-up of her body and the dress in the full-length mirror behind her bedroom door, and stood on her tiptoes. She wished she were a few inches taller, able to look Richie in the eye, just as she had done until they were thirteen or so. Those days were forever over.

Richie had told her a week earlier that he was go-ing to have just a sip of wine before picking her up. April decided to match that, even though she really didn't know where to start. She didn't especially like beer, and her parents were mixed-drink people; it was mostly gin and tonics for them. Sure, April had watched her folks drink when people were over, but she had never really taken mental notes.

Now, here she was in the kitchen, half-undressed, snooping around for the goods. She found the gin, and the bottle of tonic water was easy to get. The proportions, though, were a mystery. She poured three capfuls of gin into a squat glass, filled it with tonic, and took two ice cubes, drank up, and put everything away before the folks would notice.

April sat on her bed and gazed into her closet where she saw, on hangers, the Cousy jersey and her sweatshirt with a basketball on the front. She wondered if going to a senior prom, followed by whatever might happen this summer and then college, meant the end of playing like a boy. She assumed so. Between Jonathan Hudson and, lately, Richie, she'd spent more time musing about men and boys than splitting the defense on a fast break to the basket. At least, that's what she thought, taking a deep gulp of her drink. A few of April's friends had been obsessed with boys since seventh grade or so.

Back to the dress. Maybe it was too provocative, as she had heard. She wanted attention, specifically Richie's, but not, on this night, too terribly much. This could be a final time to get her mother's opinion, so April called for Lil to come up for a look. She quickly took off her clothes and put on the dress. It was tighter than she remembered.

"You're beautiful," said Lil.

"And too sexy?" asked April.

"You could turn some heads," her mother said. "I guess it depends which ones."

"Am I showing?"

"You mean here?" Lil motioned across her chest.

"Mom!" April took a breath and nodded.

"Yes, and it flatters you, really."

April felt her face flush and got a bit dizzy, probably from the drink.

After a moment, Lil said, "You look sensational. The best. I'm so proud of you."

April considered why and how her mother could take pride in her appearance, as if she, Lil, had sculpted her. Still, she managed to nod and say thank you. Lil hugged April and walked out of the room.

April was not one to be overly made up, and even prom night would not become an exception. April was fully aware that "girly girl" had never accurately described her. She might be ready, though, for a late dose of femininity. Richie rang the bell exactly on time, as if all of the clocks in the two houses were synchronized and he knew it would take a minute and a half to walk from his front door to April's.

She raced down the stairs as she had practiced with the medium heels several times and didn't stumble once. April was less at ease greeting Richie, even if this, too, she had rehearsed. "Act eager and pleased to see him," she had been told by friends, "but temper your excitement." Boys evidently thought over-the-top enthusiasm would lead to sex. So, she opened the front door and stretched upward to kiss Richie on the cheek. In return, he hugged her, but April kept a bit of distance. He took her hand and led her to the older car, opened the creaking passenger door, and waited while April situated herself.

As Richie slid in, April realized she had forgotten to say good-bye to her parents, who had generously stayed upstairs. She motioned to Richie to roll down her window. "Bye!" she yelled, and Lil responded with, "We love you, sweetie! Enjoy!"

April knew and adored this scent — Old Spice aftershave. She found herself putting her hand on Richie's cheek, saying "Smooth." Might as well play the part and, anyway, she liked doing so. He extended his right arm and she took it, snuggled it, so that he could reach around her. They'd been out for ten minutes or so when April realized that Richie, driving back and forth to the city, couldn't drink—at least, not much.

So she said, "I can drive, Richie. That way, you can really love the Copa."

"You're so nice to offer, April, but I'm fine. Let's remember this forever," he said, reaching for her knee but landing on her stomach. She blushed but, pleased, she left his hand in place.

Then, they were more or less silent. Richie was happy, and April felt comfortably close to him.

Before allowing the valet to take away his car, Richie trotted around to open April's door. The Copa, a few feet away, glittered. The marquee was blazing and blaring. Women strolled by, and even April saw why men were staring right down their ultra-revealing dresses. There were black-and-white pictures of Dean Martin, Frank Sinatra, Sammy Davis, Jr. and The Supremes.

She was stunned by the chandeliers, filled with glowing white light bulbs. April looked upward but was conscious that Richie had his hand on her back, then a little lower, and she wondered where he would go next. Someone was showing them to their table, and she thought there must be hundreds of people around. Everyone was dressed, as her dad would say, "to the nines." The lights, mostly reds and purples and blues, changed colors. Up front behind the stage, another Copacabana sign sparkled. Richie had moved his hand down so that it touched the low, dipping section of her dress. Maybe that was still okay, just barely. She was glad that she had chosen a long gown.

The place was buzzing. Some women had already had too much to drink and were playing up to one man and then the next. April was out of her league. She recognized a few male classmates who were leaning on either the bar or their dates. Others were blatantly groping the females they had escorted to prom, which, April thought, was way ahead of schedule.

On stage, a warm-up group, playing slow and melodic jazz, filled the air with tunes before Bobby Vinton took over. He had April, immediately, with "Roses Are Red (My Love)," then "Blue Velvet," and, finally, April thought she, herself was an angel and began to swoon. More specifically, she was leaning on Richie, whose anxiety about what to do was waning. By the time Bobby Vinton concluded with

"Mr. Lonely" April and Richie were dancing close. Richie couldn't believe his good fortune, and April, giving in to her emotions, finally ceased to question herself. She found herself melting into Richie, and that is what she wanted.

Dancing morphed into hug and sway, hug and sway and, eventually, Richie pulled April tightly into him. It was still early in the evening, and she wondered where this was going. She looked forward, eagerly, to the hours ahead.

She saw the blur of purple and blue above her, the lighting shifting to violet. Her dress was silver with a hint of lavender, and April felt the stars were aligning—with, of all people, Richie. She'd hoped he would use her favorite aftershave—it dizzied her. For her part, she had spritzed Lil's Chanel No. 5 just above her breasts and behind each ear. April buried her head into Richie's neck and wished she could nibble on his ear.

Vinton tossed his head and hair as he continued singing ballads. April genuinely believed that he was gazing right through her. She fought an impulse to cover up with her hands. He looked younger than she anticipated—but nowhere close to a teenager—and he was singing songs she loved. It wasn't hard to respond to the words. April wanted to hear more songs like "Mr. Lonely" that broke her heart.

She tried, for once, not to overthink. If she initiated a kiss with Richie, how would he take it? Would he think she was asking him for more? Much more?

Flesh-to-flesh, leading to what everyone called all the way? Most of her wished she had maybe gone further earlier, taken away the mystery, the suspense, the clinical processing. She had doused herself with perfume. If he loved it, he would say so or caress her neck or, more dangerously, navigate just above her low-cut dress. Yes, she wanted all of it, but she desperately wished not to be labeled "easy." She also did not want the "hard to get" tag. She wanted something in between, even though her impulse was to jump into Richie's arms and go for more.

He had his hand around her waist as she was leaning in, and he guided her to the bar. She remembered sipping whatever drink Richie gave her, specifically one with a maraschino cherry within. She ate it immediately, then drank, and tried to relax. Richie gulped at his drink while holding onto her. Had other kids been doing this all through high school? Had they kept it from her, or had she simply missed it?

For her first three years, she was too busy. April started with flute. She wanted to be in the jazz band, but there weren't any parts or chairs—whatever they were called—for flautists. Switching to sax was a much better idea. Then she was cast in the role of Sarah Brown in *Guys and Dolls*. Luckily, it was the spring musical and did not conflict with any of her basketball playing. Boys started to show interest, and she was definitely aware but too afraid to show her feelings. If only she had . . . What would that have meant now?

She was melting, dissolving, wishing she and Richie were alone.

Hearing Bobby Vinton sing "There, I've Said It Again," "Roses are Red," and—her favorite—"Blue Velvet," April positively thought Bobby was crooning to her, for her.

She already felt hot, and the lighting made it even warmer.

April said, "Richie, I need some fresh air." He pulled her even closer and guided them to the front door. They were in the lobby and then outside on the sidewalk.

April knew they were near Broadway and needed to shield her eyes from the blinding Times Square light show. Richie was holding her hand, clasping it tightly so that she felt protected as swarms of people surrounded them. She wasn't cold, but she wished she had anything, even a sweatshirt, to cover up from the top of her dress to her neck.

Before she knew it, Richie led her into an arcade. They were surrounded by pinball machines, and he wanted to play. On this, the night of her senior prom, she might have been drinking to excess and dancing and waiting for him to lift her onto his shoulder and carry her to a nearby hotel room. Instead, wearing her strapless dress with the purple stitching and sparkling sequins, she pulled back and let fly a silver ball designed to ricochet in a way to score points galore. She and Richie took turns. When it was hers, she felt his touch; he was attached to her, and she loved it. Still feeling the effects of the alcohol, she stumbled backward and fell fully into his willing arms. He caught her by the stomach, and it did not bother her when he brushed the upper portion of her dress that covered her breasts. She relaxed further as she landed within his strong hands and realized she wanted more. April turned and placed her hand just above Richie's belt buckle, steadied herself, then moved around in a circle. He drew her into him.

This was her senior prom, and she was in a honky-tonk back room in Times Square when she was supposed to be sipping drinks and listening to a pop song idol with people she called friends. But what she wanted was to go somewhere private with Richie, this boy who was her next-door neighbor, who had taught her how to hold and pull people's shorts while defending in a pickup game on a playground basketball court. Return to the Copa? No, April wanted to leave. She must be out of her mind.

Richie pulled back a bit and looked at April, who tilted her head toward the entryway. Holding fast to her waist, he guided her out onto the street. April felt assaulted by blaring horns, the cacophony of screeching brakes, loudly conversing passersby, and even an occasional yipping dog. She lifted one of her arms to block the noise while the other hand stayed in place, within Richie's grasp.

As they walked, April felt taken care of. She knew Richie would always be, at the very least, a close confidant. Except that she hoped he would sweep her away, maybe even carry her off. He immediately hailed a cab, and they were off—headed somewhere. She leaned against him and saw, through the rearview mirror, the driver glancing, it seemed, directly at her. April pulled up the front of her dress, which had begun to slip down. She was pleased to have Richie's arm around her back and hugging her shoulder.

April knew certain sections of the city well, but much of New York was foreign territory. She could tell now, through her haze, that they were zigzagging downtown, but she knew not where. The driver cut sharply from lane to lane. Richie held her to him. April would not have minded if this bubble enveloped them for a much longer time. Suddenly, the cabbie swerved dramatically and she fell across and completely onto Richie. The car stopped. Richie lifted her, and a wave of warm, musty air greeted them as he opened the door. Richie paid and gestured toward a ferry. *At last*, thought April. It was the ferry that left the dock for Staten Island. She had only heard about it. Now, on this occasion when her parents were just a bit concerned about her time at the Copacabana, she would get to ride it.

It was a warm night and, despite the glare of multiple lights, dark enough so that the water could not be seen. As they boarded, April listened as the splashes smacked against the big boat. While the ferry was far from fully occupied, she was still surprised at the number of people who had boarded. She'd long known that this was a New York thing to do, but on a Saturday night?

The horn blew loudly and, from an unknown source, a series of recommendations was piped in through electronic amplification. Then the horn blasted, and off they went. Richie led her to the side, and the two teenagers, in prom clothes, stood and caught spray as the large vessel slowly made its way forward.

"April," was what he said.

"Richie, where are we?"

"Let's go for a swim or, as The Beach Boys say, surf. Huh, Apie?"

"I get it," said April. "We're doing our own prom out here on the water."

"We sang this how many times as we dribbled to the park?" Richie wondered out loud.

"I used to think that we would always be little-kid friends. You would talk to me before your parents even. I was the keeper of all your precious secrets."

"I've been dreaming about this night for a while, April. At least since the beginning of this year," said Richie.

"Why then?" she asked.

"Physical."

"Huh?"

"Remember that time at the basketball court when you tripped and fell into me?"

"Not that I've been thinking about it, but yes," she said.

The ferry horn blew for a third time, and April didn't know whether this was accidental or intentional. Every so often, the boat seemed to mark its presence, to announce its significance. And then, suddenly, there was music. Seemingly out of nowhere, Sonny and Cher were singing "Baby Don't Go" and April turned and kissed Richie fully on the lips.

He lifted her so that she hadn't any choice but to conform to his body, and this she loved. April willed her mind to exercise control over impulse since this had previously worked—at least, she hadn't allowed herself anything more sexual than a bear hug and a deeply felt kiss.

The boat reached its destination, and she knew it would halt for a few minutes before turning around and heading back to the city. She started thinking about whether she wanted to return to the Copa. The party would be going on and on and on. The drinking, the slow dancing . . . then some couples would be leaving for the next phase of the evening. The hallways in school had buzzed the past few weeks with rumors and plans for what would happen after the actual event. April had convinced herself that she wanted to move beyond the usual touching and tempting, but she wasn't certain she would do it. She didn't know what her previously trusted inner voice would say. What's more, she thought she might not pay attention to it.

Lost in thought, warmed by a drink or two, clinging to Richie and so enamored, April concentrated on the sloshing of the waters around her. Experiencing soft splashes since they'd moved to a side railing, April listened as Richie began to sing "Blue Velvet" and she couldn't help but kiss him once again. He was so much taller now.

Very suddenly, it seemed to her, they were back, somewhere at the southern tip of Manhattan. That was all she could process. But what next?

"Want to go back?" Richie asked.

"Where?" April wondered, then wondered, "What else could we do?"

"We could go for a walk."

"Where, Richie?"

He had his arm around her, escorting her off the ferry and into the night. April had no knowledge of this region of Manhattan but was glad to hang onto to Richie, who seemed familiar with their surroundings. Either that or he pretended with ease and knowing conviction. April looked back quickly and across the water watched a lightning streak approach the Statue of Liberty. Thunder next and nothing more. She could visualize the looks on Bert's and Lil's faces when she returned home well past midnight, drenched in her prom dress. Could she possibly be truthful with her story?

"Heading north, April. Just in case we want to go back to the club," said Richie.

"What about finding a place to just sit?" she asked.

"You mean like a boat ride?"

"I cannot believe you took me there. I'm ready for a quiet corner table," said April.

"Come on," he said as he shifted his grip to her hand. "Pretend we're off to the court." Soon they were running, fancy outfits flying in the breeze, and April sang some of "I Want to Hold Your Hand" and shook her hair a bit like a Beatle.

"And when we touch, I do feel. even more than the song says, happy. I mean it's where I want to be," April said. Out of breath, they came upon a park bench and, together, crashed on to it. "Seriously, where should we go?" she asked.

"Home," said Richie.

"What?"

"You said you wanted a quiet corner. Our parents will probably be thrilled to see us, and we can hang out in either house. They'll just be glad we aren't totally drunk at the Copa, though we'll have to get back there to retrieve to my car."

"Can you drive okay?" she asked.

"Sure. This is not so bad," he said.

"You mean you've had more to drink and driven?" April asked.

Richie nodded, and she kissed him again. Arm around her waist, he helped her into a cab. April wondered whether she had briefly fallen asleep since it seemed they were instantly at the nightclub.

"Let's go back in for a minute, Richie. See what goes on."

"Okay, April, I'm fine with that."

Time had stopped. Vinton remained on the stage singing about kisses and love. Then, it seemed to April, it was about missing and she was sure the man was looking into her eyes.

She smiled and said, "I get it, Richie. This isn't where I—where we—should be. Let's go."

He handed the valet his parking check and, moments later, they were leaving Manhattan.

"We're here, April," Richie said. She realized she must have been dozing again. That's why Richie was gently patting her on the shoulder. "We're going to my house," he continued. "Smile." She tried to stay awake but, instead, found herself involved in a recurring dream, something about a swimming pool. If you lived on Long Island and had one, everyone came to your house. Next thing she knew, they were walking around to a backyard she knew so well and the bench seat swing she had been on so many times before. She was delighted to see her favorite three-foot-high stuffed animal sitting before her. April had had White Bear as far back as she could recall. It sat upright now, and she looked at Richie.

"I guess I did plan this out," he said. "I was hoping, sooner or later, we would find our way back here on this night."

"I love it, Richie," she said. "I wish we could just swing until we both get tired and fall asleep right here."

"What happens when your parents or mine start to worry and find us out here?" Richie asked.

"Lil and Bert aren't a major problem. They worry just the right amount, especially my dad. He'll always worry about his little girl," said April, "even though it's prom night and he told me he trusted me."

"I'm sure my parents are up," Richie said. "If we could, what would you do right now?"

"The beach! Let's go there! It would be beautiful."

"At one in the morning? It's not like a public beach is open all night, April."

"We would have to tell our parents," she said.

Richie held April close to him and kissed her, and she felt herself melting within his arms.

"Richie, you go inside and I will go to my house. Then let's come back here—and head off. But we have to say something to them first."

Against her instincts, April extracted herself from Richie, turned back, and then kissed him again before walking across the yard to her house. The kitchen lights were on. Her parents were sitting at the table as if it were noon and they were preparing for lunch.

"I'm glad you're home, sweet," said Bert.

"We just wanted everything to be okay," said Lil. "Was it wonderful?"

"Yes," said April. "We want to spend some more time together, Mom."

"Of course. Before college," Lil answered.

"No, I mean now. We're heading over to the beach," she said.

"The beach? Well, we were terrified about your spending the night in the city, so I guess this is better than that. Fine. Just no swimming, please. As for the rest? Be . . . be yourself, April," said her father.

Richie pulled into the driveway, which was visible through a kitchen window. He waved while smiling broadly. Rolling down the window, he called out, "Hi! We're going to the beach!" He received a nod and a half smile from April. He was wearing a tight, yellow T-shirt.

April said, "I'll be right back. Just let me get out of this contraption." She left the table to run upstairs and change.

"Contraption, wow," Lil said. "What next?"

"A lot—and I trust it's pretty terrific. Richie's more or less been her brother," said Bert. "It's all out of our control, anyway, from this point forward."

When April returned, all her parents saw was a basketball jersey, white and green, with the number 14 across its back. They hadn't any idea what, if anything, she had on underneath.

"You two are the best," she said, waving to her parents as she slammed the back door behind her.

Chapter Four

Beach

APRIL GREW UP GOING to the beach—Jones Beach, parking lot 4 or 5. Through the tunnel, whooping loudly in hopes of an echo serenade, to the women's changing area and excitedly onward toward the saltwater pool, the hot dog stand, the whitest sand ever, and the ocean. Ride the waves. That routine.

At times, she and her parents would turn right off the Meadowbrook Parkway and head for Long Beach and the boardwalk, games, and coupons.

Richie, on this very late night, was driving moderately and April felt safe. She edged over on the bench seat till they were touching. Nothing else mattered. She looked out the front windshield and saw stars upon stars. She was awed by the white-on-black natural spectacle.

Richie asked, "April, Jones or not?"

"Or what?"

"We could try Point Lookout and maybe we would be the only ones."

April nodded, but Richie couldn't see.

"Which way?" he asked.

"Sorry. Maybe turn right, opposite from Jones, since that's the only sign we have."

"I agree," he said. Either he was a careful driver or he was looking out for April, or both.

It was well past midnight by now. Hardly a passing car drove by, but the bright sky and moon made it possible to see. Spine-like reeds appeared amid low bushes and then sand. One animal became visible. A cat? She could not tell.

Richie reached for the radio with his right hand. April intercepted and held his fingers while she turned the knob to produce sound. There it was, a song from the past year she was positive was speaking to her. She sang along with "My Guy," the Mary Wells single that had come out during the past year or so. April only knew a few of the lyrics and, really, the title was enough.

She heard the beach before she saw it: waves whooshing, then fading away. No one was in the area as Richie parked in what must have been a vacant lot. April was too tired to think. They both needed sleep, yet the scent of the smacking sea ensured that they stayed awake. The engine shut off and the two of them, the boy and girl who had grown up shooting baskets together, the duo who had left the senior prom well before the crowning of the king and queen, giggled. Before Richie was able to open his door, April tousled his hair. He loved that. Then they were out of the car, barefoot, heading for the ocean. April tossed a little camera she had with her onto the sand. As they ran, their clothing, with some prompting, loosened. Richie was down to his boxer shorts, and April laughed loudly. His basketball shorts were much tighter and more revealing than the boxers. She didn't know what to do, what was right. She had the Cousy jersey on, and beneath it she wore a bra. That bra would stay but not the Celtics legend's shirt. She twirled it off and dropped it. She was aware, yet more accepting, of the tiny jiggle of flesh just above her shorts, then felt Richie's hand encircling her waist. April dissolved . . . They were walking and swimming for more than just a few moments. Laughing, too; this, April understood, was her senior prom—by the shore, by the moonlight, just the two of them.

A bright light, after a time, approached. Two lights, actually: beams coming from a car. A skinny, lanky man with a cap like a police officer's approached, and April knew this face too well: Jonathan Hudson.

Half-undressed, April and Richie wandered out of the water and onto the wet sand.

"Mr. Hudson?" she asked.

"You recognize me, April." He turned. "Hello, Richard."

"Mr. Hudson," said Richie.

"It's okay, you two, if you're alright. You're not supposed to be here. I'm on duty, so please stay out of the ocean. I will soon be off."

"Why are you here, Mr. Hudson?" April asked.

"Teachers need second jobs. At least, I do," he answered.

"You're my only teacher who gives me even a sense of who you really are, Mr. Hudson," said Richie.

April's head buzzed. She had been spinning fantasies about Hudson for a year, and now she was ready to take off her remaining clothes with Richie; there wasn't any way to make sense of it. Fortunately, she saw the Cousy where she left it and flipped it back on over her head.

"It's okay," April whispered to herself, as if it were noon on a school day. She saw that he had a gun fixed into a belt around his waist. "Why do you have that?" she asked, while pulled down her jersey. Even with the shirt on, April felt half-undressed. She was simultaneously appalled and embarrassed.

"Guards carry guns, April. Part of the uniform they give us. Luckily, I've never used it," he answered.

"But you could, right, if you needed to?" asked Richie.

"We were trained, if you can call it that," said Hudson. "I could never hurt even an animal. I guess, in that way, I'm not a perfect fit for this job."

The asides, these moments, during school and especially just now, drew April to Hudson. She was in awe of his compassion. Several hours ago, though, she wanted Richie to take her off to a hotel room.

Where, she wondered, was her heart? What was she to do with her fantasies?

Hudson broke the spell: "You can stay here. I never saw you. Like I was saying, just don't swim." He pivoted, walked back toward the parking lot, then turned his head and called out, "You guys are a cute couple. Invite me to the wedding in five years?"

If Richie had asked her to, April might have tossed her special shirt into the spray of the ocean, where it would be lost forever, and not cared one bit. But he did not. Instead, he played with the sliver of skin available; all the while, he hadn't moved his fingers away from her waistline. She decided she might as well accept the fact that Richie was too exhausted to go any further.

They were walking backward from the water, across the sand, when Richie surprised her by saying, "I've been wanting to spend a night with you." His mouth opened as if he had more to say, but that was it.

April laughed. "You might have said something, let on, even given a hint."

Richie shrugged and hugged her. She quickly lifted the Cousy above her head and wrapped herself around him. This was right. Richie carried her back to the car. Why, thought April, have I—have we—waited so long?

The car slowed as Richie said, "April, we're home." Her head in his lap, she realized she must have been in such a pose and position as he drove back.

"Okay, yes, I better go inside. What time is it?"

"Almost three," he said.

"Oh, no. Now what?"

"Maybe the front porch. The swing. We could just say we were there for hours," he said.

· · · ●·●· ● · ·

She and Richie, in metronome-like symmetry, were gliding back and forth, back and forth, when April, still exhausted, drifted off once again.

Always sensitive to light, she awakened at sunrise and realized, surprisingly, where she was and with whom.

"Is anyone else up?" she asked.

"Not so far," answered Richie. "Well, me, but I must have slept, too. This whole night feels like . . . like a dream or a movie."

His parents, then, were jostling the back door, trying to get the kids' attention without intruding.

"Can you stay for a second?" Richie asked at first, then decided, "No, you don't need to." Smiling, he waved to his mother and father who walked back into the house without saying a word.

"It's different with my parents," said April. "I think I should say something. Want to come?"

"Sure," he said, stretching.

But before they could get up, Bert and Lil walked out the door of their house and ambled, as if invited, across one yard to the next. The couple had similar oval-shaped faces, and they were about the same size. Lil appeared to be perpetually smiling ever so slightly, even when sorrowful. She rarely grinned gleefully but managed a sunny hello. Bert laughed and dimples on either cheek peeked through midlife creases. Both of them had remained willowy, but Bert had begun to show signs of a permanent forward tilt. As her parents approached, April attached herself further to Richie. "April and Richie," she thought, like the girls who drew hearts on notebooks with a boyfriend's name. She wondered what would happen once when they began to unabashedly, in public, cling to one another: "Richie and April."

"Hi, sugar," said her father, using a term that she found inappropriate and embarrassing.

"Hello" said Richie.

"Richard," said Bert, shaking hands as if this were a business lunch.

"We were a little worried," Lil said.

"And here we were," said April, "swinging on Richie's porch the whole time."

"I, for one, am not at all surprised that you two are together," said her father.

"Why, Dad?"

"Well, you've been hanging out together, physically, for over ten years. Remember how I told you that we tend to partner with people we know? Case in point."

"The prom was pretty glamorous but, yeah, we just wanted to spend time alone. So, here we fell asleep."

"Really?" said Lil. "Innocent?"

"Actually, yes, mother," April replied. "Clothes on. Looks like it's going to be a beautiful day. Maybe we'll go to the beach."

Richie laughed and poked her in the side.

"Well, maybe we could all use some breakfast. Some of my famous French toast?"

"Let's do it," said April.

"At this point," Richie added, "I'm more than hungry. French toast would be a dream."

Lil shifted the conversation as she led everyone inside.

"Richie, do you think you'll keep up with music at college?"

April and Richie exchanged glances before April said, "Mother, Richie doesn't play an instrument anymore. That was a long time ago."

"Well," said Bert, carrying in some food, "I once tried drumming before focusing on piano."

"What?" April asked.

"I took a few lessons, but I really couldn't coordinate the two hands. Something about the left one following the right when it should be equal, and I could not adjust."

"Let's eat," said Lil.

April and Richie were on the way to the after-prom brunch five hours later, but neither one knew why. April attached herself to Richie as he drove.

Finally, he said, "April, what is this?"

"I just want to keep this night, this day, going forever, Richie. It's the best feeling, isn't it?"

"But why didn't this happen earlier?"

"Richie, I'm supposed to leave in two weeks for Silverbirch Inn, and then we go off in separate directions. What can we do?"

"Love these days and not worry, April."

Chapter Five

Silverbirch

NESTLED WITHIN A VALLEY in the Catskills, the lodge, run by Abby and Ben Silverbirch, served as a vacation home for New Yorkers, Long Islanders, and people from places like New Rochelle, Mount Vernon, White Plains and Montclair, New Jersey, too. Silverbirch, to April, was a tree palace. She knew only these: oaks, maples, willows, and birch trees. Of course, the apple orchard by the tennis courts was a treasured spot. The accommodations were what her parents called "rustic," but she loved the smell of cabins. It meant, simply, the country.

April first went there with her parents. At home, she had always been surrounded by Bert and Lil. Not at Silverbirch, where she was with them but also able to step away and be by herself, too. They started going there when she was only ten or so: for a winter weekend, then spring vacation, then a week in the summer. July or August were best, and they began to rent for a month. She had her own room in the family cottage, romped off to summer camp on her own, and adored the free time to wander within the orchard or trek off to the pond.

The largest, sweeping willow tree, according to April, greeted those arriving at the main house. She felt comforted sitting beneath the majestic beauty. April could relax there. Three birch trees, standing like guardians, surrounded the lodge.

The program for kids was coed. She didn't have to wish that she could be a boy to play sports. Everyone was together. Basketball in the barn, gentle football on the snowy hillside in winter, softball on the field, and tennis on the four clay courts. You could swim either in the nearby pond or in the pool. Adults sat around smoking cigarettes and, every so often, one of them might refresh with a dip. Kids dominated the pool. April learned to back dive and flip over. They went to the highway overpass and waved to trucks, laughing gleefully when a horn blasted in recognition. At dusk, the kids tread softly on trips to the a nearby graveyard and returned to the main lodge for chocolate chips.

April had been too shy to dance, except at Silverbirch. She could innocently dance with a boy within the confines of the barn and so what? Nobody from back home would ever know. It would remain her secret. April considered Silverbirch a haven.

She also loved the bagel shop, the only one in the area to bake and sell bagels at six in the morning. April had begun going there at age twelve. Simon, who ran the shop back then, knew she wanted a plain bagel with butter, so she didn't have to ask. Besides, she had a crush on his assistant, Robby, who was maybe a few years older than April. He remained a mystery since he was so often at the shop. April was sure he was going to school as well. She always gained weight at Silverbirch. Her jeans were tighter when she came home. April could resist neither the ultra-rich dining room food nor the bagels.

Other kids went to more conventional sleep-away camps. Silverbirch was April's, and she did not especially want to share it. Now she felt it was fortunate she hadn't been there for a few years. It was likely that people didn't know her exact age. April, several months ago, felt okay about telling Silverbirch a white lie to get the upcoming summer job. To her, it was not complicated. She pretended she had already gone off to college and, projecting forward, would just now be completing freshman year. They didn't want recent high school grads. Silverbirch knew her and her parents were longtime vacationers. Why not believe her? When she showed up weeks later, everyone would expect her to have been there by herself, familiar with boys and accustomed to drinking.

She wrote a short story earlier that year for Jonathan Hudson's English class and mentioned Silverbirch by name. April remembered being surprised when Mr. Hudson returned her paper and said, "I know it well."

"No, not this Silverbirch, Mr. Hudson," she said.

"With the dark wooden buildings and the long pool out back? Up the hill, there are apple trees surrounding the red clay tennis courts. The pancakes have real blueberries in summer, and you can walk for a little while to get your own bagels. It hooked me right away, and I went back again and again. To be by myself, most often I went to the pond with the bullfrogs. I think when you were little and on vacation with your parents, I was working as a specialty sports counselor."

"That's it," April said quietly. "We called it Janet's Pond. One of the boys named it," she added. "The other part about you being there when I was? Maybe, probably you're right.

"I could tell from your story that we shared that special getaway and, a mile behind it, the hidden pond," said Jonathan Hudson.

April's cheeks reddened even as she tried to calm herself. "Were you always planning to tell me?" She didn't know what would come next.

"Oh, I did, but you were probably thinking of something else and not your English teacher's reaction to a short story," he said.

She so wanted to keep talking with him. "Could you say why you went there? I would be interested," she said.

"This takes me back some years. I had a friend at Williams College who said he summered there, either with the kids' camp or as a kind of maître d' in the dining hall. Very personable guy. Len Moscow was his name, but I never believed that was his real name, if you know what I mean. He must have been a Muskevitz or something like that," said Jonathan.

"What about you? I mean, a man named Hudson at a lodge where Jewish people go for vacations?"

"Not everyone who works there, April, is Jewish. More than half are not. My friend, Len, yes. Me? My mother is Jewish and my father not. Technically speaking, I am a member of the tribe, if you know what I mean."

"I don't see it in you, Mr. Hudson," said April, who had dreamt about this man's body ever since she saw him in a tank top and shorts playing in the faculty-student basketball game. He was bony, but that was okay with her. He had taught her *The Legend of Sleepy Hollow*, and she thought there should be a movie version with him in it.

"Silverbirch was all about basketball at first for me, April. Len told me that the staff had a team, actually went to a high school gym to practice and joined a summer parks and rec league. He and I had been playing together forever, and Len knew that it was a fever for me, a backboard fever. Like in the kids' sports book series that I devoured."

"What series was that, Mr. Hudson?"

"Clair Bee's Chip Hilton sagas," he said. "Chip was always the hero, the good guy. He scored the winning basket, hit a home run in extra innings, threw or caught the touchdown pass. Besides all that, he took care of his friends."

"But you taught us this year that life and art are not the same," said April.

"If you're saying that the Hilton novels aren't exactly realistic, you would be correct. Still, for a young kid growing up in the sticks . . ."

"Where was that?"

"I'm from the Albany area—a small town called Rome, believe it or not."

"Rome, New York? Doesn't sound right," she said.

"I could be myself there," he said. "No pressure. I convinced myself that I could become a pianist, so I practiced six or eight hours a day. But that conflicted with sports and, regrettably, I gave up piano and gave in to basketball. You play, don't you? I mean, play basketball."

"How did you know?" April asked.

"I've seen you wearing the Cousy jersey many times, outside in the back part of the school lot, shooting."

"Wow. You're so sure it was me?"

"Nobody else wears Celtics gear around here," he said. "Also, you lope around sometimes like you're walking onto a big-time court."

April wondered whether Jonathan Hudson had some interest in her, whatever that meant. He had to be at least thirty-five, she imagined. God, seventeen years older. Still, she wanted to somehow keep the conversation going.

"Your name is like the river or even an old car brand," she said, twirling the ends of her hair. "Do you still go to Silverbirch?" April asked.

"For the longest while, only an occasional weekend in the summer. I have a choice, sort of, when it comes to other jobs while not teaching," he said. "I like doing a lot of different things. Otherwise, I can get bored pretty easily. Till now. Silverbirch is making a nice offer, and I am seriously considering going back."

"What do you mean?"

"I'm signed up to be at the beach this summer. I do weekends there during the off season from school. Teaching, however trying, isn't like being in the coal mines, if you know what I mean. I get paid to teach kids like you about novels and short stories and even an occasional play. That's not exactly drudgery. My hands are never dirty. I don't cough up blood at day's end."

"You have me thinking about being a writer," she said.

"Sorry," he said.

"I don't understand."

"I write, but not using my real name. My nom de plume is Hudson Jerome."

"Wow," said April.

"Teaching and summer work allow me to write. I could never make it just on novels alone."

"More than one?"

"Many unpublished and two in print. April, you need to write more. How about you come in after school and show me what you're doing?"

"Sure. I mean, if you think I'm good enough for you to spend the time."

"If someone had nurtured me, my world would be a very different one. When I was in school, the whole idea was that everyone was held to the same set of rules and tests. It was called favoritism if any student was treated as an individual."

"Not all that different," she said, "from now. Especially when someone's a girl and her teacher is a man."

"Let's not allow that to get in the way," he said as he stood.

April realized that he was both taller and less angular than she thought. "Sure. I will write something," she said.

For a long time, April wanted to talk about her life as what she phrased "a one but not only child" since her parents never, not even once, referred to her as an only child.

So, April met Jonathan Hudson in his classroom every other Wednesday. Never would she have thought it possible at the beginning of the school year. Simultaneously, she was becoming even closer to Richie. In fact, she was unable to resist him. She could not and certainly wished not to deny the emotional and physical pull. Still, she found herself daydreaming about Hudson as she looked forward to her conferences with him. Two men. April wanted Richie every moment of the day. But she knew that in a few months, they would be separated by college here and college there. She was also looking forward to spending time with Jonathan Hudson at Silverbirch.

It would soon enough be mid-June and a couple of weeks away from departure for a Silverbirch summer. She had told the white lie about her age and experience to get the job. Her parents understood her job. She would teach both basketball skills and swim strokes to kids.

Now, however, she and Richie, hand in hand, pressing together, found places to be alone. The key retreat was the finished basement in Richie's house. The land on the way to the high school included the rolling soft hill, some brush, and the path going through. At this point, they ignored anyone who happened to see them.

April was ready for more than fondling and kissing, but Richie was reluctant. He held her, carefully caressed her, tracing the contours of her body. He was gentle, sweet, and considerate, and he wanted to explore—but only so far.

Finally, snuggling against him in his car, parked at the edge of the new development of houses, the road having been paved days before, she took off her T-shirt, undid her jeans, and pulled him to her.

He responded, but April wondered why he didn't rip off his clothing that very instant. Did he not find her attractive?

Richie knew she was disappointed. "I love you, April, but I don't know," he said.

"What?" she asked, pulling her shirt back over her head and bra. "Don't you want to do way more?"

"Yes, yeah," he said.

But they did not, and April, staying near because she adored him, did not question further. She now acknowledged the reality that he and she would be in separate places through the summer and into the fall. Her thinking turned toward fast-approaching Silverbirch.

As far as she knew, everyone would assume she'd been at college for a year. The application said you needed to be nineteen. She had fabricated a story about her first year at college just in case that was necessary. She thought her face looked young and worried people would be suspicious. But when she had interviewed there, no one had questioned her age. Maybe she was wrong and actually did seem older. Her experiences, though, were limited to Richie. She didn't drink—not much anyway—and she was never interested in cigarettes. Jonathan Hudson would be coordinating all sports at the inn. He knew this much: that she had occasionally vacationed there with her parents, that she would probably like being there, and that she would be terrific working with little ones. April told herself not to anticipate. Soon enough, she'd understand her specific staff responsibilities. April, realizing that Hudson did know her age, knew that somehow she needed to get this across; she had to tell him that he was the only one who would know the truth. April had about a week to square her story with him. She had thought Silverbirch would be all hers. Now, she would be sharing it with Hudson.

Finding him would be easy: the courts behind the high school. She needed a strategy. As seniors, days at high school were lame-duck ones for the most part. Sure, a few wayward, marginal students were in jeopardy of failing, but these kids had been on the edge, for one reason or another, a long while before. Nothing new.

The next day, at 3:00 p.m., when the bell rang, April, dressed in comfortably loose clothing, waved good-bye to Richie, who seemed puzzled. She made her way to the rear playground, where, pre-dictably, Jonathan Hudson stood methodically and carefully shooting from the free throw line.

"HORSE?" April asked.

"Better than PIG," he said. With that, he ambled to the left, turned, and hit a bank shot.

"No need to jump or spin. Just off the backboard," he called.

April, as instructed, stood flat-footed, took a deep breath, and calmly sank the same.

"Are you going to play in college?" Hudson asked.

"I want to," she answered, even though she hadn't thought about it. "Do you think I'm good enough?"

"Hand and eye, definitely," he said. "A lot of practice this summer, you're in. Where are you going again, April?"

"NYU. I wanted to be in the city," she said.

"They still have a team?"

"I, I guess so," she said, "but, honestly, I never looked. It was either that or Cornell and, you know, everyone is going to Cornell. Why are you out here every day?"

"Gives me hope every time the ball goes through the net. That represents possibility. Otherwise, I get slightly discouraged but just tell myself to keep shooting," he said.

"I've been playing since I was a little girl. Mostly with boys at the park near my house. It's always been a part of my life, and girls still don't get as many chances as boys do. Also, it's a lot more fun to run around the basketball court than some other forms of exercise," she added. "I mean, way before you knew me at school, I was always outside. The weather didn't stop me."

"Answer to your question: You could play on many college teams. Shoot hoops all summer."

April nodded and said, "I have to talk to you about something else. I'm going to be working at Silverbirch. Or did you already know that?"

"Oh, that's a good thing. You mean before college? Like for spending money?"

"True on both counts, but I need to tell you how I got the job," she said. "I pretended I would be nineteen at the start of the summer when I'm really eighteen. You think I look old enough?"

"I guess, sure. Last two years of high school and first two years of college, I'm not sure I can guess the ages of kids like you."

"Just what I want to hear, really."

"It'll be an interesting summer, April," he said.

April felt he took the news as if he expected it. No exclamations, just more free throws. Calm and easy; never off-stride. He wasn't like anybody else she'd ever met.

• • • • • • • • • • •

April and Richie were in denial—about the end of childhood and the fact they would be apart for the summer. How could it all crash down so suddenly upon them? A dozen years or so could not be so easily erased. They agreed that this was only a suspension of the relationship.

"Time out, April?"

"Okay," she said as they sat entwined, swinging on the back porch just as they had several hours after the prom. The stars seemed to be jumping out of the sky, hurtling toward them. April blinked as if a star might actually drop fully and splash directly in her face.

Suddenly, Richie yanked off his T-shirt and, bare-chested, turned to her. April thought this was finally it, an evening she had long awaited but could not, at the moment, believe to be real. What was she supposed to do? Would it be too much to grab the ends of her sweatshirt and lift upward? She knew this was not likely, not with at least one and possibly two sets of eyes peering out from one of the two houses, through a window, the homes separated by a thin strip of grass that never grew. Instead, she turned toward Richie, soothed his face with one hand, and placed the other upon his taut stomach. She knew, immediately, that he was aroused. It would be their last night together for a while. Who knew when they would see each other again? He pulled her onto him and hugged her whole body. Still, she was unsure. Richie relinquished his grip, kissed her, and told her he would always love her. Nothing more.

"You're so sweet," she said because it was so. He was the sweetest of boys.

It wasn't difficult to persuade her father, Bert, to drive her to Silverbirch. He always leapt at an opportunity to spend time with his daughter. As the two of them walked to the Pontiac on a sparkling late June morning, April had to wave good-bye—to the only home she had ever known well; to her recent boyfriend and everyday companion whom she adored and might love; and to her mother, who, attempting to hide her tears, smiled through them.

April could barely believe the quantum leaps before her: Silverbirch and then college. Yes, she would return for vacations and maybe even a summer or two, but only as a visitor.

On impulse, she ran to Richie's house, rapped four times on the side door (their signal), and fell into his arms when he appeared.

"This cannot be happening," she said. "I mean, we said forever."

"We are, April. It's just something you wanted to do. Go."

April understood. If she didn't break his grasp, she might stay forever. "I have to leave now, Richie. I will call when I get settled." She kissed him and walked back to the car as her eyes watered. She looked back and saw that he had not moved. Richie stared off in her direction, but he seemed not to be looking directly at her. Weeping openly while spreading her hand over her face, April opened the passenger side door and slid in beside her father.

Bert looked at his daughter. "You okay?" he asked. When she didn't respond, he added, "Don't answer. Talk to me if you want to. Otherwise, I know."

Nearly an hour later, as the Pontiac headed north, April said, "It's a lot. Leaving you and Mom and whatever happens with Richie. I'll be, what, an hour-plus away from where I grew up, from everything, and who knows when I'll be back?"

"It's a summer job, sweetheart. And, of course, school. You're not going across the country, so you can come home any time. Many of the kids are around even in September."

"Right and right, Dad. There are just some things I haven't been able to make peace with. I don't want Richie to be thinking of me every living second but, on the other hand, I do," she said.

"You might find me ancient, April, but my memory is fine. I remember when I first thought I was in love," said Bert. "The young woman—not your mother—dropped me. It was deserved, but I'm able to say that only now."

"It's just that I'm thinking maybe I should have stayed at home instead of going to Silverbirch."

"Listen, you know the grounds, April, and the special Silverbirch gems, too. How bad could it be? Money before college and memories close to your heart."

"It took Richie and me twelve years to come together, and tossing it away isn't so easy, Dad."

"We can still turn around, but I don't think it's the best idea," he said.

April put her head back and tried to relax. She did not want to turn around. Besides, the time away would grant perspective. With distance, she would better understand the past few months. No reason to look backward, peer out her bedroom window, and wonder about her fate. Instead, she would work each day, pose as a college student on summer break, and experience something of the larger world.

"Drive on, Dad," she said. "Thanks so much, and of course you're right. I have to take a big breath or three or four and get out of town."

With that, she alternated between dozing, conversing with her father, and musing about her impending arrival at Silverbirch. She knew nothing, and starting from scratch would be an improvement. As it was, April was behind—in age, experience, and savior faire. She was young, and her circle, until now, had been small, filled only with people and stops she fully understood. It was uncomfortable to thrust herself, boldly, into uncharted territory, and she squirmed as they exited the Thruway.

Silverbirch, however, was nature's treasure of apple trees and weeping willows. April took in the greenery, her senses awakening and her body unwinding as she stretched in the front seat. The air was different here, sharper and piercing even as temperatures were much the same as back on Long Island. *Give the next month and more a chance*, she told herself, wishing for peace of mind even as she struggled with her recent departure from home, with the final image of Richie, who seemed, in retrospect, puzzled and even stunned.

"We're here," Bert announced. "Where to?"

April stiffened before reaching for the car door. "Around the back of the main building, Dad," she said. That's where her assigned room was. Bert carried her two duffels and then went back to the car to grab the record player, albums and two of April's stuffed animals — a bear and a puppy. She handled the large food bag jammed with pretzels, the chocolate chip cookies Lil had baked, oranges, and a seeded rye bread.

Her unit and one other were attached to the primary lodge as if these rooms had been an afterthought. She picked hers because she remembered, having been inside during a family stay at Silverbirch, that it smelled like a pine forest and, for April, scent came before sight—always.

April was only mildly surprised that Silverbirch looked as she recalled it: the same outside chairs—some metal, some aluminum, some twined together, and the beautiful white and blue Adirondacks—and the willow and three birch trees that framed the lodge itself. While she was certain that the buildings were either painted or stained (she didn't know which), every structure looked occupied, lived in—as if isolation were anathema. Silverbirch was created for enjoyment, talk, games, sports, casual walks, and sumptuous meals. The silver birch trees could not be ignored. April thought of a two-week family vacation years ago, when she and her parents had listened during dinner one night to a man who explained that white birch was the more common name but that either was fine.

"April," her father called, "where are you?"

"Thank you so much for driving me, Dad. You should go. It's better if I try to adjust by myself," she said. "I'm just thinking about how lucky I am to be here among the trees, with this job, and in the most special place of my childhood." Still, April had to convince herself not to back out. This had been her idea nearly a year before. She knew she couldn't and shouldn't give it up.

"Okay, sweet," he said. "If it doesn't work, just call and you'll be back home later that day. Silverbirch was perfect for us as a family, but it's now solo for you. Call. Yes?"

"Sure. Tomorrow. Give me a day and tell Mom I love her." April raced to him, hugged him tightly, and suddenly let go. She watched him walk back around the main building and saw him turn toward her as he opened the driver door of the Pontiac. He seemed to be gesturing with one hand and shielding his eyes with the other. She couldn't fully decipher.

April did not go back inside. Instead, she walked up the rear hill toward the grove of apple trees near the clay tennis courts. When she saw her favorite tree, she ran and then scaled it swiftly. From this vantage point, she could see the swimming pools, ball fields, paradise. Flashes of her childhood flew toward her: pretend football in the snow; back dives at sunset; apple picking (who could gather the most in three minutes); the crush she had on one of the waiters, Randall, who went to Amherst College. For a long while, she wanted to go there, too, even if he would have long ago departed. She knew at the time nothing would ever come of the crush: She was a ten-year-old kid with her parents, and he was practically a man facing the world. That was even more true the last time she, Bert and Lil were together at Silverbirch during her sophomore year in mid-winter. Still, she allowed the reverie to continue. It was during that final visit that Randall had personally asked her if she could help with a meal when they were short a staff member. Listening to all the talk in the kitchen, she felt privy to a different world, one in which workers playfully or pointedly commented about the visitors, the renters, people like April and her parents. She remembered her forced laughter and inner defensiveness when the remarks turned to money and pretense. April was caught—she could not say a word on anyone's behalf.

Now, she was voluntarily joining the brigade of those who were employed during the summer and hoped for tips that could enhance a basic salary. Since April professed to have had a year of college, she had to have been out of high school before the previous summer. She thought that was what it came down to: In order to be hired, she claimed to be an experienced young woman of the world, not the sheltered daughter who grew up in the suburbs. Could she live up to her fabrication?

April descended the tree, branch by branch, until her feet reached the ground. She thought of walking to the pond but decided what would make her most comfortable would be the swishing sound of the net after a basketball fell through it. She knew where balls were stored in the barn and so she ran there, grabbed a basketball, and trotted out of the annex toward the newly positioned freestanding hoop. This was a recent and welcome addition. April snapped her sweatshirt to the ground and, wearing an old Silverbirch T-shirt, began shooting.

She had long ago made it part of her routine to sink three straight makes before she could move to another spot. She drew, with her foot, an imaginary free throw line in the dirt, bounced the ball two times, took a deep breath, bent her knees, and swish! Same routine and same result the second time. Then she missed a couple and punished her body with laps.

Her next shot clanged off the rim, bounced away, and rapidly rolled downhill. As April turned to retrieve the ball, she recognized a familiar profile, complete with a one-of-a-kind body, headed up the hill toward her. *All bones*, she thought when she saw the figure. April blinked as if she could hardly believe this was Jonathan Hudson. Here. Now. Wearing nothing but a white undershirt and some gray gym shorts. Not why; rather, why not?

April bounded after the ball, which sped away from her and made its way, jaggedly, toward Mr. Hudson. Nearly losing her balance, April wondered just what to call him. "Mr. Hudson"? That seemed too formal, considering they would be co-workers soon enough, but "Jonathan" was out of the question. Something else? "Hudson"? That wasn't really appropriate. She hoped the answer would come to her—and fast.

Hudson snagged the basketball and called out, "Hey, Cousy, take this!" Then he whipped a pass over his head directly toward April, who was running downhill. Initially surprised, she managed to catch the ball without toppling backward. "I thought you were a shooter," she said. "That's what it looked like in the faculty game."

"Nice to know you've been tracking my moves. I thought my value came to a stop with literature and writing."

April blushed but thought quickly. "Remember that time you drew an analogy between the way actors and a director—and basketball players and a coach—actually run parallel?" she asked. "You were the one who told me that the best thing someone in charge can do is get people working together. 'In sync' is the way you put it—running like a smooth device or something like that. In sync."

Hudson nodded. "When I played at Williams, we were not only good but we had a great time, too. I try for that in my classes, not always with success. April, thanks for noticing. I just shortened what my college coach said. He was always calling to us, 'Synchronize, men! One for all!'"

April laughed. "Mr. Hudson? Well, first of all, what should I call you?"

"Jon? Jonny?"

"You're my teacher."

"I was, and now we're colleagues. Was there something else you wanted to ask me, April?"

"Go for a walk?" she asked and wondered whether he thought she was a simpleton.

"I'm dressed for the gym. If you don't mind the attire, sure. Where to?" he asked, grabbing a light jacket he had brought with him off the ground.

"The pond and maybe the loop behind," she said, remembering that there was a gentle trail that led to a meadow.

April was filled with emotion. This could not be more awkward. A walk into the woods with Mr. Hudson? On the one hand, she was thrilled; on the other hand, she was uncertain. And what would Richie think of the two of them strolling along, side by side. Perhaps because Hudson was really bony, April had never realized before that he was so tall. He towered over her. She stood on her tiptoes and only reached his nose. He sidled forward on his feet, and April needed extra strides to keep up with him.

Eventually, though, she skipped ahead and said, "Follow me." April led Hudson around the still water and through what she simply called "the purple flowers" since she never knew what they were. The grasses and reeds were matted down slightly; it appeared someone else had already been there. April's imagination took over: They would stroll along for another ten minutes until reaching the field and then . . . and then Jonathan would take off his shirt and she would lie down and . . . and what was she thinking? He was in his mid-thirties! So what if she'd begun this fantasy months before? *Get real, April*, she told herself. He surely had a girlfriend or wife or someone more in his age bracket. She was still a teenager. And Richie, whom she adored, truly loved her.

They sat opposite one another, Jonathan twirling a lengthy piece of grass as April did the same with a couple of long strands of her hair. He smiled at her and then said, "April, you have to continue writing. Keep a journal this summer. You will never be able to recall everything that goes on unless you have some notes."

"Thanks. I was thinking, maybe, at the end of each week, I could write two pages. Would that be enough?"

"Not a matter of length, April. Just give yourself something to go on." He paused before adding, "When I was in school, one of my teachers insisted that I read Kay Boyle. I had never heard of her, but it seems that she's a pretty major writer whose personal life is, well, complicated. Anyway, her book *The Crazy Hunter* opens at a lake not all that unlike the pond back there. One young woman, a few years younger than you are now, is putting on her bathing suit and about to go for it, jump right in."

"I like it when you're my teacher again," said April.

"Not positive I should take on that role just now. Maybe I can be more like a senior writing buddy. Okay?"

"If you say so."

"I noticed in class that you get a glazed, faraway look when you're really concentrating. Someone might think you were spacing out when the opposite is true."

"What about you? How do you look when you're concentrating?" she asked.

"I tend to fidget."

"I've watched you do that, with a pen or with your shoelaces. I always thought it was nerves."

"Makes sense to assume that, April. Just the opposite. When I squirm, I'm actually concentrating harder. I know that doesn't exactly make sense."

April looked directly at Jonathan, realizing she was staring past his shoulder. "Why are you an English teacher and not a writer?" she asked.

"Only because I like to afford a decent dinner every so often," he said. "Go to a movie."

April was prone to crushes: the waiter at Silverbirch, Jonathan Hudson, even Richie. Once, earlier in the year, Lil had asked her if she'd ever thought she had "fallen" for someone. "What's the difference between a hard crush and falling in love, Mom?" April had asked.

"Well, I think you will know, sweetie, when it's more than a crush."

"That's not an answer," said April.

"Okay, well, a crush stays in your mind, but falling in love involves much more than that," said Lil.

Now, as the temperature soared on a late June afternoon in the Catskills, April, facing Jonathan, thought of that conversation with her mother and wondered whether this thing with Richie was actually her falling in love with him.

Hudson snapped his fingers and asked, "You okay?"

"Yeah, because I like the way you are both kind and strong with students. I thought that I could try that," she said.

"Oh, I thought maybe you admired my jump shot."

"That, too," she laughed. He always managed to make fun of himself. He was self-deprecating, April thought—one of those terms she had learned from an SAT prep book. She always confused it with self-effacing. Maybe both of these words described Jonathan. She imagined being on a high school faculty with him, thought he would run interference for her, anticipating and knocking away various hurdles. Was this way-older-brother/much-younger-sister love?

April, out of nowhere, said, "Cousy was my favorite player, and I haven't picked anyone else since he retired two years ago. I can sort of shoot the way he did, even though it would be nice to jump into my shot. It's hard enough to imitate his runner."

"I can teach you that," Jonathan said. "I have the Havlicek version since I'm more his build."

"Okay, sometime let's do it."

"How about now?"

"I really haven't even unpacked."

"Where are you staying, April?"

"Just around the corner from the court," she said while pointing.

"I'll walk you back. You're right: You should get settled. Maybe later?"

"I'm not saying no," said April.

They left the pond and found the dirt road leading back to the main building. April was glad to go to her room by herself, open the two duffle bags, and begin putting away her clothing. All the rest was happening too fast. She wasn't sure if she was ready for a tutorial on how to replicate Bob Cousy's running shot. On the other hand, wasn't this the best dream: shooting baskets on the Silverbirch court with Jonathan Hudson, who would be in a T-shirt and shorts?

A greater problem was her own outfit. Of course, she had the Cousy. Maybe that and a white T underneath would be appropriate. Or just the jersey with some Celtics green shorts? Would she be showing too much? Or was showing too much exactly what she wanted to do? She spent time in front of the mirror adjusting the Cousy over a white T.

That was who she was, the way she went to the park most of the time with Richie. Why change a good thing?

When she arrived at the dirt court, though, she found again a bare-chested Hudson standing at a free throw line he had drawn with his foot. April stared at him.

"Is my elbow pointing out?" asked Hudson. "I can usually make at least eight of ten, most swishes. Right now, I'm only hitting six or seven, including rattlers. What do you think, April?"

"I'm hardly a shooting coach."

"Are my elbows next to my body?" Jonathan asked.

April hadn't any choice but to respond. "Well, your left one is in, but the right one kind of points on an angle," she said.

"Show me," said Hudson. "I couldn't possibly know that unless someone watched and demonstrated. That's what I do when I occasionally coach kids."

April awkwardly took his elbow, which felt crackly in her hand, and pushed it toward his body. She felt his upper half relax, heard him sigh, and then took a step away.

Jonathan acquiesced. He smiled at her and said, "Thanks." Then he turned his attention to the hoop—a new, orange, shiny one fixed onto a wooden backboard that could use a paint job and reattachment. He wondered why Silverbirch didn't go modern with everything basketball. Hudson drained nine free throws in a row before missing. "Damn," said Hudson, more to himself. He tossed the ball to April, who threw it back to him, cut for the basket, took a return pass, and gently put the ball through the net.

"Two," said Jonathan. "In your sleep."

"Thanks," she said and drew a deep breath. "I think I need to take a nap or something. I just left home this morning, and the drive was kind of long. Want to get together at dinner?"

"Sure," he said. "Nice knowing you in this other role; not teacher/student."

She smiled. "It's strange for me," she said. "Strange but great." That was the truth. "Bye. See you later," she said, as if she and Jonathan Hudson were long-time friends. April ambled around the main building toward her room. *I'll never be able to tell anyone how handsome he is*, she thought to herself. And then *What's fifteen plus years?*

Approaching her room, she saw a note, on yellow lined paper, taped to her door. It said, "Call Richie." April was perplexed. Who had taken the call and attached the message? She began to walk toward the main desk to find out the origin but realized it did not matter and returned to her room. Richie was trying to reach her. She was here, in a known land she had convinced herself to be her secret, and he was home. That morning, though, just before sitting on one of her bags to get it shut, April had tossed in a prom photo from Point Lookout. She had asked Hudson to take the picture with the small camera she had carried to the beach that night. She and Richie were wet and happy, and she wanted that drenched memory to travel with her. Her impulse was to immediately call Richie, but, exhausted, she resisted. Instead, she laid down on her bed and stared at the ceiling before falling asleep.

The nap lasted all of twenty-five minutes or so, but April felt she'd slept for half the day.

She was conflicted: Should she get ready for dinner or call Richie? How would she reach him? The old pay phone in the dining hall was available, but she would have to reverse the charges. She didn't have enough change to pay for long distance. Still, this was a priority.

She wanted to look fresh for dinner, so she first put on a clean, sky blue, collared shirt. This was a moment to toss the jersey, which was old and still true to her. Even though the Cousy no longer fit the way it once did, she would still wear it at Silverbirch. With forty minutes until dinner, April took the path up the hill toward the dining area.

She put a dime in the slot of the pay phone and awaited a response. When the operator came on, April gave the number and asked that the charges be reversed. Nervous that Richie's parents might answer, she was thrilled when she heard Richie accept the call.

"April," said Richie and nothing further.

"Richie, I already miss you," she said. She was certain that this was true, but it confused her to say so.

"I only want the best for you." He paused. "Would there be a time when I can visit, maybe in three or four weeks—or two?"

"I think so, but I have to be here, to do my job here, and actually begin Silverbirch summer, Richie, before I can say for sure," she said.

"I just don't want to erase what we had this spring, April."

"Me neither."

She was about to continue when the operator interrupted. Something about stopping or reversing the charges.

"Yes," said Richie.

"Richie, I have to go soon. It's dinnertime, and everyone's coming in."

"Okay. See you?"

"Yes," she said, and then, "Bye for now."

She sat with the other support staff at a long table. April would be teaching swimming and basketball to the kids. Other counselors would be covering baseball, dance, tennis, crafts and ceramics, and more swimming. They seemed near her age—upper teens or maybe early twenties. She was excited to meet a few people who had been there for previous summers. She kept reminding herself that others thought she had just completed a year of college.

Senior staff members sat in the front of the room, and that is where she saw Jonathan Hudson flanked on either side by a pretty woman around his age. *As it should be*, she thought. She was staring at him when he looked directly at her and smiled. He moved his head backward and to the side as if signaling something.

Before she could decipher what Hudson was trying to say, the camp director, Denny, began addressing the group. "Welcome, all, to Silverbirch summer," he said. "This will be the best ever, my fifth here. Look around and know that you are a member of the highest-quality group of leaders in the Catskills. Let's do self-introductions and, after we eat, talk more." One by one, each of April's new friends stood and identified themselves.

After the meal, which included roast chicken, sweet potatoes, and vegetables, the staff helped themselves to dessert and coffee before Denny talked again. This time, he was full of spirit and energy and catering to the clientele. "We serve those who vacation here, group. My father is a retailer, and he frequently advises me that the customer is always right. You've each been hired not only because you have skills but also for your warmth and ability to relate. The kids—some of them are boys and girls of privilege—have been given a lot, and they expect that to continue here. Ultimately, they pay your salary. Without them, no program, no camp. Okay?"

Pretty much everyone in the room nodded at once. Jonathan, again, looked at April, this time rolling his eyes. He gestured, with his thumb, toward the side door and porch. When the staff was dismissed, April walked outside to the porch, where Jonathan Hudson awaited her.

"Hokey, huh?" Hudson asked.

"Is this the way it usually goes?"

"More or less. Party line for a summer resort: We are here to please and pamper. I have to tell you, though, that I like it here. Reasonable money, excellent company, and even a few patrons who have become my friends."

"Wow. I don't know," said April. It was all so new to her.

"Could we go for another walk?" Jonathan asked. "It wouldn't be, well, inappropriate? I keep asking you the same thing, huh?"

Thinking that some people would find this idea questionable, she was, nevertheless, eager. "Where to?"

"Follow me."

April expected a return to the pond, the likely and nearby getaway spot. Instead, Hudson led her up the hill toward the tennis courts. The red clay was smoothed out, and the lines were neatly drawn.

"Do you play?" he asked.

"Not well," she replied. "Pretty much only when we vacationed here. It's mostly basketball for me these days."

"I grew up near a playground where the tennis and basketball courts were adjacent. We would play twos and threes on a hoop and, exhausted, knock around the tennis ball after we could barely stand up. It was fun and, since we weren't any good, not nearly as competitive as hoops. Come on," he said.

As they walked down the slope beyond the tennis courts, April wondered why she had never explored this area before. It was dusk, and the sky was deep purple. Jonathan pointed to a couple of blue jays that seemed to await them. April thought she saw horses in the distance. Is that where they were headed?

Then Hudson stopped. "You've intrigued me because of your writing, April," he said.

She thought it was a great line but did not respond.

He continued, "It's a combination of imagination and lack of fear, isn't it?"

This time, she knew he wanted a reply. "I've been making up stories since I was very little, maybe seven or so. My dad, who is good with his hands, built a miniature stage for me in our basement. My parents found little figures to go along with this playhouse. So, I wrote lines for different characters I was thinking about."

"You were writing plays when you were seven years old?"

"I guess."

"That's why you have your unusual feel for conversations in the stories that engaged me." He then shifted the conversation. "I call this tree Methuselah. I'm not a scientist, so I'm not good at specific analysis in this area. I just say it's a thousand years old."

"You teach and talk and write," said April. "You should be telling this story. Jonathan, it's getting dark. Shouldn't we get back? I'm totally exhausted. I can't believe this morning I was on Long Island. It feels like days ago."

"Sorry, April. I wanted to show off this view and the tree in this light," he said. "I sometimes do Christmas break vacation here. I'm sure you know about non-brutal tackle football in the snow. Well, one winter we devised a game within the tennis courts, taking advantage of the poles and also avoiding them. It was a continuous game of tag during which the markers were home bases, just for relief. Talking about it now, I'm amazed no one skidded into a pole or something. Where I'm going with this is that a few years ago, we strayed beyond and someone had decorated that tree with silver bulbs and bangles. Blazing white on white. Incredible to behold. I wish you could have seen it!"

April, enthralled, was also overly tired, and she knew it. "I need sleep," was all she could say.

"I can see that, and I've dragged you here. I apologize," said Jonathan Hudson, her former teacher and current peer.

• • • ● • ● ● ● • • •

Silverbirch summer, during its first week, did not disappoint. April loved the routine: breakfast, morning classes or workshops, lunch, afternoon games, dinner, and then maybe listening to records or a square dance or time to read. She and Jonathan Hudson were on different schedules, except for meals and ball games.

They would meet on the dirt court. He liked to pass the basketball to her with precision. He was so tall, but she could see that he must like to control a game from the top of the key. An accurate shooter, that aspect of the game seemed of little interest to him. It was all about flow and sharing the ball—even when it was just the two of them.

April could not help but muse about him. She was certain he must have a life partner. She remembered the time he took her on that walk, how excited he was and how he pushed the pace to the tennis courts and the glorious, special tree. She kept thinking about him, wishing she knew more about him. He was often so calm yet, as a teacher, excited.

The second week was even more fun. April took a group of kids to the highway overpass. They waved to speeding cars below and received as responses flashing lights, loud horn toots, and friendly gestures from the drivers. The goal was to score a massive blast of noise out of one of those massive trailer trucks from a guy who might be motoring all the way to Canada. Recognition!

• • • ● • ● • ● • • •

Richie called on a Thursday evening and asked if it would be okay for him to come up and stay from Friday till Sunday. Although she was unsure if that's what she wanted, April said, "I would love that." She didn't know where he would sleep, where she wanted him to sleep, with whom (if anyone) to share the news, or how to handle the visit. The Silverbirch policy was that staff members could have visitors. April decided not to ask for more specifics. She didn't know what to wear, if she should plan anything, or where to go. What she did know was that she had to say yes, and she convinced herself she would be enthusiastic when he arrived.

April then reconsidered and chose to tell Jonathan Hudson, at Friday breakfast, that Richie would be there that night.

"Your boyfriend, you mean?"

"I don't know."

"I saw you two together all the time during the lame-duck days for seniors. Lovebirds," he said.

April saw ducks and birds before her eyes. "We've been friends forever," she said. "This other thing just happened. I don't know."

"It only gets more complicated, believe me."

She knew nothing of Jonathan Hudson's personal life except that many months back a beautiful red-haired woman, sitting in the stands, came up to him at halftime and after the high school faculty game. He could be married, divorced . . . April could not believe that he didn't have, at the very least, a girlfriend. When April mused about Hudson, this was a fixed part of the equation.

April was lost in thought when he continued, "Could you even consider growing right along with him, adapting, accommodating for a few years, maybe a long time? I wasn't so good with that."

Was this man, her teacher, about to spill details of his intimate life to her? April definitely wasn't ready for this. Her focus was on trying, without enough time, to prepare for Richie's arrival.

And yet she asked for more. "We probably have different definitions of love, Jonathan. I mean . . ."

He interrupted. "You mean to say that I'm a lot older than you are. I know. I've seen more. Well, seen isn't exactly the word for it," he added. "You clearly have affection for Richie."

"It would be fine if it was just dinner," she said. "But all weekend?"

"I get it," Hudson replied. "But it's hours away. First, we have this day to get through."

It was almost 8:00 a.m., and workshops began in thirty minutes.

"Thanks," said April.

"For?"

"Saying lovebirds. It's true. Or it was. Or it might be."

"We can sit together at lunch, too," said Jonathan.

She reached out and touched his wrist, and then they went separate ways.

April's mind raced with everything that was going on: being in a familiar yet new place, on her own for the first time; the undefined but closer relationship with Jonathan; the easy job responsibilities; the husbands she had watched coming, staying a night, and then leaving; the kids, some of whom were delightful and others spoiled; and maybe a few new friends. Now this: her first love—but what, really, is love?—arriving at day's end. He would stay in her room and probably end up in her bed, too. How could she possibly process all of this?

Images swirled in her head as she made her way from the dining hall to the volleyball court. Her job, when asked to assist with this game, was to teach the kids how to set and serve; a couple of them might be able to spike the ball. Not that April was ever all that proficient with the sport, but her exceptional hand/eye coordination on the basketball court was an asset. As a little girl, she had enjoyed watching others pop the ball, overhand, above the net and onto a vacant patch of dirt. The day was glorious: high sun, just a few clouds, deeply set trees in the background. If only she could paint, but that was not one of her talents.

Then it was time for swimming, which meant a bathing suit. She was self-conscious about her appearance. The food at Silverbirch was both plentiful and delicious, and she could not resist the nearby bagel shop. April refrained from looking in a mirror, heeding her mom's advice. Hudson, observing her each day, could see she was bigger. If she ever asked, April knew he would say something like, "You're a woman now."

April imagined herself replying, "Very different from the girl who was your student?"

She squirmed into the suit, which she knew was snug, and decided that this was a good look. She did not live at home anymore where the phrase cover-up carried more than one meaning.

Swim, as she expected, was joyful. Kids splashed in the pool, and, every so often, one would emulate April, who was demonstrating the crawl and a basic breathing technique. Other children hadn't any interest whatsoever. April was glad she had completed senior lifesaving, which was an essential now, allowing her to teach. Water was a tonic for most everyone, and that included April, who was glad not to ponder men and boys for that hour. Playing in the pool, working with little ones—this was fun.

Chapter Six

Richie's Visit

HUDSON SOUGHT HER OUT at lunch. "I shouldn't have been so jokey or whatever about you and Richie. So sorry," he said.

"I didn't feel that," said April. "It was kind of nice, actually, to get your reaction. Who could have guessed that Mr. Hudson would be my best friend at a summer job?"

"Watching kids grow from ninth grade through senior year, well, that's a mini-lifetime. You probably can't imagine what it's like to observe the changes. I would think you would be more than thrilled to see Richie."

"We know each other from our houses and the park and school. This is different. I'm suddenly an adult, which, in some ways, isn't that hard to get used to. It's not like we were boyfriend and girlfriend for a year at a college. We were brother and sister, sort of." She pressed her hands together. "Then, suddenly, we were like this. I don't know what he expects." April was eating leftover breakfast for lunch. The cooks always offered morning goodies, and she loved omelets. Hudson took two hamburger patties and put them between a water roll: his meal.

April had an hour before successive sports blocks. First, basketball for kids thirteen and under. It was perfect: April was close enough in age to remember what it felt like to be that young, and she was confident that she could be helpful. Basketball would be followed by an all-camp jog around the property. Several different courses had been developed and marked. By groups, all the kids would trek through. It wasn't a speed test or competition. At the end, everyone participating received something: a feather, a lanyard, a bookmark, a tennis ball. Nobody left empty-handed. Of course, one always wanted what another one had: "Your rabbit's foot is bigger than mine." "Yours is fuzzier." It was tough to satisfy everyone. On the other hand, not one child got left out: Each person was rewarded.

An hour or so until dinner. April opted for a lengthy shower, hoping the driving spray and solitude would bring clarity. No Richie, not for a couple of hours; and no Jonathan, either. Standing there, soaking herself within the pounding, silvery beads, April thought she heard a knock on her door. She flew out of the shower, tried to dry herself, covered up with the white terry cloth robe, and went to see if anyone was there.

"April?" She was both startled and relieved to hear Richie's familiar voice. He was at least an hour early. "What should I do? Is it you, April?"

Standing on the other side of the door, dripping, April said, "Of course. You know it is. Come in, Richie."

He walked through the door, and April, her robe coming loose, lunged into his arms. The heat from his body radiated as sweat from his forehead rolled down his cheeks.

"Looks as if you've been playing one-on-one for an hour," she said.

"I wish—with you," said Richie. "You're beautiful. I'm sorry, but I've wanted to be with you since you left, April."

She felt that part, too—missing Richie. If Jonathan were not here, April admitted to herself, she would have been absolutely longing for Richie.

She blurted out, "Jonathan Hudson is around. He's always shooting foul shots."

"Wow. Is he still talking about downers like *Long Day's Journey into Night*, which we had to read in school?"

April leaned further into him and said, "You're tall."

He laughed and said, "April, I'm exactly the same as I was two weeks ago."

"I see you differently," she answered and wondered exactly what she meant.

"It might take me more than ninety seconds to assess you. I'm just relieved to see you."

"I know," said April, not knowing what to do next—other than hold him. She pulled him to the bed.

They bounced and wrestled, and April made a halfhearted attempt to fasten the terry cloth robe. Within seconds, it fell away as Richie grappled with his T-shirt. They embraced and kissed one another until April, within Richie's arms, said, "I have to go to dinner soon. You, too; I told them a friend was coming."

"My stuff is in my car, April. What should I do with it?"

"Bring it in here, Richie. Then wash up and walk up the hill with me to dinner."

Within moments, they were slowly making their way, hand in hand, toward the dining hall. Jonathan was standing on the porch with others, as they arrived.

"Richard," he said.

"Mr. Hudson," Richie replied.

"From now on, call me Jonathan—much friendlier, and this isn't school. Thank God it's not," he said. "Another familiar human makes it even better here. It's already pretty great, right, April?"

"Better by the day," she said, her head spinning as she watched the two of them together.

"Hey, let's go in and eat," said Jonathan. They followed his lead.

When everyone was settled in, after evening announcements, Jonathan introduced Richie to the rest of the table, calling him "a rising star—on the court and in the classroom. He could start for many college hoops teams, and he's a young essayist. Welcome to Silverbirch, Richie."

Richie blushed, unsure whether he should respond. He nodded his head and said, "April and I have been friends since we were little kids."

"Sister and brother," April added. When she touched Richie's wrist, she realized that this calmed her. "We met when we were six, and we're three weeks apart in age. Neither of us has brothers and sisters."

"We just happened to be a boy and a girl," added Richie, "and even that didn't keep us from being apart. Just now, we're figuring out what it all means."

"She can really play. That's what I have to add," said Jonathan. "You probably know that." (He nodded at Richie.) "I'm flipping the lights on after dinner, just in case either of you or both want to join me," he said, finally.

Beginning the actual meal was a relief. Seated between them, though, April found herself barely touching her food while she worried that Richie or Jonathan or both might get up and walk off. That was not the case as a lively conversation began, about college, sports, and life beyond adolescence, that was both informative and fluid.

After dessert, April took Richie's hand and Jonathan said, "I saw the beginning of this at school—and then came the Point Lookout moment. A treasure. See you later." He smiled at each of them.

April led the way back to her room. When they got there, she said, "Put your stuff over there," motioning to the closet. "Let's walk and figure it out."

"I drove up in my car," he said. "*The* car."

April laughed. "Are you suggesting a repeat of the prom, Richie?"

"They have ferries up here?" he asked. "Want to go for a ride?"

"I sort of do. Haven't been off the grounds very much aside from making my way to the bagel shop and back. It's perfect on the weekends. I love the atmosphere there."

As they walked behind the main building, April wondered if people were watching and what they might be thinking.

She opened the passenger door of the car and caught the familiar whiff of sweat and his Old Spice aftershave — so Richie. She felt at ease and as Richie settled in, she slid next to him. It felt like being home. The car, too, had a distinctive personality, rumbling and grumbling as he turned the key, slightly misfiring, then slowly rolling forward. April relaxed and watched as he drove along the bumpy road, which passed the horse farm and the random, dissimilar houses that were so unlike most of the developments and clusters she knew from the Long Island suburbs. The sky was still light, a robin's egg blue. She hugged Richie, and the car swerved but he steadied it.

"Stop on the hilly side of the road," said April.

When Richie did, April said, "Let's slide down."

"Sure, whatever you say."

After exiting the car, they stood at the top of the hill, grabbed each other's hands, and, entwined, began to roll down the gentle slope—laughing, clinging to each other, and collecting grass as they descended.

When they stopped, April jumped onto Richie, kissed him deeply, and said, "I'm so glad you're here." She hoped this would finally become the big moment for the two of them.

"Me, too. I'm wiped out, though, April."

Arriving back at Silverbirch, April led Richie to the main lodge where they swiped three large cushions that they placed on the rug in April's room. Richie slept there as April snuggled, with confounding and conflicting feelings, beneath her quilt. Before sunrise, she awakened and found him sprawled beneath an inadequate, threadbare blanket, April touched Richie's shoulder and motioned for him to get in her bed. He did so without hesitation.

His familiarity was welcome, and April watched Richie breathe softly while his arm rested on her stomach. It wasn't until 8:00 or so that he began to stir.

"Wanna get breakfast or walk with me to get bagels?" she asked.

"Orange juice or coffee or both and then walk?" he responded.

"Good plan. You can shower first."

She watched Richie, whose body was now taut, as he ambled into the shower wearing only his undershorts. He stretched upward, and she smiled. April then took off her clothing and joined him.

Richie stayed an extra day, making it four. He held back tears when, after dinner on Monday, he left.

April tried not to show her emotions. On the one hand, she felt certain she would marry him. Why not? They had been close and newly closer, and she expected this would continue forever. "Marry your best friend and you will live happily into old age." At least, that's what her mother always advised.

April, though, was still only eighteen, even if almost everyone at Silverbirch was certain she had just celebrated her nineteenth birthday. If someone asked her a question about college, she just made up an answer. Like a game.

She was in love with Richie, but she told herself things with him wouldn't be a slam dunk until each had navigated college. By then, if the bond had been sealed, why not confirm its longevity with a wedding? That part could very well be in the script.

April watched as Richie drove slowly down the dirt road, which soon merged with pavement. She thought he just might make a U-turn and stay. She knew she needed more time, more space. Yet, if he had stayed, she would not have been upset. April's imagined story line saw them coming together till the end of time—eventually. As the car disappeared from view, she sighed deeply and her shoulders relaxed. This really was better.

• • • • • • • • • • •

"I'm sorry," Jonathan said in his familiar baritone. He was walking toward an Adirondack chair shaded by a grand willow as Richie drove off.

April shrugged and looked away. She wondered if Hudson had witnessed the previous scene.

"Want a hug?" Jonathan asked.

He was too caring and respectful to be true. Almost saintly, thought April. But what about another aspect of his personality—the passion he spoke with when helping his students interpret a Thomas Hardy novel for AP English?

Suddenly, without taking the time to contemplate what she was doing, she blurted out, "Have you ever been married?"

"Yes," he immediately answered. "College sweetheart. Things were perfect for five years, and then . . ." He hesitated. "Well, it ended."

April heard regret, and she looked him in the eye. "Five years is more than a quarter of my life," she said. "Richie and I—we've lived next door forever, but this . . . this part between us only began, really, in early spring."

"Yeah, but I've had the two of you in class for a few years. You've always exchanged these knowing looks, like you're in the same family," Hudson said. "Sensing each other."

"Or when we were playing pickup and I was the only girl, he and I had this eye contact thing," she said.

"You probably won't believe this, but the woman I married was named June. Then there's you—April."

She couldn't resist asking, "What about May?"

"I had a cousin named May, but I haven't seen her in at least a dozen years and I cannot imagine our paths crossing again. She married an Orthodox Jew. To each her own, but it's hard for me to embrace such rigidity."

"Again, back to your teachings, Jonathan. English literature was obviously your favorite. We kept hearing about freedom of expression and, to use your phrase, 'no dogma, please.'"

He nodded and smiled. "I guess, April. Well-worn."

"What was June like?"

"A tennis player. One of the reasons I first came here, to Silverbirch, was because she knew of the clay courts. No other hotel had both green and red. I was—I am—just a hack when it comes to tennis. So, she would use me for a practice wall since all I could do was feebly try to get it back over the net. Len also spoke so highly of this place."

"Going to June, here, when we read a play, you taught us to 'Use adjectives to describe her character.'" April paused.

"One would be strong and two would be rational."

April said, "So, the first applies to you and the second, too. Keep going."

Jonathan motioned to a nearby green wicker two-seater. "Would it be too uncomfortable if we sat together?" he asked.

"I'm so exhausted that standing is a chore," said April as she plopped down.

"The difference between me and June? You might find me thoughtful and, as a teacher, perhaps I am. Otherwise, though, she is level and I'm not."

"Level?" April asked.

"I'm high drama. She has way more control."

April looked at him and saw that, up close, he seemed younger. His face had fewer lines, in reality, than it did when she stared at him from her seat in the classroom. He could be nearer to thirty than forty. Spending the next several weeks around a much older brother she never had? That potential reality was calming.

"You and your wife are not officially over? Spell it out?" April asked.

"Together, not together . . . this has gone on for years. I do not advise it, April." He stood, then sat again. "Like that: one moment up and the next down. I don't know except that I wish she were here," he continued.

She took his hand, and he held hers. It felt natural, right. April wasn't about to overthink the possible implications. She had long fingers that were in proportion to his. Jonathan's grasp was gentle and warm. April began thinking about palming a basketball. Not likely for him nor for her. She had wished and wished to be able to and only recently had accepted that this would not happen. Richie was closer, which meant he could dunk a tennis ball.

April and Jonathan sat quietly together. He gestured toward the sky and a silvery moon sporting a tinge of blue that was making an appearance. April's shoulders relaxed, and her entire body followed suit. She told herself that her former teacher would now be a caring, nurturing friend. This was reassuring, a relief.

She turned to him and asked, "Do you wish it was June and not me sitting here with you?"

"Yes, no," he laughed. "You have this softness about you, always have. Keep it forever, April. June is blazingly smart, but sometimes her intellect gets in the way." He looked directly at April. "I know that you are able to analyze, but it's that creative side, the searching part—like when I saw you looking past me in class—that is unique to you. I would stare at you, as I am now, and you were in another place."

April was surprised and flattered as he continued to hold her hand.

"Jonathan, I was thinking of going to the barn to listen to the music they have tonight."

"Let's do that," he said.

"It doesn't start for an hour," she replied.

"I'll take you up on the catwalk."

April had wanted to be both on the stage and behind it, so there was no way could she refuse Jonathan's offer. They were setting up on the makeshift stage for two folksingers. Hudson seemed to know everyone at Silverbirch, including one young man she hadn't met, someone around her age who was checking sound.

"Good to see you exploring, Samuel," said Hudson to the smiling boy. "Have you met April? She's teaching swimming, basketball and helping elsewhere as necessary. This is her first year working at Silverbirch."

"I've seen you," Samuel said to her. "Whatever I can do, please call on me."

She smiled and nodded, then leaned toward Hudson and whispered in his ear, "Who's that and what does he do?"

"The real question is what *doesn't* he do. He's a handyman for the inn, and it is almost impossible to stump him."

The area above the stage extended to a third of the partially refurbished barn. Before April knew it, Jonathan had one hand around her waist with the other glued to her palm. She was aware that he was guiding her across rickety beams that were none too steady. She welcomed his touch, which was both comforting and assuring.

"Let me show you something, April. Hold onto me till we get to the spot," Hudson said, moving forward very carefully on the beam. The two of them then shifted so that she could get both of her hands behind him, on him, as he navigated. She was fully aware that she was gripping the waistband of her former teacher's pants, but she hadn't another option. Besides, it was fun. They inched along until Jonathan stopped and pointed. The initials A & B were etched into the ceiling above them.

"Whose initials are those?" April asked.

"The Silverbirches before they were married," he said. "A and B for Abby and Ben. I don't know what her last name was. He was always Ben Silverbirch. Did you ever hear him call her Bea? That's his name for her."

April said, "Yes, I always thought that was her actual name."

"Sometimes when you're around them, it's B and B. Confusing, but so romantic."

"You almost cried when you tried to explain the Romantic poets to us. I felt sorry for you since no one else seemed moved and some of the boys snickered behind your back."

"No matter. I reach one kid and that's reward enough," said Hudson. "Look here, it's a red A & B with a heart and an arrow through it all."

"The Silverbirches were around and visible for a Valentine's Day weekend when our family was here," said April.

"You are a young lady with imagination, so I should tell you that the Silverbirches couldn't do much up here. It's about keeping balance or tumbling to the floor, which must be painful and embarrassing and maybe both," he said—and then slipped. April grabbed him, they tottered, and he steadied both of them.

Just a few seconds later, they were laughing loudly as Jonathan shushed her. He led her across the catwalk till they were near a none-too-stable heavyweight ladder that stretched from a beam to the floor below. Slowly, rung by rung, Hudson and then April descended. At the bottom, his hands encircled April's waist and he drew her toward him. She gladly acquiesced.

April, with a calm that surprised her, walked with Jonathan back to her room, where she explained that, given the events of the day, she needed time to herself, time to consider.

Hudson, with a courtly demeanor that became him, immediately bid her goodnight and ambled off, his gait accelerating as he scaled the hill to senior staff housing.

Finally, April was alone, able to shut her door, plop down on her bed, and cuddle with White Bear, her childhood stuffed animal who had survived April's adolescence. Here, she found a true and long-lasting confidant. As a girl, she had grown up very much by herself—with her parents, Richie, and a handful of friends. Now, she wasn't sure to whom she should turn. Even if she wished to avoid making a choice between Richie and Jonathan, April could not help but compare the two. She had foreseen a summer of complexity, given her outright lie about her age and experience. Six months ago, to state the obvious, Jonathan was her favorite teacher and Richie was her best friend. But she had never expected all this.

She tried inhaling deeply. Bert had instructed her about breathing since he was trying a technique to lessen stress: in through the nose and slowly out through the mouth. One of his guidance counselor friends had read of this.

Moments later, though, April wanted conversation. Richie might be home by now, and she could try calling him. Or, she could track down Jonathan Hudson—and hope that she didn't knock on his door and interrupt something.

She went after Hudson. He answered and, as if anticipating April, ushered her in with a sweep of his hand. He was wearing gym shorts, and that was all. Jonathan looked around for a top and, opening his middle bureau drawer, grabbed an old, frayed collared shirt, bright white, with an embossed brown bear positioned so that it lay flat upon his chest. As he flipped the shirt over his head, April could not help but watch and note the tapering V formed from the line of Hudson's shoulders to his midsection.

"Sorry about that."

"What?" Classical music filled the room, and she knew it but could not decide if it was Beethoven or Tchaikovsky.

"I was half-undressed."

"No, it's . . . it's free time. I'm fine with that," said April, inwardly dismayed with her lame response.

"Well, this is surprising for me, too—that it's not awkward, I mean. When you told me you would be here, I was glad, really happy. I mean, when you told me you'd be coming to Silverbirch."

"Your wife, though," said April, bringing this up once again.

"Time and distance help," he said. "April, I am still the same man you see at the front of the classroom," he added.

"It's already different, though, Jonathan," she said and realized she was easier using his first name. "Like the rafter walk. I mean, you know."

"It was confusing to me as well," he said, "the part when we fell into each other, not as teacher and student, April."

"That's the problem. Maybe 'problem' is the wrong word, but it was easy and sweet. That's why I came here."

"To answer your question, I'm not seeing my wife and I don't love her anymore. I do miss her. We were together here a few summers. So, there's that—the usual spots like the apple trees and the pond and more remind me of her.

"And the catwalk?" asked April.

"No. That was only the second time I've been up there, and it's been a couple of years. First, it was by myself and now with you."

"You made it seem like this is a routine you know well."

"My style with women, I confess, is to pretend to be knowledgeable."

April was unaccustomed to being referred to as a woman. When people from her parents' generation greeted her, they called her a girl or maybe a young lady. Still in her late teens, she was in between: a college kid but no longer in high school.

"I'm not used to someone so . . ."

"Old?" he interrupted.

"No, just not in my age group," she said. "Maybe it's not great for me to be in your room."

"I'm harmless, April," he said. "Not a threat."

She had known as much but appreciated the reassurance nonetheless. "Walk me back?" April asked.

"Sure."

They were silent until they reached her room. It was nearly 9:00 or so and just now fully dark. April said, "Jonathan, come in but just for a little while. It feels like the sun just went down." She motioned inside.

"Twenty minutes sound about right?"

She nodded, and he walked to the bed and sat at the foot of it. Even though she would be there for just a couple of months, April had meant to buy one or two things for her space but hadn't yet found time to do that. Besides, were there the right stores around here? As it was, she had an old wooden chair, a matching desk, and the bed. She took the chair, faced it at Jonathan, and sat cross-legged on it.

"Don't worry, April," he said.

"Thanks. This is a bit awkward."

"To thine own self be true," he said.

"And as sure as night follows day, thou canst not be false to any man," concluded April.

"Or woman," he said, and they both laughed.

"Ten more minutes," said April.

"You were an exacting young woman, and I noticed this when you were first in my class a few years ago."

"What do you mean?"

"I would return a paper with compliments on it, and this didn't especially please you. If I said 'excellent work,' that wasn't nearly specific enough. You wanted criticism."

"I never thought much of my own writing, and I guess could not believe that you did," she said.

"You write natural dialogue, April. You cannot teach ear," Jonathan said.

"Thank you, I guess. You never put it that way," she said and felt stupid for sitting with her legs crossed beneath her on a wooden seat three feet from the teacher she had fantasized about.

"Time's almost up," he said, checking his watch.

"Nine-thirty," April said. "I will get bagels really early tomorrow morning before camp begins." She then yawned. "It's not you, Jonathan. These days have felt like a week, with Richie, the walk over the barn floor, slipping, now this."

"Yes," he said. "Time for me to go, April. Good night." When he extended his hand to her, she took it, pressed it between both of hers, and let it go.

"See you soon, Jonathan," she said as he stood and walked out the door, shutting it gently behind him.

April slept from ten at night till nine the next morning, when she awakened to music. Her schedule granted her a bit of a break: a day off. It sounded as though Bobby Vinton was singing "She wore blue velvet" right outside her door. That could not be. She quickly put on her green Celtics sweatshirt and pulled the door open. With no one within view, she wondered about the source of the tune while listening to the verses. April went back inside, quickly splashed water on her face, pulled on shorts and tennis shoes, and walked back outside. This time, no further Vinton. She suspected the noise had come from the barn, which must have been a hundred yards away. Silverbirch's main buildings were compressed together, while the far lodge (appropriately named) was out of earshot. The birch trees seemed to shine with illuminated white and black.

She heard voices within the barn, then "Embraceable You" with Frank Sinatra. The music made her think of her father. The rickety door was propped open, so she went inside, where she saw someone new to her: Lee. She had heard of Lee. He was always just "Lee" without a last name, and he was an Elvis impersonator who also did Fats Domino. She didn't know much about Fats Domino other than his song "Blueberry Hill."

April thought about her preference for the color blue in songs—"She Wore Blue Velvet," "Blueberry Hill," and there were probably more. With a handheld microphone, Lee was sashaying back and forth, mouthing lyrics as he watched his feet. His black hair was slicked back and formed a V at the rear center point of his neck. Lee was glistening from exertion, and it was only then that April remembered he was headlining in the barn that night. Starring at Silverbirch?

Smiling, she turned away.

Chapter Seven

Bagel City

WITHOUT RETURNING TO HER room, a half-dressed April began the thirty-minute walk toward Bagel City. She found this a comic name for a place in the rural Hudson Valley. It was easy enough to remember, though.

April especially liked going there to see Viv, who operated the store. April had never really given much thought to it before, but it was certainly true that, for the most part, men ran businesses back home: the ice cream shop, the deli, the bakery. The hair salon was an exception, with a husband and wife co-managing.

She liked talking to Viv, who had a given French name of Vivienne and had lived a bit of her life in New York. To get to Bagel City, April walked down the main road, where she soon came face-to-face with a soft-looking deer just about her height. The deer looked directly at her without flinching, and April stared into the animal's eyes for perhaps a couple of minutes. Instead of turning, the deer slowly crossed the road and suddenly sprinted past

April into the woods. A few more turns till Viv's place.

Golden sunshine enveloped the shop on this Tuesday morning. To her delight, April opened the door and Viv, behind the counter, smiled. It was a relief to have a friend who wasn't a boy or a man.

"Plain with butter and toasted, April?" Viv asked.

"You know," said April.

"You've only been coming here for a few weeks, and already you're a regular," said Viv.

"Is that Vivaldi?" April asked of the lovely music filling the Bagel City confines. Viv had the screen door open. The orchestral sound of strings streamed outward.

"I often put the LP on my record player, yes," she answered. "Not that much that begins with V, you know."

"It's one of the few classical pieces I can identify. My English teacher, Jonathan Hudson, every so often had it on for first-period class. Not only was it beautiful, but he absolutely blasted it. His students liked him, but maybe not so much when he urged us to read classic American and British novels. Before too long, though, I looked forward even to that."

"Well, it's relaxing and also driving—the beginning section," said Viv, who soon had April's bagel ready.

April took the bagel, and Viv gestured to a counter seat. April was more than pleased to be invited to stay and talk.

"Viv, how long have you been here?" April asked.

"Eight years—the first four with my husband and almost four more running the shop all by myself. I was here, I'm pretty sure, when you and your family came for vacations," she said. Before April could ask, Viv said, "We're still friends, and every so often we talk about getting back together. He works at Silverbirch, so you might know him. Lee?"

April was stunned. She had just watched the man, caught by his energy and physique. "When I was I was about ten, we came to Silverbirch just for a weekend to see the place and the next summer for a great week." She paused. "Before walking here, I saw Lee practicing in the barn."

Viv continued, "When we bought Bagel City from a guy named Simon—it was partly for the shop and partly so Lee could perform at Silverbirch on the weekends. He sings."

"I just saw him working on an amazing version of 'Blue Suede Shoes.'"

"A long while ago, he was a dancer who was just learning how to sing," said Vivienne.

"And then?"

"He's a beautiful man," said Viv. "We grew up in adjoining towns, suburbs of Boston. I was a cheerleader, and he was a quarterback. We were at rival schools, and the two of us came together."

"Richie and I were in the same schools all the way through," April said. "We lived next door to each other, and neither of us had siblings."

"He's your boyfriend?"

"Best friend for sure and boyfriend for the past few months. Now, I'm confused."

"I know what that's like," said Vivienne. "When things are not clear, murky, you don't know where to go, how to navigate. Part of the time, you think he's Mr. Right."

"What happened with Lee and you?" April asked and then said, "I can see why you were attracted."

"Exactly. He would perform at Silverbirch, and girls—young women–literally swooned."

"I would imagine that's not the greatest for a marriage," said April.

Viv shook her head from side to side and shrugged. "It wasn't like he was having an affair or a couple of them. I was so jealous, though. Now, there's this part of me that wants to be openly envious of you. It's easy to see why men would fall for you."

The Vivaldi continued as April felt the sun's warmth seep in the screen door, a dry heat permeating Bagel City. She was most accustomed to shorts and a T-shirt and felt overdressed and overheated.

"You don't happen to have a plain white T-shirt that I could change into, do you?" April asked.

Viv started laughing. "You think I just have a supply of clothing back here? Wanna wear a Bagel City T and stand outside the door? You'll bring them in—men, that is."

April blushed. "I'm just overheated," she said.

Vivienne tossed her a white T with black lettering across the front, and April took the shirt to the restroom and changed. "I think it's a fit, huh? I love it," she said.

"If Lee saw you, he'd be jumping your bones in a flash," said Viv.

The Vivaldi was winding down and, as Viv bent to flip the record over, April asked, "Did you know Lee was the one?"

"Until he wasn't, sweetheart. Even now, a small voice inside of me has hopes. It was better here with him, and he isn't much more than a mile away."

"I do know what it's like to miss someone who is a part of you. I mean, Richie and I have been together since my earliest memories. What we've been to each other can never be erased."

Viv sat down beside April. "Woman to woman, April: If you never open up, you lose possibility."

"But just what is real?" April asked Vivienne.

"For me, this. The store. What I do each day. Seeing you now. If I can touch it, it exists. A bagel and a beautiful young woman are real," she answered. "Of course, this was a joint venture, with Lee. If it all worked out, we were going to expand into a restaurant or a café with books—one of the two."

"Your place is so cool. Bagels, like from the city or the suburbs, up here in the Catskills. I think it's about how warm and friendly you are, Viv. That's why people come in."

"How did you become such a sweetheart? Richie's lucky. I can say that for sure. Stay and talk with me for a while? What do you want to hear?"

"Okay. Do you have any Beach Boys?"

"'All Summer Long' from last year is so great. Yes?"

Viv put on the record, and they began to dance—first separately, then together—and took turns either singing or mouthing the lyrics. Soon, they were outside the shop as two cars drove up. The morning patrons seemed enthralled with both women who appeared to be having the best of times. Viv took a break to prepare a few bagels and then resumed her conversation with April.

"It's just comfortable here," April said. "Not that I don't like Silverbirch. I do. The job, working with kids, it's totally fine. More than fine. And I'm good at it: Teaching swimming is different, and basketball is my passion."

"So is it the social stuff?" Viv asked.

"Yes. Richie just visited, and I'm positive that he'd move right into my room if I just nodded my head. But there's Jonathan."

"He's my age, April."

"I know. He was my most influential high school teacher. Besides, he's kind, and he just gets it. I mean, he just sort of understands a lot about me. Richie's a Hudson fan as well."

"Consider this an oasis; get away from overthinking when you come here for a bagel. Dance to the

Beach Boys, and I have The Beatles, too. The Vivaldi was on to calm me down," added Viv.

"Keep playing music, and we can dance and sing," said April. "I don't have to be back at Silverbirch—my day off."

April spent the rest of the day and part of the evening, well after the shop officially closed, with Viv. Viv kept the door open after hours and, to her surprise, half a dozen people wandered in and, even more unusual, asked for several bagels to go—not sandwiches with spread.

The following Sunday, encouraged by Viv, April was back at nine, beaming, happy to spend a mellow morning with Viv, the store copy of the *New York Times*, and a pitch-perfect recording of the *Brandenburg Concertos*. April wore a lime green T-shirt with AAU embossed on the front and Cousy's number 14 on the back.

"Bright suits you, April," said Viv, who had on a light blue denim, short-sleeve top and khaki shorts. "Don't say it. I know I'm wearing a nice outfit for a bagel store proprietor. I would say you are looking a little today like private school."

"You're not one type, Viv. Each time I'm here you style differently."

They were laughing when Jonathan drove up and parked.

"Wow," said April to Viv before going to greet Jonathan.

"I'm not a stalker," he said, rolling down the driver side window. "Just a transplanted New Yorker in search of a plain bagel with cream cheese schmear. Oh, my. Brandenburg. What a perfect choice on a day like this. My mother used to tell me I could find my reflection in the sky on a cloudless summer day. No truth to it, but I would try. It seems that romantic."

"Come in, Jonathan," said Viv, walking behind April.

"Sure, thanks. You don't mind, April?"

April knew the morning would be different from the previous time she was at Viv's—not necessarily better or worse, just different. She had, however, envisioned another relaxing day with just Viv and some bagel buyers.

"Vivienne, have you heard that very young British cellist, Jacqueline du Pré? Her first LP is out. I'm just wondering if she was part of a Brandenburg recording session."

Viv, preparing Jonathan's bagel, shook her head from side to side. "I've heard of her, sure. Not aware of a record. I'm the first to admit that my world, these days, begins and ends up here in the Catskills. It was a little different in the city."

"What borough? You don't have the accent, but you don't have the upstate twang either," said Hudson.

"Both of my parents grew up in the Bronx, but we moved to the Boston suburbs just before I turned four," Viv said.

"I lived up the block from Washington Square Park after my family left sleepy Rome, New York," said Jonathan. "We next moved to the Island." He turned to Viv. "I spent most of my boyhood in Long Beach. Those connections eventually got me the job at Point Lookout. Remember, April?"

"Unforgettable," said April. "You had this foot-long gun hanging from your belt. Teach us about plough shares and then show the pistol," she added.

He started to laugh. "I'm not the strongest-looking guy, so they needed to give me a weapon," Jonathan said. "The two of you, on that evening? You might as well have eloped."

"That obvious?" April asked.

"It was impossible not to notice that you both were practically undressed as you waded in and out of the ocean. I let you go but was actually worried. Drunk on love or whatever. It was sweet but, given my job, I probably should have shooed you away."

"Not totally sorry but a little bit?" April said. "I was a little shocked to see you. Actually, a lot. The whole night with the Copa, the Staten Island Ferry, and then someone who looked just like my favorite teacher but couldn't be, really. Well . . ."

"You could have been swept out in the riptide or an undertow. Nobody ever believes it can happen. Neither did I until I was caught in one."

"Tell me, Jonathan," said April.

"A few years back, I was lifeguarding at the beach. It was at the beginning of the season, end of June. After my shift ended, I decided to swim and maybe a hundred yards out, I got caught," he said, shaking his head as if it had just happened. "I thought I could swim my way out of it even though I was the one who told everyone not to fight but try to just stay parallel until help came."

"So?"

"After a brief panic, since it had me and not the reverse, I decided to tread water. And it worked. My fellow lifeguard, who was a woman, summoned another guard from a chair down the way. They got me onto what is a kind of lifeboat, and I was fine. Shaken, as you can hear in my voice even now, but unharmed. Physically okay."

"You still swim way out there?"

"I'm mostly an off-season guy now, April. I suppose it's safer to be up here in the hills and valleys," he said.

Viv, who had brought Jonathan his bagel and a ginger ale earlier, silently listened.

"We would go to some beach at least every other late spring and summer Sunday for years," she said. "My mother pushed for this, and my older sister acted as if we were going to jail. As soon as we got there, Mom and Valerie would head for the snack bar."

"V for the children's names, huh?" April asked.

"Yes. My father and I would swim in pools, too. I loved chlorine, the way it stuck like paste to my body. I felt it would help my tan. Dad claimed he was a lap swimmer; maybe between one and three was his limit," Viv said. "How are you, Hud?" she asked after a pause.

April knew about the movie of that name since it had come out during her sophomore year and she had gone to see it with Richie. This was well before they were a couple, but she remembered that he had put his arm around her shoulder at her seat at the theater. Vivienne calling Jonathan Hudson "Hud," though—that meant something, it seemed to her.

"You know each other," April stated rather than questioned.

The pause spoke for itself.

"Yes. We met quite some time ago when Lee and I were roommates in the barn," Jonathan said.

"Only natural for me to call him Hud," said Viv. "Jonathan is a long name."

Vivienne stepped away and, since the classical music was over, placed an LP on her turntable, dropping the needle to allow for Bob Dylan's nasal voice to issue forth with "It Ain't Me Babe" and, soon enough, she and Jonathan sang along.

April was certain there was more to be said when the words were about, really, a relationship that was no longer. She thought it best to be quiet.

As if anticipating, Viv said, "We're not involved in the way you might imagine, April. It was an emotional time for each of us when we met." She eyed Jonathan. "Lee was, I thought, completely absorbed with his work. It was his life."

"And my marriage," said Jonathan, "well, it was long over. I was just so tensed up all the time. I still think it was about more than me. I don't know if she wanted to be married. I came to Bagel City a couple of times, and pretty soon Viv and I were close."

"I would see him coming and douse an egg bagel with cream cheese, pour a coffee, and . . ."

"It would be a couple of hours before I left," said Jonathan. "An oasis for me."

"These records, April? Hud brought in a lot of them, and he just left them."

Finally, April asked, "What about now?"

Jonathan said, "Each of us is unattached. I guess we're seeing what happens?"

"What about you two?" Viv asked.

April, her face immediately reddening, quickly said, "He was my favorite teacher. Classic American and British Novels was my favorite class. Mr. Hudson—Jonathan—would lose himself in books so different from each other, like *Middlemarch* or *The Sun Also Rises*."

"What about you, Jonathan?" Viv asked.

Seemingly unfazed, he said, almost matter-of-factly, "April, if she wishes, can be a fine short story writer; maybe even more."

"Come on," said Viv. "I saw the way you two looked at each other when Hud pulled up. I know because I've been there."

April tried to change the subject. "Mr. Hudson first interested me in plays, too," she said. "So, I became obsessed with Ophelia."

"Ah, I can understand that, April, since I played Ophelia in college."

"Wow," said Jonathan. "Explain, please. I know that April, too, was Ophelia in a high school production."

"I went to a certain women's college not all that far from here, which, by the way, might have something to do with my comfort level in this part of the state. Anyway, I thought I was going to be an actress. They were auditioning for *Hamlet*, and the best actress—the most capable—came down with mononucleosis. She wanted to go through with the play, but Vassar wouldn't allow it. They looked around for anyone who could do it and settled for me."

"How did it go, Viv?" April asked.

"I was at my best being crazy. I'm not sure about the more normal sequences she had. But Ophelia going mad? Yeah, I admit I nailed that pretty good," she answered.

"That is impressive, Vivienne. It's the role every young performer wants. Well, it might be a challenge for some to separate reality from the role, but anyone serious about an acting career would treasure that opportunity," Jonathan said. "You are fortunate to be gifted."

"I had had a little practice already when it came to losing boyfriends. I just didn't know the extent of what would follow," said Viv.

April wasn't certain she wanted to hear the rest, but she was trapped between Viv and Jonathan Hudson, who sat so near on either side of her that she could almost feel their knees touching hers. Not that this was repellent. Just a bit much.

"Why don't you guys go outside and talk about that?" said April. "I'll stay inside, with the register, in case someone comes in." Viv was comfortable letting April, who had briefly worked the counter at a Long Island deli, make change as she served customers.

Besides, this would give April the chance to pick out a record to follow Dylan. She flipped through the LPs before settling on Mozart's *Jupiter Symphony* with Leonard Bernstein conducting. Her parents had an identical copy at home. She knew the beginning by heart, and she thought it would calm her to hear something so familiar. She sat on the stool behind the counter and felt the persistent sliver of flesh pushing over her jeans. Not serious, she thought; at least, not yet. She pressed in her stomach.

Bernstein was her father's favorite, and April, who considered herself overly quiet and sometimes subdued, appreciated and envied the conductor's flair. Even on the court, making the winning shot or pass became an understatement. April would toss the credit to someone for having set her up or downplay her assist. Bernstein soaked up the spotlight. Just now, though, it occurred to April that she had never seen a woman conduct a symphony orchestra.

April liked sharing the morning intimacy within the store and the sunlight, just outside, with Viv and Jonathan. She was just now pleased to be inside by herself, however, and finally able to imagine Richie. She wished he were there. He was comfortable, and, she had to admit, very much family. Except for the part about his body. Each time she saw him, she wanted to leap into his arms. Well, part of her wanted to tackle him, but she kept that impulse to herself. Still, he probably knew, given the way she barreled into him.

April didn't want to admit it, but she couldn't help but be jealous of Viv. April was sure Viv and Hudson had been to bed. Was it crass of her to think like that? No, that was the way Hudson had put it when they read the two Tennessee Williams plays. "Don't mince words," Jonathan had advised. "It's carnal. We all want it."

April, who had already seen Hudson shooting foul shots while wearing only skimpy gym shorts, easily visualized the man wearing nary a stitch of clothing. She was lazily dreaming when Viv and Hud, as Viv called him, came inside for coffee refills.

Jonathan was beaming.

Viv said, "April, could you cover so that Hud and I can take a pleasant walk to the gazebo just past my yard?"

"Sure," she said, with mixed feelings.

Viv grabbed two Cokes and off she went, nearly skipping to keep up with Jonathan, who, at well over six feet, appeared to be a foot taller than she.

As soon as they were out of view, April reached for the phone.

She dialed zero and, when the operator came on, asked for a reversal of charges. April was trying to reach Richie. She was certain he would be there on a Sunday morning when, typically, he pored over the *Times* if not the *Sporting News* for Yankees statistics. April smiled as the phone rang.

When Richie answered, she told him she loved him and he said he would drive up the next weekend. April, smiling, simply said, "Good." She heard a cello in the background, the instrument Richie's mother played. A sterling musician, Marianne appeared with local symphonies and performed by herself in churches, synagogues, and libraries, as well as at the high school. April was certain this was Marianne playing now, and she recognized the only cello music familiar to her: Bach Suite no. 1. She heard it all the time when she left her own bedroom window open during summer months. This was almost like being home. Except upstate didn't feel like home and Bagel City carried the delicious scent of bread recently baked in the oven. She liked arriving when Viv's bagels were still warm.

Her conversation with Richie over, she munched on a banana and a bagel. Viv always perfectly positioned fresh fruit in a large cobalt blue bowl on the counter—her gift to her customers. Healthier than a cheese Danish. April was nearly woozy with delight, listening to the Bach, pleased to be running the store by herself.

April's reverie quickly shifted as Lee opened the screen door and, smiling, walked toward her. "Hi," he said, "Viv around?"

Lee clearly did not recognize April, and she was relieved.

"She went for a walk," said April.

"You're on for the rush of customers?" Lee asked, sitting opposite her.

"You probably don't know me. I work at Silverbirch. I started two weeks ago. I teach basketball and swimming."

"I think I saw you leaving the barn a while ago. So I guess I do know you," he said.

April blushed. "I didn't grow up with Fats Domino on our record player. Where did you learn all of that?"

Lee said, "It seems like a hundred years ago that I was in high school, decided to perform, and thought if I had a variety, that would make me different. Combining Sinatra with Fats or Tony Bennett with Elvis—you know: back and forth with styles and sounds. That's my concept. It works up here, on this circuit. Not sure if this translates as well in a big city." Then he began singing Fats Domino's "Blueberry Hill." He edged closer to April, making it seem like he was performing for her, a rapt audience of one.

April knew some of the tune and began singing.

"You weren't in the barn long enough to hear me singing that."

"Not inside," said April. "I stopped on the other side and listened for a while."

"My voice isn't all of my act. If that were the case, I wouldn't be anywhere," he said.

Suddenly, he was up, gyrating, shuffling his feet, smoothing back the hair hanging over his brow, launching into "Blue Suede Shoes." He motioned for April to come around the counter. She did, and he grabbed her around the waist, spun her 360 degrees, and let her be. April loved the move. She had long wished she could do this with a basketball but had never mastered it. Now, the dancing thrilled her.

"See? It's not about my voice, sweetheart. What's your name?"

"April."

Lee turned her one way, then another, then stepped away and dazzled her with his solo footwork. "Look," he said.

She saw that he was wearing blue sneakers. "Where did you get them?" she asked.

"Special order," he answered. "I couldn't do the number with conventional footwear."

Viv and Jonathan, hand in hand, walked into the store. They quickly disengaged when they saw April and Lee sliding, sweating.

"Well, this is awkward," Viv said, breaking the silence.

"Hey Viv," said Lee. "The shop looks fantastic. I see you have a star here so you can take a break. Hey, Hud."

"Lee. You're knocking people's socks off every night," said Jonathan. "Elastic Man should be your moniker."

Lee smiled. "Keeps me in shape, and as long as I'm trying to be someone else—Fats, Elvis, even Sinatra—I'm okay."

April was surprised and pleased that they all seemed to be getting along so well. Jonathan moved away from Vivienne, who replaced April behind the counter.

Lee, sashaying back and forth and then over to her, said, "Viv, you still have the Elvis single we used to play?"

Viv nodded, scooped the record out of the wooden crate, and said, "You're going to dance by yourself?"

Lee winked and beckoned to April, who, without hesitation, joined him. He put his arm around her, and they were slowly moving together to Elvis pretty much crooning "Love Me Tender."

Viv and Jonathan, who turned his stool to watch, did not join in.

No one sang, although April thought she heard Lee, once or twice, whispering lyrics.

At the end, she listened carefully to the part about dreams.

Lee kissed her on the forehead, and she wondered why she found these older men so enticing.

Jonathan snapped his fingers several times and nodded his head. Lee smiled broadly and bowed; he still had April's hand in his. Viv walked into the back room and returned with a bottle of red wine.

"You're how old, sweetie?" Viv asked April.

"I'm nineteen," she said, keeping up the story she had told in order to get the job at Silverbirch.

"Good. Then you can have a drink with us," said Viv.

"The kids definitely drink at after-prom parties," said Jonathan.

"Hud, you're spilling secrets," said Viv. "You're how far away from senior prom, April? Give us a snapshot."

"Richie brought a flask with him to prom, and we shared it on the Staten Island Ferry," she answered, telling the story for the first time. "Every moment was magnified or maybe like looking through a kaleidoscope with all the colors: lights, water, even people on that boat with us," she said. "It was all sur-real. They were playing a Beach Boys record over the speaker system. We were singing." April realized she was beginning to ramble with her thoughts. She sat on a stool, pulled her shirt down, and took a deep breath. April felt partly like a high school kid and partly like a young woman. So this was what the next two months were going to be like.

Lee broke her reverie. "Why don't we all dance? Come on, Hud," he said, and Jonathan, shrugging, sauntered in that toe-to-heel walk of his to Lee.

"I get the cute kid," said Viv. She went to the record player and said, "Let's twist. I got the sweet-est girl," she said, pointing to April. "When I was a dancer, this maneuver was just a bit easier but life begins at what age?"

Chubby Checker was just beginning to implore anyone listening to go for it, to twist and twist some more. Each of them corkscrewed, and Viv had the toughest time returning to an upright position. Hudson, long and lanky, took his time but did so smoothly. Lee was all fire and attack, and April slid into a crouch and then, by fluid increments, shim-mied upward. She softly shook herself, as if discard-ing water after showering, from head to foot. Why not skip college, she wondered, and go straight to this?

"Fun. Let's keep rolling," Jonathan said. "Switch it around." He took April's hand, his long fingers enveloping hers. "More music. What else, Viv?"

"I do have a couple of great Motowns. Listen to this," she said.

Mary Wells sang "My Guy" once again. April had heard the song a few months back as it played in the Copa lobby before she and Richie made their way to Bobby Vinton. She loved the song which was also on the radio that night after they left the Copa. Now, though, Jonathan was spinning her, spinning with her. She followed him as he rotated, waving his hands high. She was happily dazed. Viv followed with The Temptations, The Supremes, Smokey Robinson.

"Break for lunch?" Lee asked.

April hadn't any plans for the day, except simply to stop at Bagel City, spend some time with Viv, and walk back to her room. She thought she might begin one of the novels perched on her nightstand.

"Sure. Then we could all go to the pond to cool off," said Jonathan.

"Maybe after two?" Viv asked. "I need to stay open for a while." A couple of people were just entering the store, wanting to pick up bagels to go.

April felt she should contribute to the conversation, so she said, "I love the dancing, being here." Once the words were out of her mouth, she thought them lame and predictable. No one seemed to mind.

"Okay, then. One free bagel for each of you on the house," said Viv. "If you want cream cheese or lox, I'm afraid I'll have to charge something."

"Your intuitive business sense floated this place to start with, Viv. You are even sharper now," said Lee. "Many moons ago, you knew a lot even if you weren't quite so savvy," Lee added. "That's what's different on this day."

"I don't know if we want to spoil this glorious day by going there, Lee," said Viv.

"I meant it as a compliment to you, Viv," said Lee. "No one else could have turned what was formerly pretty tired looking into a successful bagel shop."

"I should go," said April.

"Drive you back?" Jonathan asked.

"Thanks, yes."

Chapter Eight

The Pond

WITHIN MINUTES, AFTER BROWN-BAGGING the bagels, they were out of the shop and on the winding road back to Silverbirch.

"Still want to go swimming?" Jonathan asked as they approached the main building.

"I forgot," April said. "Sure. Let me change. Meet me outside my room in ten minutes and we'll walk over?"

"Sounds good. I will try to find something stylish to wear," he said.

April had three bathing suits: a brown one-piece and two bikini styles, one a bit more revealing than the second. She chose the brown one-piece. She was aware that it was snug and decided that was okay. The temperature was in the mid-eighties but not muggy. Still, the air was light and April did not wish to be chilled after a swim, so she tossed on an old beach sweatshirt. She pulled her hair into a ponytail, washed her face, and saw in the mirror a young woman who was clear-eyed but pensive. She remembered the many times her dad had said,

"Smile, April. You're gorgeous." Her mind formed an image, and he was immediately grinning back at her.

Jonathan rapped three times on her door, and April opened it to greet him. "You look so graceful," he said, carefully choosing the word.

Unlike the day when Jonathan had preceded April to the basketball court for some easy shooting, he now sidled next to her and timed his steps to match hers.

"Lee is a magnet for women," said Jonathan. "Women of many ages."

"That obvious?" April asked, smiling again. "I mean, I don't feel anything romantic. Nothing. It's about the way he slides and shuffles and moves—and his voice tumbling on and on. He's like a coffee brewing machine: constant, seemingly endless energy."

"I happen to know that he's a solid sleeper," said Jonathan, and April immediately wondered what that meant. Were they really roommates?

"We came to Silverbirch at different times," he said, as though he knew what she was thinking. "There was just a little confusion one summer about accommodations. So, for a few nights, we shared a place. That little hideaway inside the barn. At a certain point, they squeezed in two beds and, briefly, it was home base for me."

As they walked, April had the sense that Jonathan might take her hand. She had been down the sandy road countless times by herself but, at this moment, would have happily welcomed his touch. She had feelings for Jonathan but what, exactly, did that mean? Out of nowhere, a knobby branch tumbled several yards in front of them. Jonathan grabbed her, then apologized. "Sorry. If it hit one of us . . . bam! Who knows? That kind of thing happens in English novels."

"I'm fine, really. Ten-foot branches fall out of the sky every day at my feet," she joked. "Any other deep, dark secrets I should know about Lee?"

"I can tell you something about Vivienne: She is a very attractive woman," he said.

April daydreamed as Hudson escorted her over the fallen piece of wood. She eagerly went to Bagel City as much for the talk as the food. Viv, so sweet to April, was easy and casual with advice. Once Viv had said, "Men in their thirties are very often on the rebound." Of course, April always assigned another connotation to the word rebound—as in, box out. Because of her dribbling skills, she was always the ball handler on various teams. Still, coaches wanted her to rebound, too. How to do both when she was often at the top of the key and nowhere near the basket? They seemed not to care about that part.

I would love to try those hoop earrings, April thought to herself. Each time April visited the bagel shop, Viv showcased different color earrings: turquoise, magenta, silver.

April initiated the hand-in-hand with Jonathan. She knew that she was the one to reach out, but it felt comfortable. *Both easy and right*, thought April. Hudson slowed the pace.

"Look," he said, raising a finger to his lips. "Blue jay." April, who saw similar species each morning through her bedside window, played along as if in awe of the bird that sat and watched the two intruders approach.

"She's a beauty with such perfect symmetry," he said, and April found this an unusual assessment. Did he judge humans' proportions as well? Wasn't someone in one of those old novels he had them read a birder? Is that where he got this?

They arrived at the pond, and April was uncertain what to do. She waited for Jonathan to take the lead. In a way, he was chivalrous, always watching out for her. Richie and April were equals; Jonathan was from a generation before.

He looked down at her, right through her eyes, and said, "I didn't mean to get between Lee and Viv. It just sort of happened."

"Between?" April questioned before she could stop herself.

"Well, not exactly. I came here, and—I know I'm repeating myself—Lee was one of the first people I knew at Silverbirch. We shared that room, worked on staff for a summer, became pretty good friends. Viv was visiting on weekends. Mostly, they spent time together. I did get introduced, found out that she was, I think, a theater major at Vassar. You know how much I like family generation novels, closely followed by plays: Shakespeare, Greeks, Eugene O'Neill, musicals. She was hoping, eventually, to direct but not yet. To get there, she had supporting parts in college. She told me about playing the lead, Alma, in *Summer and Smoke*. Said it changed her life, and she began to crave acting roles. That was about all I knew of her then." Jonathan sat on a large rock, and April found one nearby. "Viv and Lee were soon gone, and we didn't stay in touch."

"Doesn't sound terrible so far," said April.

"Quite some time later, I guess, they moved up this way and opened the bagel place. I was up here on some weekends. Lee was working here but living in a rental house with Vivienne. It's like some of the books we read, April. Friendship, love, lust—it all gets confusing."

"I know," she said.

"You do?"

"Well, not personally. I'm still a little short on experience."

"But you were always ahead of everybody else in getting character motivation in both novels and plays."

"Sometimes I wish I could freeze in time as a dumb teenager," said April.

"You get the teen part just because of your age," said Jonathan, "but you perceive so accurately. That is what sets you apart from so many of your class-mates."

"It's easier when I think of you as my teacher," April said.

"That aspect doesn't change, April," he said. "I'm just adding a new layer to my identity."

"Every kid wants to get you as a teacher, Jonathan. I still have trouble calling you by your first name," she said.

"Try JT."

"Why?"

"I'm Jonathan T. Hudson. Don't ask because I don't know why they just gave me T. But I will respond to JT. Or even TJ. Basketball friends reversed the letters." He shrugged.

"You mentioned playing in college and I imagine you were something special in high school," April said.

"Yes is the answer. I was a starter as a high school sophomore and a college freshman, too. Same story each time. They, or maybe I, couldn't find a position. I was long enough but not strong enough to play forward. I played guard and when I wasn't required to handle the ball, that was good. If I had a really skillful point guard beside me, it all could have wo

"Cousy?" April asked. "I mean, someone like Cousy to set you up?"

"Yeah. Anyway, I always had the wrong combination and ended up at the end of the bench.

Great practice player, but not much success during games."

"Pickup ball is so much more fun," said April. "It's always been more competitive to hang with boys, too." She blushed. "I really didn't mean it that way."

"You never worried about getting hurt?"

"Being a girl doesn't mean being delicate," she said. "It was sometimes but not always a problem with girls' games, not mixing it up. I grew up playing one-on-one. It's kind of impossible not to be physical."

"Am I a problem?" Hudson asked.

"Yes, but it's not your fault," said April. "Anyone else in my position would be thrilled. And, to be honest, so am I."

"But . . ."

"I'm eighteen, and everyone here thinks I'm nineteen. Having men in my life is kind of new. I'm not ready to say you or you or maybe even you are Mr. Right. Far from that."

"I guess I'm not second but third?"

"It could turn out to be Lee. Just going on impulse. The way he moves," she said and shook her shoulders. "God, I talk to you like you're my best friend."

"Let's swim," said Jonathan.

April peeled off her sweatshirt and pulled her bathing suit forward. She was perspiring, and the fabric was clinging to her. She pried it loose, and the suit snapped back. It was all just too embarrassing, especially since lanky Jonathan's shorts nearly fell off his frame. She wished she had the same problem. She liked bagels, and she liked the pancakes and French toast Silverbirch presented each morning. Her clothes fit, more or less, and she was able to get everything on. It just wasn't like when she was growing into her wardrobe five years ago.

Jonathan grabbed the rope hanging from the oak tree and was about to propel himself into the water when he paused.

"One of the kids just the other day did this with me. Want to?" he asked.

April immediately realized they could be skin-to-skin. "Definitely," she said. She was not exactly sure why she was that declarative.

"In front of me or behind me? Which is better?" Jonathan asked.

"Behind," was her quick reply. She would be in control that way, which made things feel less risky.

He put both hands on the rope and nodded backward, over his shoulder, for April to join. She placed each of her hands around his waist, and he said, "Come on, April. You have to be more or less attached to me for this to work." She pushed up against him, grabbed his torso, and clutched his ribs. "Better," he said. "Ready?"

"Yeah," she answered.

He leapt forward and upward from the hilly area, and April knew they were flying—but where? A few seconds later, they splashed down in the deepest part of the pond. Having been a swimmer here as well as group swim leader, she knew they were landing in a ten-foot depth. Both of them submerged briefly before popping upward. Jonathan was laughing and she was gurgling, clearing her throat. They made their way through the water to the sandy beach.

"You good?" Jonathan asked. He faced her, grasped her shoulders, and began massaging April's back. She did not want this to end. Relaxed, she leaned into him, turned, and, with water dripping off her limbs and bathing suit, hugged Jonathan Hudson.

Comfortable, he took a step back. "Is this okay, April?"

The spell broken, she smoothed her hair and wiped her eyes.

"I think yes." April paused. "It's a lot at once. Let's swim," she said.

He took her hand, and they walked, slowly, into the pond. The water, benefiting from the sun's heat on an almost ninety-degree day in July, was temperate. April swam easily, on her back, and Jonathan, beside her, moved fluently hand over hand. The configuration was rectangular, and they gracefully made their way from one side of the pond to the other.

As they walked, this time hand touching hand, to the shore, Jonathan said, "I love Janet's Pond."

April asked, "Any idea of how the pond got its name?"

"The first year I came to Silverbirch, Janet was still ruling. She was a large, bellowing bullfrog who seemed to announce the arrival of swimmers here. Her status grew and grew."

"Where is she?"

"Evidently, the frog died. I was up here that winter and the following summer, but no more Janet."

Jonathan spread two large beach towels on the gritty sand. Beneath the shade trees, the two of them rested on a hot, toasty day.

"What else can you tell me about Janet?" April asked.

"Well, this was handed down to me, April, so I can't really vouch for its authenticity. But I guess she had a higher sound than the usual bullfrogs. A summer before I was here, Barry—I think his last name was Gould—named the frog. Barry taught crafts and some ceramics the next summer, and I overlapped with him. I gather that Barry was also an opera buff, and he liked Jan Peerce, a tenor who sang with Toscanini and Metropolitan Opera. I think Gould also heard Peerce sing the role of Rodolfo in *La Bohème*. The frog had an upper octave, I guess you would say, so Barry named her Janet for Jan. Do you believe any of this?"

"My father had some opera records around, and I know he played *La Bohème*. I had no interest, but it could be that Jan Peerce was singing on it. I don't know," she said.

"The myth around Janet grew. She could sing 'Oh, Susannah' in the summer and, if it wasn't below freezing at Christmastime, a celebratory 'Jingle Bells.' I never heard that one, but I was once certain she was humming and bellowing along with 'Swing Low, Sweet Chariot.'"

"We came here a number of times for vacations, but I never heard that story," said April, tugging at her sweatshirt. "This little treasure was known simply as the pond, and that's all. Never knew of the frog."

"It's a legend at this point. Gould is an embellisher, sure, but I think Janet did live and make some noises, even music. And that's why we have her name for this sweet spot." He looked straight ahead. "I guess we ought to go back," he said. He carefully draped his long arm around her shoulder and neck, gently placing his palm on her far shoulder. April moved with the awareness that she was enabling and encouraging his hand to move downward a bit to her arm. It was easy with this man, perhaps because he was older. Richie was her contemporary, equally inexperienced when it came to sex. Jonathan had been through it and survived. That part was encouraging.

She wished the walk back to the buildings could be extended. It was the weekend; her time was her own, and April wanted to spend it with Hudson. If she said so aloud, what would that indicate? She kept her thoughts to herself. When they neared the main building, April said, "Let's go to the apple orchard."

"I'm free," said a smiling Jonathan. "Trot?"

"Good idea. We've done a few swim laps. This is next."

They ambled up the hill, each of them breathing harder at the apex.

"Too bad we're at least a month early," he said, looking at apples that were not yet fully red.

"I like McIntosh when they just appear," said April. "Tart and crunchy."

"April, nature does its thing, unless we humans keep ruining the earth," he said.

"I know," she replied and then changed the subject. "It's a confusing time for me."

He bent down, and she stood on her tiptoes and kissed him, gently, on the lips. He held her, stepped back, looked at her as if trying to interpret a photograph, and smiled.

Neither of them moved; neither spoke.

A strong gust of wind dislodged a single McIntosh apple, which glanced off April's shoulder before tumbling to the ground. "I told you how confusing all of this is," she said.

Hudson picked up the apple and fired it at a nearby willow tree. The reddening apple disappeared among the green boughs. "Magic, my sweet," he said.

Bert often referred to Lil as both sweetheart and sweet. April loved being called sweet by Jonathan.

She responded by using his first name. "Thank you, Jonathan." She picked another apple and wiped it on her shorts till it began to shine. She took a bite. "Not sweet—the apple, I mean—but perfectly sharp," she said. "Want a bite?"

"Forward of you to ask. Yes," he said, brushing her hand with his as he took the fruit. "Is this an Adam and Eve moment?" Jonathan asked.

April felt her face redden. "I'm not exactly sure what that means," she said.

He took a chunk of apple and, as he sat under a majestic tree, motioned for April to join him.

"I don't know what's going on either, April."

She nodded. "Time, Jonathan? You spoke of it often when we read novels. You talked of patience, not rushing."

He rose and stared far beyond— where they had been. "The pond is still and calm today."

Hand in hand, they walked toward the main Silverbirch campus. April glanced at him and noticed that his eyes were focused upward. Jonathan Hudson was one to spot a cardinal or a more exotic bird. He was ever vigilant, and April watched him. When they arrived at her room, he opened her door, then took her hand in both of his. She wanted to kiss him again.

Chapter Nine

Masked Ball

T HE RECENT TRADITION AT Silverbirch was to celebrate the midpoint of summer as July beckoned August with a celebratory dance. Who, other than Hudson, a man introducing *Romeo and Juliet* to high schoolers, would think to incorporate a theme recalling a Shakespearean highlight?

• • • • • • • • • •

April had seen Richie just once during the past month. He called from home the second Saturday morning of July, told her he could not wait to see her and asked if she wanted anything. She requested, from her mother, more gym shorts and a few tops. April's feelings were mixed: Hearing Richie's voice on the phone catapulted her backward toward childhood, when they were always speaking, house to house, or preparing to walk to the park. Then she flashed forward to the memorable prom excursion. Now, pining for her, he had to be there. She was ambivalent but, she admitted, a portion of her could not wait for him, for the new, blossoming Richie.

He was her best companion, always. Jonathan was in her life now even if she could not define or categorize him and the implications. Each time she tried to think it through, April gave in. He was a good man and she cared for him, but how deeply? She could not answer, but she could not ignore her question.

Richie wanted to be sure he and April saw each other often in the fall. She would be in the city and he in upstate New York. They had talked about the moderate geographic distance when they applied to colleges. They would have separate lives, and each wondered what that would mean.

When Richie came to see her that second time at Silverbirch, he said, "April, I'm still used to looking out my bedroom window and imagining you in your kitchen." She remembered how she quite recently began to pick out V-necks to wear when she knew he would be looking down at her—longing to touch and embrace him.

Currently, April was preoccupied with two older men. She found Jonathan's grace and gentility impossibly beguiling. Lee, too, had a magnetic field about him. April could feel it. His flying feet dazzled her. The way he dressed caught her attention: various pin-striped vests and half a dozen solid color T-shirts, paired with tightly pegged jeans. His marriage to Viv was also interesting.

Viv saw right away that the boys were taken with April, her new, youthful friend. She was at ease with the fresh and fetching teenager. She cared about the girl and noted that Jonathan always seemed to be with her, even when he wasn't. Jonathan and April liked each other. He was nearly twice her age but she somehow found him sexy. Viv was curious—and also concerned for April.

When Richie arrived, he and April drove to Bagel City. April watched Viv, whose eyes popped out of her head when Richie shed his T for a collared shirt, one of many in his collection of faded Lacostes. He turned toward April with a quick smile and wink before smoothing the yellow shirt down over his chest and stomach.

This was her prom date, the guy she thought she might have been if she were not born a girl. Easy to imagine. She knew his body, having played basketball with him day after day. Whoever said basketball was a non-contact sport? The last few months of senior year, the romance, and particularly prom night, had heightened everything, perhaps forever.

At first, Viv stayed behind the counter, which was unusual for her. No dance music, no conversation. Instead, Viv simply observed. April whispered into Richie's ear, then said, "Two egg bagels with cream cheese, Viv, please." Straightforward and direct.

"Not toasted, I assume? Regular, yes?"

"Thanks, Viv. Richie and I used to have this all the time at home. For years. On Sundays, our fathers would get more elaborate and we would be in the back seat of one of the cars tagging along. They would come out of the deli with white fish, baked salmon, lox, bagels, bialys and more. Sometimes our families shared brunch together."

"Not that our parents were totally alike," said Richie. "Good neighbors, sure. And there's us," he said.

"Us day after day, year after year," said April with a smile.

Viv presented the plates, each with a strawberry and a slice of cantaloupe framing the bagels. "Voilà. Drinks?"

"Two Cokes," said Richie. "Pretzels?"

"I have the long kind," said Viv.

"Those are good," said April. "Good for dueling."

"So I heard you two went to prom," Viv said. "Back in my era, we were told to be home by midnight. Can you believe it?"

"Luckily, we didn't have that. I don't think any of our parents really believed that we were, well, involved more than as lifelong buddies," said Richie.

"My father either knew or suspected," April said. "He would focus on us, and I looked up and caught him one time. My eyes locked with his."

Whether the revelation caused it or not, Richie dumped Coke all over himself. Viv quickly tossed him several paper napkins. He had his shirt off immediately, and Viv stared first at him, then at April, who dabbed at his tight midsection, then his shorts.

Laughing, Richie said, "You don't happen to carry an extra pair of shorts, do you?"

"Actually, I have the ones I wear when I'm cleaning this place," said Viv. She looked him up and down and added, "The waist might actually be okay but not the rest."

"He's practically fizzing," said April.

Richie went to the back room, stripped to his boxers, which were pale blue, baggy, and not very revealing.

"What do you think?" he asked the two women.

"Nice look," said Viv.

"I'm not about to be surprised," April said as if this was not something new. "Except for that on the bottom. What is it?"

He lifted the side of the shorts. "A frog," said Richie.

"There was a legendary one around here," said Viv. "I know that, and I've never really stayed at Silverbirch. Well, I sort of stayed there once."

"Mr. Hudson told me all about Janet," April said.

"She's in the cemetery," said Viv. "You two love-birds ought to go. It's very romantic."

April and Richie gazed at one another.

Viv continued, "What I've heard is that people walk there with a little wine, maybe. You know."

"Okay," said Richie. "I don't even know where the graveyard is."

"It'll be better at night, Richie," said April. "Not now. But maybe we ought to go back so you won't have to parade around without pants."

"I don't care, but sure," he said.

Before, when they were in her room, April wasn't certain whether she should go outside, stay in the bathroom, or just watch as Richie shed his clothing. She told herself the obvious: She knew what his body looked like. Not that he had ever stood naked next to her. Should she stare? She did.

Watching her watching him, Richie said, "Same me, wouldn't you say? You're changing, though."

April didn't know what he meant, so she said, "I weigh the same. Well, maybe two pounds more."

"I've known you since you were a little girl, when I called you Apie. You're a woman now. No more Apie."

He placed his hand upon hers, and April appreciated the familiarity of his fingers.

• • • • • • • • • • •

Now, at the Bagel shop, Viv returned from the room behind and gave each of them another Coke. "For the road," she said. April and Richie talked with Viv for a bit, and then April indicated that it was time to go. The trip back to Silverbirch was a quick one.

As soon as they were in her room, April went into the bathroom and tossed on the old Celtics jersey over her underwear. Caught up within her thoughts,

April knew that Richie should not, as he had a few weeks earlier, sleep by himself curled up on the floor. She was ready to share her bed with him.

She and Richie sat together at the foot of the bed.

"I don't want you to feel pressured, April," said Richie. "It's time for me to admit that competing for you with someone older is getting to me. And I do know I'm the one talking about our colleges being several hours away."

"Not the same town."

"Not houses practically adjoined," he said.

"When we were little, I drew a picture with me as a bride and you as a groom, Richie." She leaned into him and kissed him. "Let's shower," she said and removed her top to accompany her best friend to the bathroom.

• • • • • • • • • • •

Richie dried April's body, and she pressed her towel to his. Draping his arm around her, he gently walked April to her bed. It was only natural, following the script of their lives, that the first time for each of them would be with one another. April was surprised only that it was at Silverbirch amid shadow presences of both Jonathan and Lee.

April, first to awaken, found herself intertwined with Richie. The masked ball was the featured event of an otherwise quiet weekend, and she wanted to be there, wanted Richie to be with her.

Richie opened his eyes, and April said, "Richie, that was amazing." She paused before adding, "There's a dance, a ball, to celebrate summer tonight. Everyone is going to wear a mask. Want to go?"

"I love you," Richie said. "Amazing doesn't come close to what I feel." He paused before saying, "Is it okay to say I want you?"

He really means it, April thought. In the past, they had playfully closed out conversations with "Love you" or some variation. This felt different.

"I know. I feel the same," said April, uncertain whether this was true. It could be, but to declare it? Well, April wouldn't start that. "Could we go to the dance?"

"The last one we went to cost each of us a lot of money, but we didn't stay all that long. On the other hand, it was pretty much the best experience of my life," he said. "With you."

"There are masks in a wooden chest inside the barn. We probably have an hour before they get the place ready. It's on a theme from *Romeo and Juliet*."

"One of Mr. Hudson's favorites. I remember him explaining it and actually calling it a wonderful example of the dream world his man, Shakespeare, created," said Richie. "I mean, I see why everyone loves Shakespeare so much, but I don't."

"The best, for me, are the imagination times," said April. "Like in *A Midsummer Night's Dream*. Fairies and the drug potion."

"Not tragedies," said Richie.

"Except that this dance is out of another play," she said. "Let's get two black masks." April hoisted Richie up and dragged him out the door and toward the barn. His arm and hand held fast to her waist.

They entered through the rear door and found Jonathan Hudson in gym shorts and a baggy black T. He was hanging lights.

"Hey, great surprise! It's Richard the Lionhearted," he said, smiling at April and Richie. Neither responded, so Jonathan continued. "He was King of England and known mostly as a warrior, but he was also a poet."

The young people felt as if they were back in a Hudson class.

Richie said, "I only know of him because I was interested in finding out about his name," he said. "What I discovered was that he was strong but not the nicest person."

Hudson said, "They could have called him Richard the Meanest and not have been far off. But you don't remind me of him. Lionhearted just jumped into my brain." He looked at both of them. "You could be brother and sister but I sense a different kind of relationship."

April was simultaneously surprised and relieved. She and Richie had thought of themselves as brother and sister for a dozen years. The romantic part was new.

"How can I help?" Jonathan asked.

April wished he weren't there but he was, so she said, "Black masks," without finishing her sentence.

"Ah, going to the ball?" Jonathan asked.

"After taking your class, Mr. Hudson, it's kind of required, yes?"

"Once a teacher, a teacher forever?" Hudson asked. "Let's see what we have," he said and walked toward the old, wooden floor-to-ceiling ladder. "Follow me."

April had noticed a landing when she and Jonathan had been navigating high above it on the day of the catwalk adventure. Armed with that knowledge, the current endeavor was even riskier than the previous time. This makeshift room, perched precariously above a wooden floor, was a costume shop?

"It's supported, from the rear, by pillars. I was thinking the same thing," said Jonathan.

"I'm the last guy in the room when it comes to engineering," Richie said. "I can't even think about how bridges stand up."

Jonathan led them to an old, battered, heavy-looking trunk with latches unlocked and said, "Presto!" It was filled with wigs and masks.

"Try this," he said to April and tossed her one that featured deep red fabric with black piping. "Richard, here," he said and presented an opaque mask. "Play it as you wish for those who don't know you: strangers bumping into one another by chance or longtime lovers having fun."

April was conscious of the two men flanking her. Part of her wished she were invisible; the other part implored her to take each one's hand. She impulsively took only Richie's before thinking further. Trust.

He picked up four masks and said, "Mr. Hudson, can we take these and bring back the ones we don't want?"

"Sure. No one else has ever shown an iota of interest."

April and Richie looked at one another and started laughing.

"The joke?" Jonathan asked.

April calmed herself sufficiently to quickly say, "Mr. Hudson, an iota?"

Hudson, too, began to laugh. "I do it so often that sometimes I'm not even aware. 'No interest at all'—that's what 'not one iota' means."

"You taught us how to figure out meanings by, as you said, circling the word and, with context, understanding it. Yes, I might have gotten it," said Richie, "but not right now."

"Will I see both of you later?" asked Jonathan Hudson. "At the ball?"

"Yes," said April. . "Don't leave us here, though. We don't know how to get out. Also, I don't want you to go."

Hudson suddenly remembered she was just eighteen even though most at Silverbirch thought her to be nineteen.

"This is awkward," he said, for once seemingly the slightest bit flustered.

"I just showed up out of nowhere," said Richie. "Maybe I should be the one taking off."

"No! Both of you!" shouted April, stomping her foot. "Each of you is in my life. Please."

Jonathan situated himself between them and, this time, assisted on the dismount from the ladder. When they reached the floor, he said, "Remember, when they had masquerade balls in the fifteenth and sixteenth centuries in Italy, Spain, and France, these were dances as well. The wealthy wore elaborate costumes, too. You know the story of Romeo and Juliet. Enter Richie and April?" Neither April nor Richie responded. "Listen, if you want wardrobe, we have that, too. They used to do plays here in the barn. You go beneath the ground to find those outfits, and it is not nearly as scary as up above." He motioned with his hand. "Follow me."

Hudson brought them to a dingy, dank spot—concrete for the most part, edged with old dirt. A heavy wooden door, latched with a black clasp, once protected the interior. Jonathan quickly ushered them into the room. It was more like an expanded closet, just big enough to hold a few clothing racks. He tossed a black leotard to April and, to Richie, black tights and a white shirt with ruffles both down the center and at the sleeves.

"Seriously?" asked Richie.

"This is the dress of the day for such an occasion," said Jonathan. "April, the leotard will flatter you and you it," he said.

Feeling her cheeks flush, she nodded. "It's only a few hours away. Jonathan, how does dinner figure in?"

"There's food, April. Hors d'oeuvres glorified, with some chicken from the outside grill. They disguise the drinks to be Elizabethan. It's actually a Champagne-based punch. If the chef feels like it, he will provide a meat dish, too. And dessert. No one starves around here," he said.

"Richie, come on," said April. "We have, what, like three hours to get ready?"

"Sure, Ap, I'm into it; I'll go," he said, and waited.

Hudson interrupted the silence and pointed to himself. "Third wheel, no question."

Hand in hand, April and Richie left Jonathan Hudson in the clammy region beneath the dance floor. At April's urging, they jogged down the hill leading to her room.

"Okay, let's try on the costumes," said Richie, who began unbuckling his pants as April watched. "What do I do about these boxers?" Richie asked, knowing the answer.

"Off with them," said April as Richie stripped down.

He pulled on the black tights, which clung to his legs, and tugged them up to his waist.

"What do you think?" he asked as he fastened his blouse together.

"You're bulging, Richie," she said and started laughing. "I'm not sure what people will think."

"Well, try on your things," he said.

April took off her clothing, moved her arms upward for a moment as if to cover her upper half, then let them drop to her side. She put on the black leotard, then pulled it forward before it snapped back as if magnetically drawn. She sucked in her stomach before realizing this wouldn't work for more than a few moments. April exhaled and sighed.

"Totally works and looks delectable on you, April," said Richie.

"You really think it's nice that I'm popping out of this thing?" April asked.

"Short answer? Yes."

"That does mean a lot, Richie. I'm not used to this newer body. It might be with me for a while, no matter what I do. Around here, there's a lot of French toast, too, which isn't helping."

He hugged her and she embraced him, kissed him fully, felt him press forward. She leaned into him. His midsection was now taut; she remembered, again, that had not always been the case. She was told to defend, on the court, by touching an opponent's middle. When she and Richie played one-on-one for years, his belly was softer than expected, jiggly. Now, she could feel his stomach muscles. No more Jell-O–like covering.

"I have a black skirt," she said. "Maybe I can wear that and it will make me feel better," she added. "Plus the mask."

He fastened his face covering and smiled.

"Come on, Lone Ranger," April said and put her arm around his waist as they walked back outside. "I feel like I need a wand or something," she said.

"Princess April," Richie said, gently placing his arm around her shoulders, then letting his hand slide down her back.

• • • • • • • • • •

Even before 6:00, people were congregating in the barn. Lee shimmied around and about them, lip-syncing Motown tunes like "Baby Love." While in mid-shake, he saw April and called out, "Sweetness, you would never do that, would you? Let's hear it for The Supremes," to a smattering of applause.

He signaled to April, who looked at a smiling Richie. He pushed her to the dance floor.

"Flip on 'The Twist,' will you?" said Lee, nodding at someone to his right who sat by an old record player.

"The Twist" blared forth. Lee winked at April, who tugged at her leotard. He spiraled downward, and April followed his lead. A moment later, several people surrounding them chimed in as everyone began singing at the top of their lungs.

Lee placed his palms down and asked that the music be lowered. Then he sang, "Come on, April, let's do the twist. Come on, April, let's do the twist. Just follow Lee, now, and go like this." Lee waved to Richie, beckoning him to join. The three of them, corkscrewing up and down, took center stage. When the song ended, Lee bent at the waist and swept a hand toward April and Richie.

"Folks," said Lee, "give us a few moments for final checks and we're ready to go."

"I'm sweating, and this thing is totally clinging to me. Probably a size too small," April said to Richie. "Let's go outside."

"Sure. Me, too. The tights are, well, they're too tight," he said.

Richie undid the clasps on his shirt as soon as possible.

"Wish I could do that with my outfit," said April. "I'm trapped. It's not possible to take a deep breath. If I do, the whole thing might snap and I might provide a show for anyone who wants it."

He laughed. "Some revelations—now that's a Hudson phrase—are better than others. For example, mine would be boring."

"I wouldn't say that. Take off your shirt, Richie," April said.

He quickly responded and stood outside of the barn, bare-chested, in black tights. "You should go to the dance like that," said April. "Silverbirch would never forget you."

"This doesn't feel like a dance from 300 years ago, April," he answered.

"Lee is a guy and girl mover, in more ways than one," said April. "You can't help but watch him. Also, I've talked with Viv and heard a number of Lee stories. She's given me snapshots, through her telling, of their time together. Not actual ones, but she talks with her hands and I can imagine him through her. He's a little scary."

"Meaning?"

"He's in his thirties, and he kind of comes right at me," said April. "I don't mean that he is a threat. But he is a powerhouse. His energy, when he focuses in, is hard to resist."

"There's Hudson, on the other side. Pretty different approach," said Richie.

"He's like a big brother or maybe a half-brother. A generation up, but caring. Way more mellow. Yes, I do like him and I'm sometimes over his being our teacher."

"Not me," said Richie. "Both times I've visited, the guy refers to something we did in class. I'm trying to remember whether I was paying attention or staring out a window."

They were busy talking, too preoccupied to notice the single amplifying black rain cloud, which was lowering and taking dead aim on the barn. A succession of claps and booms sounded; suddenly,

the cloud released buckets of water, dousing anyone foolish enough not to have noticed.

Instead of running inside, April and Richie, nailed
to a spot, simply laughed—at the rain, at the sky, at
themselves. A large and animated golden retriever,
hair flying about, burst through the screen door and
barreled into April. "God, what are you doing here?"
April asked.

"God?" Richie said.

"Lee's dog who goes everywhere with him. He
reversed the d-o-g and called her God."

"Lee is god of dance, wouldn't you say, Ap?"

"He actually practices, Richie. Can you believe
it?"

"How many hours did we spend in the park playing HORSE? It's the same."

"You're right. You saw him twisting with me. I
know he comes here or somewhere else late at
night and wills his body to maneuver into those
almost contortions," she said. April knew: She had
gone back to the barn close to 11:00 one night
to retrieve two bracelets she had taken off while
dancing. "I found Lee and God here one night," she
explained. "I'd lost something and came to get it.
There they were with Elvis and, if you can believe
it, 'Hound Dog,'" she said. "Lee was here saying,
'Listen, God, you have to be the dog.' Every time he
said it, God would jump up to lick his face. I'm not
kidding."

"What now, April? We have these outfits on, and we're half-soaked."

"It's stopping. We can walk around, dry out a little, and go back," she said.

"They have towels by the pool, right?"

"Yes, but what does that have to do with anything?"

Richie said, "Let's walk down the hill, wipe off a couple of chairs, and wait. It looks like an incredible sunset could happen."

"Okay. Just by ourselves. Good idea."

Off they went, hand in hand. This felt familiar to April. She had memorized the configurations of Richie's body and the feel of his fingers. She had always known his hands were long and slender, but it wasn't until prom that she realized his grip enveloped—pretty much dwarfed—hers. She had to admit, just now, that she enjoyed the way their limbs and everything else fit together. April and Richie quickly arrived at the pool, and a dark cloud loomed above. As she looked upward, it began to defuse and split apart, revealing an early evening burnt orange sun. April smiled to herself. This might be better than a rainbow. That would be startling—always unexpected and unpredictable—but they had their own motion picture in the sky.

"I see it, April," said Richie as if he understood what she was thinking.

She pulled on the leotard, which snapped like it had before, with a squish, back onto her skin. "Nice," said April.

Richie laughed and rolled up his puffy sleeves. "People actually walked around like this?" he asked.

"And went to the equivalent of proms, too," April added.

"Want to go to the World's Fair again, Ap?" Richie asked.

"It's back home, Richie. I'm here and then we're both in college."

"You could get away for an overnight, right?"

"Sure. I have some days coming to me. If not, I could always take one. But this is where I live now." She hesitated. "I don't mean to hurt you," she said softly, taking his hand.

"Nah, just an idea of the moment. Colors up there get me dreaming," he said.

They both stood. "What's that?" Richie asked.

"It's classical: Beethoven or Tchaikovsky, I always get them confused," said April. She walked toward the music that seemed to be coming from a nearby shed where towels and buoys were stored.

She peered inside, and there sat Jonathan Hudson beneath the hood of his sweatshirt. April turned away, hoping he did not see her. She looked to Richie and said, "I don't know."

"You never could lie. You just saw someone you know. Lee or Jonathan? Which one?" Richie asked.

"Hudson. He didn't see me. He's lost in his music—you know, the way he was when he taught romantic poetry."

"I never did understand Keats or Coleridge," said Richie. "Or like either of them."

"One way to get around that was to pretend," April said. "Plus, it helped that I was a girl. When I first met him, I was a girl."

"Meaning?"

"We had great years with him. I was young and then, by the time we were finished, I felt more mature," April said. "Wrong word. I mean, I wasn't so intimidated. Now, not so much—which is part of the problem."

"Were you always more mature than me, April?"

"I think maybe I was, at least until this past year when we became more involved. Everything's different now, isn't it?" April looked directly at Richie as she spoke.

Just then, the door to the shed opened and Jonathan Hudson, smiling, emerged. He quickly walked to April and Richie and said, "I was listening, before, to a Beethoven sonata, one that sounds a bit like Mozart, and I thought someone maybe looked in. Was it one of you?"

April raised her hand.

"April, don't just stand there. Come in," he said.

Situated between them, she gazed up the hill toward the Silverbirch campus.

"Why not?" April said, realizing that her response described the summer so far and might as well apply to the remaining weeks there.

"Richie," she said and waved at him to join her.

Hudson opened the door and, when they entered, April and Richie were greeted with soothing chamber music.

"What is that, Mr. Hudson? Sorry. I mean, Jonathan," Richie asked.

"From Bach. 'The Well-Tempered Clavier,'" he said. "I keep some of my favorite records down here. This is where I go to lose myself."

"I thought this was just a storage shack for towels," said April.

"I am a hideaway kind of guy. In school, and I might as well tell both of you now, I don't tend to hang out in the teachers' lounge. There's this annex, though, to the basement boiler room. That's where you can find me, more often than not," said Jonathan. "The only other person I know of who is aware of this spot is Lee."

"Next, you'll tell us he dances to Bach," said Richie.

"Actually, he comes here after everyone's asleep, especially if he wants a small place, not like the barn. He brings his music and, yes, practices steps and small moves inside the shed."

"Seems pretty confining," said April.

"Or he might dance outside, around the pool," said Jonathan.

"What now?" April asked.

"We could all swim or I could leave and just you two swim," he answered.

"'You're both better than me," said Richie.

"If you can teach swimming, there's a place for you at Silverbirch," said Jonathan. He turned to both of them. "Can I escort you back to the ball? As you know, I am, in theory, the host. I told Lee I would step out from time to time, and he is fine with that. Just needed to get away for a few moments to collect my thoughts."

So Jonathan led the way as April and Richie, hand in hand, followed. As they neared the barn, they heard delectable piano music emanating from within.

"Masked ball music?" asked April.

"Lee accentuates it on when people begin streaming in," said Jonathan.

The music stopped and, after a pause, began again.

"Now what are we hearing?" asked Richie, as Jonathan opened the screen door.

"This one is called 'The Goldberg Variations,' by Bach," said Hudson.

Richie said, "You're still teaching us. It just keeps happening."

Hudson bowed. "Come in," he said.

Various people in various costumes ranging from the eccentric to the everyday, milled about.

Richie whispered into April's ear, "Not everyone looks bizarre—or maybe unique, I should say, like us."

As if he knew what Richie was thinking, Jonathan said, "Not everyone wants to go Elizabethan. It's okay for people to come and just do nothing. We do have some who revel in this fantasy, though, and choose it as the time to look strange and still fit right in."

A masked man wearing a black leather vest and pants to match suddenly appeared, and April immediately knew him to be Lee by the contours of his upper half. She was certain he winked at her before saying, "Welcome to the masked ball, 1965 vintage. Think backward to 1600, give or take." He grabbed a handheld microphone, sang a few lines from "Blueberry Hill," and jumped onto a rear platform.

Richie did not know whether he should cling to or release April.

Lee winked through the eyelet of his red mask and summoned April to the stage.

"Here's a sweetheart who will dance 1965 instead of 1600," Lee said. "For a beauty like you, let's really get into it," he continued and nodded behind him to a young man working the turntable.

The voice of Fats Domino was resounding on "Ain't That a Shame" and April found herself simultaneously enthralled and energized.

Lee bowed to April and said, "Not you, no," and spun her around before sending her back in Richie's direction. Richie hugged her hard, placed his hand on her head, and smiled. She touched her stomach where it had been drawn to Lee's. April, again, did not know what to think or whether to think. A couple of months earlier, she considered Richie her forever boyfriend. Then, soulful and sweet and fatherly Jonathan. Now there was Lee; she didn't really know what to make of him. For certain, he was on fire.

"Richie, maybe we should just go for a walk. I mean, you're only here until tomorrow and this dance, I don't know, it could be a bad fit for me—for us."

"Like the prom, April? We can't get to the ferry from here," he said.

"Come on," she said. "I've heard of this special place but never been there. It's way beyond the tennis courts up over that hill." She waved behind her.

"Not in these clothes," he said.

"Good enough." April led Richie to her room, and they both quickly changed into jeans and sweaters.

"Should we leave the masks on?" asked Richie. "Just in case an animal comes along, we can scare the crap out of him."

April laughed and was relieved at the opportunity for release rather than consideration. It was a lot to take in, though. After all, three men? She knew her mother would have a very mixed reaction to that sort of attention. April was happy that none of them would ever become doctors.

As they walked, Richie slipped his hand into one of the rear pockets of April's jeans.

"I know," said April. "About enough room there to fit in a thin dime and that's about it."

"You're not fat, April."

"My mother predicted this," she said. "Your shape, she told me, changes from straight drinking glass to something closer to a Coke bottle. Not the most poetic way to say it, but right. Right?"

"If you say so, Ap. I love this you," Richie said.

April looped her arm around his waist but could hardly find skin to grasp. She was envious. April marched uphill—directly toward the clay courts. Richie just a little faster and prodded April to match his pace. When they reached the crest of the hill, April signaled for him to stop. She motioned toward the woods, where several deer sashayed and stared.

"Here's a budding master of ceremonies," said April, pointing to a deer that did not move.

"And this one is either scared or measuring us," Richie added, nodding toward a much larger deer that then walked gently toward them. "I'll sweet-talk him away," he said. Richie, speaking to the animal as he would talk to a human, explained that he and April needed to be alone to explore, "so please leave." The deer, as if it were a broken-field football running back, lurched at Richie, then April, and, gracefully skirting both of them, disappeared down the hill. The rest of its contingent followed.

"They took a left," said Richie. "Guess that means we stay right."

"The large one seemed just like a teenager to me," said April. "I think they're heading into poison ivy. I know that much. The right fork has a path. Let's go." She pushed Richie in front of her. The hill was sharply angled, and they needed to slide down on their bottoms to navigate.

"At least we're not in costumes," said April.

Richie tumbled, while April used her hands for balance.

"Tire tracks?" Richie asked.

"Looks like a wagon or maybe one of those older baby carriages rolled in here," said April.

The branches had been cleared well enough to allow walkers through. April thought someone had actually manicured the edges with ferns. How else would they form such a distinct boundary? Just a few months back, she and Richie had peeled off their clothes to swim in the Atlantic at Point Lookout. Now, as darkness blanketed them, she could only see where they were going thanks to the fireflies guiding them. There seemed to be hundreds of the flashing little creatures.

April sang "This Little Light of Mine" and implored Richie to join her. They happily joined hands and smiled at one another.

"Till the promised land," added April.

Richie stopped and said, "You're suddenly a fan of religion?"

"One thing I'm learning this summer is that it's personal. Jonathan is a spiritual man, and he never goes to a church."

"April, if we ever did get married, would our children do Hebrew school?"

She was caught fully off guard, unprepared to answer, so she said, "It just doesn't matter to me, even though my parents did stress Judaism until recently. I think maybe they've finally given up."

"I wasn't forced," Richie answered, "especially since my mom never went to a synagogue. At my bar mitzvah, I wanted to hang out with friends and with the cantor. That guy was kind of cool."

"Hudson is actually Jewish. His name doesn't sound it, but it could have been changed," April said.

"It sounds so WASP-y. You know, like those old cars: Hudsons."

"The thing about you, Richie, is that you can always get me to laugh," she said.

"Even when I'm not trying, like now. And how many times did you nearly have me falling off my chair in bio lab?"

"Just because Grainy used to be giving away what he had for lunch on that little black beard of his? Not my fault," April said.

"We called him Grainy the Goat because of the goatee," said Richie, setting April off once again.

"Hey, people think I'm nineteen here, already through one year of college, too old for adolescent humor."

"Excuse me, Miss Sophisticate," he answered.

"Follow my body," April said and resumed walking through the soft leaves and branches on the ground. She didn't know why she said it that way. She decided it was because he was no longer simply the boy next door. Obviously.

Taking the cue, Richie wrapped one of his arms around her middle, under her sweatshirt, and she invited his touch. She so enjoyed having his hand pressed to her flesh.

April, with feigned assurance, walked farther down the path as Richie pressed against her. He was like a cocoon, hugging her to prevent them from falling down together. She knew what was on his mind. And why not?

"Richie, do you want to head back?" April laughed from within his grasp. "You're not giving me a whole lot of breathing room."

He dodged the question. "Does this wilderness walk end up somewhere or is it kind of like the march through, what, a land of brambles?"

April wasn't ready to run back to her room, take off her clothes, and follow his script. Not yet, at least. "What I've heard is that you walk for about 15 minutes and then you come to a clearing and an upward slope. Filled with blueberries."

"I'm good. You know I'm not really Nature Boy, but this seems fun. Who told you about it?"

"It was Lee."

"'Blue Suede Shoes' and swivel hips?"

"That's the one," said April. "He told me he wore the shoes there once and they turned two shades darker in the midst of the berries," she added.

"Okay, sure," said Richie. "Let's go."

They crunched and rustled broken branches on the ground, then heard a noise coming from a few yards away.

"What is that?" April asked, leaning against Richie.

"Shhhh, it stopped; it's scared of us," he said. "But maybe it's a sign that we better get out of here."

Within his arms, April shrugged and said, "Let's try to at least make it to the clearing. I've never walked through to see the berries, which are supposed to be legendary."

"Okay," he said, and this time he took the lead and pulled her forward. He could feel her muscles tense. "Fats Domino would be proud."

Suddenly, without a hint, the woods parted and, to the left, a pristine pond, perfectly appropriate for a picture postcard, lay at rest. At this sundown moment, nothing moved.

April squeezed more tightly to Richie and whispered in his ear, "Here or Point Lookout? Don't think; just answer."

"The beach at midnight," he said.

"I don't know. That time, we were both almost drunk," she said.

"And wearing pretty much nothing, given how we started the night—in an evening gown and tux."

April took off her sweatshirt and faced Richie. "Well?"

"What if somebody shows up here, April?"

"Who would?"

"Mr. Hudson. You told me he knows every inch of Silverbirch."

"He's hosting the masked ball, remember?" April said.

A crackling limb on a tree startled them.

"What is it?" Richie asked.

April, her T-shirt hanging loosely over her, took his hand and pointed upward. "We have owls here," she said.

"What do they do?" Richie asked.

"Hoo . . ." answered April.

He touched her stomach, and she welcomed and covered his hand. She relaxed. "I guess this is me now. I'm not thirteen-year-old April anymore," she said.

"You're ahead of me. You're fast becoming a woman, April, and I'm still a teenager just out of high school, on the way to college."

Above, something twitched once again.

"I know: owl," said Richie.

"Exactly. They come out when the sun goes down. They tend to move upward on the trunk, maybe to a branch higher," April said. "Swoosh," she whispered. "Look, kind of orange and yellow glow to its eyes."

"April, there are fireflies around the its eyes. They're glowing like suspended jewels or something," he said. Then, after a moment, "Let's go back to your room."

"I'm almost ready," said April. "When I'm with you, I want you all of that time, Richie."

"I'm leaving tomorrow, April. What happens next?"

"My job is to teach the kids to swim, show them how to dribble on the dirt basketball court, all of that. I actually love it, could do this forever."

"I'm tempted to come back every weekend, April."

"It's totally confusing. I would like that, but this is also my time to, well, be me," she said.

"So, be yourself."

"Men drop their wives and kids here on a Sunday and come back a week later. Well, I suppose I've been sheltered," said April. "I guess maybe these marriages just don't work out or . . ."

Richie interrupted, "Or maybe some women would rather be here with the slate wiped clean. You know where I'm going with that thought?"

"I'm a quick learner," April said. "I have eyes. There's a part of me that wants to just go up to someone and ask what went wrong and when. It couldn't have always been so boring that you go off to the Catskills for sex."

"Like me?" Richie asked.

"Are you referring to the fast study part or the sex part?"

"I trust my brain more than my body, April."

She drew him to her and embraced him. He was her closest friend, but how do you define friend? April released Richie and stood in front of him. "Can you find your way back to the room?"

"Sure," he said, "but why?"

"I just have to figure it out—by myself, Richie. Give me thirty or forty minutes to meet you there?" April asked.

Richie responded as he always had, as she knew he would: "You want time and space, April. I love you. I'm off, and I will wait up."

"Like when we waved good night window to window from our bedrooms, Richie."

He quickly and decisively walked the other way on the path. "Later, April."

She continued on another trail, with the hope that it would lead to a clearing and a blue-green pond. During all of her time at Silverbirch, she had heard of but not seen another body of water on the grounds. Not five minutes later, the wooded area split and the ripples of Lily Lagoon, as it was called, caught April's attention.

Chapter Ten

April

*S*UGAR? HOW CAN THAT *be so? My dad eats rye bread with tons of butter and sugar on it. I might be addicted to donuts. Viv sometimes makes cinnamon sugar bagels. Soda's good sometimes, but when I think about swimming in sugar water, that's enough.*

April slowly began to walk around the lagoon.

Sugar cone, sugar cookie, sugar is sweet and so is Richie. Or Jonathan? Maybe even Lee? I'm eighteen, and everyone here thinks I'm a year older. "Take a risk and you make the shot," as my coaches always said. Let's play it out and leave the sure thing for last. The greatest leap would be Lee. He's divorced, and I like his wife better than I like him. But he wears these clingy shirts that make me think about James Dean. Or, really, anyone with a pack of cigarettes in his chest pocket or, better yet, tucked into a short sleeve right where his muscle is. Dancing with him that day, it was hard not to jump him. Hey, I'm a girl, right? I get hot just like guys. I grew up sweating because of sports. Even getting near this man, my shirt sticks to me. He has that effect, and I can share it here, by myself with the trees and owls and, pretty soon, darkness.

I have to start walking in the right direction. It wouldn't be great if the swimming teacher couldn't find her way out of the woods on the night of the masked ball. Some teacher I am—here I am spending my time thinking and fantasizing about men's bodies.

Talking about teachers, I fell head over heels for Jonathan Hudson when he took his T-shirt off that day we were shooting free throws. A lean man, you can see his ribs. God. I had a hard time not putting my hands on his stomach. Richie's is almost as flat, but Hudson's a grown man. It's different. Are girls supposed to think like this? Comparing multiple midsections?

Richie is my good friend, no matter what, and the night of the prom I was positive he was it, this was for real, we would be married in a year or two. He wants me and knows me better than anyone. If he comes up here one or two more times, I won't be going back and forth: slam dunk that he's the one. So, what's my problem? Too easy?

"I'm going back to find out," she sang, to the trees, the owl, the moon, and the few stars that had already appeared. April thought she heard a hoo in response. "It doesn't matter what you think," she said. "I'm tired of just going so far. I mean, Lee would have taken me home that night we were sweating and dancing. I owe it to Richie."

The decision made, April began to trot back through the trail in the woods, hoping to at least see the tennis courts, from the rear, before it was fully dark. Fortunately, the moon was white and bright, assisting her through some rough ground cover.

Emerging from the woods, she was caught off guard by the thwack of a tennis ball. Who could possibly be practicing in the dark? April walked up the grassy slope that led to the court—and found Richie, in the dark, smacking one ball off the tattered green practice wall.

"I should have known," she called. "I have questions."

"Ap, I really was going back to the room to wait for you. I found the racket and this one ball at the front entrance. It's like it was set up for me to try. I never did play much tennis," he said. "At this point, it's sort of by feel. The moon's getting just bright enough, though, so I can make things out a little bit." He tossed the ball in the air and caught it.

"Well, I'm on my way back. Are you coming?" April asked.

Richie put down the racket and ball. "With you? Yes," he said.

She put her arm around his waist. "Here, let me lead. I know how to do this."

"Sure, whatever you say, April," Richie replied.

So many times when they were little, he would dribble the basketball, leading the way, as they walked to the basketball courts at the school playground. April was glad to be the one in charge now. Even if Silverbirch wasn't exactly her place, she was more familiar with the terrain.

It was an uneventful walk past the dining room and main lodge. April was relieved that Lee wasn't standing outside the barn, looking for them.

Soon enough, she was opening the door to her room for Richie and pushing him through.

He stood awkwardly, ramrod-straight, in the middle of the room.

April started laughing. "I like the way you look," she said.

Richie glanced down at himself and saw that he still had the old sweatshirt and dungarees on. April had stretched her sweatshirt to make it fit - sort of. The neck was loose, the body of the shirt tighter. The three-quarter-length jeans she had pilfered from her mother's closet.

"Shower?" April asked.

"Sure," said Richie. "You go first."

"I meant together," she answered. "Come on," April said, taking off both of her tops. Richie pushed his pants and boxers downward till he was able to step out of them. Clinging to one another, they went into the bathroom as April remarked, "Classiest part of my room—a Plexiglas shower door. Can you imagine?"

"I really didn't notice, April," Richie said and kissed her on the lips.

The steam had fully consumed April's tiny living quarters by the time they waltzed out of their lengthy shower and back into her room. She walked to her old phonograph and put on a record. Rhythmic piano playing filled the room.

"What is that?" Richie asked as he rested on April's bed.

"'Waltz for Debby' I told my father I was taking it. I also swiped one of my mom's sweaters, and the jeans I was wearing earlier are also hers. I have a special music simpatico thing with my father, so I knew he wouldn't mind if I took one of his favorite jazz records. If I know him, he bought another one at Abe's Records already."

"That's incredible. I wish I had learned to play piano," said Richie.

"You still can, Richie. We're young, remember?" she said. "Although you may not be able to become the next Bill Evans." She snuggled next to him.

"I knew you loved music, but I guess I didn't realize the jazz aspect."

"It comes from hearing the instruments. Jazz was always on in my house, thanks to my dad. You couldn't help but listen."

"And now? Whose voice do you listen for?" Richie asked.

"Yours?" April answered with a question.

"And after I go home?"

"I will still listen for you."

"Not all that convincing, April."

Wearing just her underwear, April leaned into Richie. "We were the best at prom," she said.

"I feel like I would have to live here not to lose you, April."

"We agreed that it would be okay for me to do this, Richie. Then we'll be, what, five or so hours apart when fall comes? Our colleges are that close." She got up, walked to the record player, and put on a new song.

Richie immediately recognized the trumpet beginning. "Satchmo," he said.

"You know something, at least," said April.

"I saw him on *The Ed Sullivan Show* more than once. It's like a religion in our house. I know—yours, too. Each Sunday night, we're all glued to that program. Who is that singing?" Richie asked.

"It's Ella Fitzgerald. We have albums of the two of them blending together," she said.

"Were they on television together, too?"

April said, "I'm not positive, but they must have been. This one was 'Summertime.' Want to hear it again?" April wore nearly nothing as she crossed the room.

"Yeah, and then can we go to bed? I have to drive back tomorrow."

"I did not forget. Did you ever go hear music at Jones Beach?"

"Yes, some old band," Richie said. "I don't know who. Listen, can we get stuff to eat somewhere?"

"We can sneak into the dining room. I did that with Hudson one time," April said.

"Let's go," said Richie, pulling on pants and a sweatshirt.

"Give me one second. It looks like I'm still in the shower," said April. She flipped her hair into a ponytail and covered most of it with a Celtics cap. "Okay," she said.

They took a route around the main lodge in order to come up to the rear dining room door. Unexpectedly, Lee greeted them with what April knew, by now, was one of his favorites: "Love Me Tender." He lifted his guitar to greet them and said, "Hello, sweetness and sweetness's boyfriend."

"Hi, Lee," said April as Richie extended his hand to shake Lee's.

Lee said, "You went for a swim."

"More like each of us needed to rub off some of the stage makeup. You know, someone heads up a masked ball around here and he gives out paint that won't fully wash off. You almost need a blasting device."

"I have stuff to remove it, but no one ever asks," he said.

"Lee?" April asked, touching his arm.

"Your boyfriend is one step away, April," Lee said.

"Would it be possible to lift a box of the Oreos stashed behind the cage in the kitchen?" April asked.

"I'm a champion thief," said Lee. He opened the screen door and bowed as he let Richie and April through. "Watch," he said.

Within moments, Lee had scaled the wire, held together with wooden slats, and was waving to them below. "Piece of cake compared to negotiating the catwalk, sweetheart," he said to April. "Just one box is hardly worth it. How about Mallomars, too?"

"Yes!" Richie shouted, a bit loudly.

"A single," said April.

"You can't eat just a cookie at a time," said Lee. "If you like bagels, and I know you do, cookies are upscale from that."

"Exactly," said April.

"She wants to be the same weight as when she was ten," said Richie. "We've known each other since we were six."

"April, may your grace be with you forever," said Lee. "You've probably been protected closely for these nineteen years of yours. Maybe you can outrun some of the difficulties life seems to present to all of us. The two of you make for a very cool couple. What's next?"

"I get some sleep and drive back to the Island tomorrow morning," said Richie.

April did not want to comment, so she changed the subject. "Lee, the ball was amazing," she said. "Are you in charge of it every year?"

"Not officially. If people like it, I keep doing it."

"Lee," said Richie, "I have to go. A few hours of sleep and then head for home. Thank you for including me," he continued while smiling at a man he suspected to be competing for April.

Within the confines of April's room, April and Richie were now all about tossing clothing on the floor and easing into bed.

"Maybe we better talk, April," he said.

"Okay, I guess I can't get out of it now," she said.

"When can I come back?" Richie asked.

"It sounds lame, but I need a little time. I've settled in here, but when you come, I almost feel like leaving. I promised myself to give it a good try," she said. "You need to get some sleep. Can we talk a little more tomorrow morning before you leave?"

"I love you," he said.

"Me, too," answered April as she cuddled with him. Richie pulled her closer, hoping this was forever.

•••••••••••

April did not wish to spend the early morning in the dining commons.

"Let's drive to Viv's," she said to Richie. "People come there early on Sundays for hot bagels, and then we're not exactly at Silverbirch. Close in miles, but that's all."

"Sure," said Richie, as he stretched out in her bed. "What time is it?"

"Past eight o'clock and I know you need to be on the road before noon, yes? We can shower before or not," she said.

"I would rather not," said Richie. "Shave? Yes. Give me ten minutes, give or take."

"Easy. Don't cut yourself," said April.

Off they went, soon enough, as the sun beat down upon them and Richie's well-traveled car, groaning, seemed to already beg for more rest. April liked talking to Richie about the rolling hills, light blue sky, and horse farms. One large jet-black animal looked up and smiled at them.

"I take that as a good sign," said Richie.

"This is God's day of rest," April said. "And pastoral."

"What?"

"On the seventh day, He rested and the other part is Hudson talking about the English countryside," she said, as Bagel City came into view. Viv was outside, talking animatedly with Lee.

"Does he spend all his time out here?" Richie asked, pointing toward Lee.

April looked around. She was relieved that the other men were not there. It was easier to deal with Lee than with Hudson. April wished she and Richie had Viv all to themselves.

That notion was not realized, for, as they parked, Lee shouted out, "Well, the princess and her Prince Charming! What better on a Sunday morning?"

"Where did you learn to dance like that, Mr. Lee?" Richie asked.

"Don't exactly know. Growing up in suburban Boston surely had nothing to do with it," said Lee. "Sister April, dance with me?"

April looked to Richie, who nodded and smiled.

"Viv, spin 'Hound Dog.'"

Moments later, Elvis was driving yet poignant. His music could stir emotions through the man's passion and ability to very his delivery. Lee lip-synced the words while April, twirled by the swinging dance master, sang along. She remembered when it played through the lobby sound system as she and Richie were approaching the Copa a few months earlier.

"We were married and he was dancing on the city sidewalks, even along our fire escape," said Viv. "Hard for me to resist swivel hips." Everyone heard Viv, but no one responded. She continued, "There was an incentive award for people who could bring people together on their blocks." She nodded at Lee.

"Both of us," he said. "Viv had these twirly skirts that made men dizzy."

"It wasn't so much the outer skirts but the fact that they flew around and guys looked away and pretended not to be sneaking peeks," she said.

"Little has changed, Viv. You still slay them—even more so without me," said Lee.

"April, I packed earlier and have to go pretty soon," said Richie. "It's a trip back, and I told my dad I could help him tomorrow."

"We just got here, Richie," she said. "I wanted to talk with Viv."

"Hey, I can stay here as long as you want and just drive you back to Silverbirch whenever, April," said Lee. "Take it from me. Let the boyfriend do what he needs to do. I spend too much time hovering. Right, Viv?"

April nodded, and her eyes seemed to well just a bit with tears. Viv looked away.

"I can do the bagels and the register," said Lee. "Kid, get in your car and head for home. You two"—he gestured at Viv and April—"go for a walk or something. I'm fine."

"Wait," said Richie. "April, we need to talk before I go."

He took her hand and led her around Bagel City. They sat beneath a small willow tree, the scent from its boughs wafting in the summer wind.

"I don't really want to go," said Richie.

"I just wish you were going back to the room with me," April said. She paused before adding, "It's like prom night, which I never wanted to end. I want to extend the weekend."

"My dad's expecting me, and you know I've always been the good boy," he said. "What if we just ran off and got married?" Richie asked.

"Now, you mean?" April asked.

"I don't know. There's a part of me which says to just go for that." He thought for a minute and tried to switch topics: "You are supposedly a year older than me, having been to college and all that from what you told me. Mr. Hudson just plays right along?" Richie asked.

"I actually think he feels it's kind of neat. Like a short story or something. He likes the plot—at least, so far. Richie, if you don't get in your car soon, we'll find an excuse for you to stay till tomorrow."

Rising, he led April back around to the front of the building, where they found Lee and Viv seated outside, laughing as if they were long-lost friends.

Lee jumped out of his chair while waving to April. "Let's go back," he said.

"He's always been like that," Viv said, "with a spring in his back so you can wind him up and off he goes."

Richie gave April a bear hug, pulled open the creaky driver door of his car, and slowly turned the vehicle around before heading for home.

"One thing I know," said Lee, "is that this kid will be back. You know the song, 'I Only Have Eyes for You'? Well, that's him. You ever hear of The Flamingos? Their version is the coolest, the one I learned from. Anyway, Richie is convinced you are the only one," Lee said. "I'll drive you back."

Without notice, April felt tears welling. Before Lee could sweep April into his car, Viv pulled her close enough to lightly touch her forehead. "It'll be okay. Later, we'll talk. Let Lee get you home and maybe I can come visit you late in the afternoon after I close. Yes?"

With a sigh, April nodded her head; she was too choked up to speak.

For a brief moment, Lee was silent and it occurred to April that this might have been a first, at least in her presence. Most of the time, he was a gyrating mechanism, eager to dance; even when walking, he became a man who bounced from heel to toe. He put down the top of his car while driving, and she loved the way the wind whipped her hair in front of her eyes. It served to shield the soft current of tears. The embrace with Richie lingered. Lee eyed her and, to his credit, played the radio and gave her space.

April expected Lee to suddenly blast the volume. Instead, he asked her, "Do you know the folksinger Dylan's 'Blowin' in the Wind'?"

"Only because Mr. Hudson played it for us in class. He's actually seen Bob Dylan in The Village and just goes on and on about him. He's so young he almost still looks like a teenager," she said. "I mean Bob Dylan, not Hudson."

"With heroes like Fats Domino and Elvis, you wouldn't expect me to get into Bob Dylan, but I do," Lee said. "I can also just sit in a corner of the barn at two in the morning and say or sing that final line where Dylan gives us his answer. He gestured upward.

"You must love your car, with the top down like this," she said and waved her arms like a propeller.

"I memorize the lyrics of this young Dylan guy when I'm alone and by myself and the air's swirling about me," he said. "It's like I'm in my own wind tunnel."

"You mean like at Jones Beach parking lot 4 on the way to the pools? An echo chamber or something in your brain?" April asked.

"Which is odd since the guy might show up with his guitar at Gerdy's or someplace like that and play. Not what I dance to, as you know. The impact, though, is amazing—maybe because I saw him at The Gaslight. He was just sitting there, on the floor, between sets. Just a skinny, curly-headed guy, but when he opened his mouth, it was hypnotic," Lee said.

As he spoke, Lee accelerated, the speed of his car matching his excitement. April knew about Dylan's folk and protest singing only because Hudson had played "The Times They Are A-Changin'" in class. Even though Dylan sounded like he was holding his nose during the song, she remembered being completely taken in by his boyishness and distinctive twang. Hudson talked a lot about equality in the country. As a second-semester senior, though, April still thought more about Richie than human rights.

Lee drove April to her door, pulling up on the dirt path as his brakes screeched.

"You take care," he said, "and if you need me, I will be in my barn apartment."

Given the afternoon to rest, regroup, and rethink the past two days, April chose to go for a swim. She put on her suit and topped it with the Cousy jersey and a pair of cutoff shorts. Grabbing a towel, April hoped for solo laps, even just a few, at the pond. She took a longer route, behind the dining hall and through the woods, again wishing to be alone with her emotions. April kept her head down, trying to avoid both poison ivy and brambles since she was wearing tennis shoes without socks.

Then, a large deer jumped onto the trail about twenty-five yards away.

Chapter Eleven

April Revisited

"Hey," said April, as if greeting an old friend. She walked directly toward the animal, which did not move. As if conversing with the deer, April continued, "Sure, I don't mind sharing this path with you. If you totally hated me, you could have run away already. My dad used to tell me a story about a deer outrunning the wind. I was in the story because my father always made me the focus, if not the hero, of these things. Anyway, it seems that a little girl named June—yeah, I know, April gets changed to June—well, June pretty much skipped forward instead of walking in a straight line."

"Several blocks from our house, behind another development of half-built homes, we kids had a cut through that led to the playing fields at the high school. This part is real, by the way, not what Dad made up. It was always swampy there, and after it rained, you could step into muck and it would cover your ankles. Still, for teenagers, it was a nice break from the usual walk up to the head of our street, taking a right and then half a mile to school. There was the possibility of small adventure if you cut behind Zucky's yard. Some of my friends were a little nervous about being in what we called The Patch by themselves, but no one would admit it. I really liked this marsh, complete with snakes and who knows what else, but I didn't get there until this past year. Until then, it was home and basketball and school for me.

"My best friend, Richie, has definitely become more than that. At first, I thought it was too much too soon. I can get emotional about it because just maybe he's perfect.

"Anyway, one day in late May, when light lasted much longer, I decided to take The Patch to the high school after dinner. I think I just wanted to be alone. What I remember is walking along and wishing I had my basketball. They had just installed lighting on a court by the school, and I wanted to try that out. So I guess I was lost in thought when a deer, out of nowhere, just exactly like you, showed up five or six feet from me. I took a step toward it and sank into mud. Away went the deer and there I was, nearly up to my calves in sticky gunk.

"By the time I made it to the high school, it was pretty dark. There wasn't any reason to stay, and I took the safe way back. When I got home, Dad was swaying back and forth in the wooden swing on the front porch."

• • • ● ● • ● • ● • • ●

"I figured you'd show up at some point, Apie," Bert said.

"Dad, there was one beautiful deer and . . ."

"Where were you, April?"

"Just on a walk through The Patch to the high school. A deer came along, and I was thinking about the Junie story you used to tell me when I was little. Junie was my made-up very wonderful friend, even before Richie," she said.

"I have a June story that actually did happen," he said.

April sat next to her father in the clickety-clackety wooden contraption that he had put together. She was repeatedly amazed at his construction aptitude. The swing groaned each time they pushed it forward.

"The time I took you to The Catskill Game Farm," he said. "It was within a week of when we moved here," said her father. "Do you remember that trip?"

"Was there a pony ride?" April asked.

"Yes, that was part of it." He smiled broadly.

"That's all I can remember. Sitting on a pony."

"That you did, sweetheart. I was holding you since I was afraid you would slip off. Well, we walked you around that ring and you were laughing so hard and I was caught in that moment in time. But then in an instant, Junie disappeared. I looked for her, and she wasn't there."

"What did you do?" April asked.

"I totally panicked," Bert said and pushed off on the swing with greater force. "Didn't know what to do. I had to stay with you, but where was she? And the game farm backs up into the woods. I was terrified."

"Yikes," said April, aware that she had said this word probably once or twice before in her life. "What happened next?"

"Well, you were just over six. For some reason, I brought an old backpack I used to carry you around in when you were really little. I had made holes so your legs could dangle through. It wasn't really built to tote a six-year-old about. But I grabbed you off the beloved pony, which caused you to scream and scream. Without giving you a choice, I jammed you into the carry and just took off up a hill while yelling for Junie. After a minute, you joined in.

"It was hot, too, which didn't help. I immediately thought the worst—that Junie had wandered off and how could we possibly find her. There was a main trail, so I just followed it since I couldn't possibly reason out what might or might not be logical."

"So I'm actually in the story, wow. How long were we doing this, Dad?"

"A while. I can't say how long exactly. Then I thought we might get caught in a thunderstorm. I remember that. Finally, there was a fork and I took it. Otherwise, it was just too much of an uphill. Racing downward, it twisted and turned. With you on my back, we came upon what must have been six or eight deer—like a family. They were startled but then held their ground. I stopped, not knowing what to do. After a few minutes, a doe split off, looking back at me once or twice, and, for whatever reason, I followed. That deer was running fast, toward a house in the distance."

"Chasing after one deer in the middle of the forest with your own growing six-year-old on your back? Is this a real story, Dad?"

"I just tell cool things I remember, April."

She did not know what this meant, but ever since she was a little girl, she found it joyous to listen to him as he knelt by her bedside. His impersonations of animals were the best.

Now, he resumed: "I sprinted after the deer—the fleet and graceful creature who seemed to beckon. The animal ran directly to the cabin below—and then stopped perhaps fifty yards away. I saw a little girl with sky blue barrettes in her hair, and I knew it was Junie. I tried to get you to stay quiet, but you, too, recognized her and started to say her name."

"Sorry, Dad."

He laughed. "No, sweetheart. We inched closer and discovered her playing in what seemed to be a miniature village. She was surrounded by characters out of fairy tales."

"Come on."

"No, really. I walked softly and approached. No one seemed scared or fazed or anything. Junie smiled and kept playing."

"So far, it actually sounds partially believable, Dad."

"I meant for Junie to sound real, be real. She was your creation, and I just put her into stories," he said.

"You're telling me this was a place for Minnie Mouse and Daisy Duck and such?"

"They were talking with Junie. I came nearer, and the deer ran off, again looking over at me, as if to say good-bye. Junie was in the middle. Maybe there were actually people wearing costumes and I didn't think of it at the time. I was out of breath, worried about you, stunned with relief to find Junie. So, I just bought into the fairy tale of it all."

"A happy ending. You and Junie and me, the three of us together, and you were able to leave the village and find the game farm. Right?"

"More or less." Her father shrugged and nodded, a combination he used when there wasn't anything more to say.

• • • • ● ● • ● • • •

At the pond, April lay on her towel and stared at the boughs above her. Thinking of her father and home, she wondered whether it might be best to depart Silverbirch—to fully resume with Richie. Could she possibly come up with some story and leave the resort early? She was always the good girl, little Miss Perfect. This particular summer dizzied her. There were too many choices. Her eyes were opening to a world beyond that which she knew. Richie would be back home for a month or so before packing up and going to college. April realized she hadn't left herself time for transitioning. Everything had happened so fast: prom, end of high school, working at Silverbirch. And then there were the men: Richie, Hudson, Lee. She was just eighteen. It was all too much. April shut her eyes and slept.

Later, she was glad to quickly walk, by herself, to her room. No people, no television, no phone. Alone, she was pleased to immerse herself in *Middlemarch*, the novel Jonathan Hudson had recommended and kept referencing. She recalled him saying, "It's a coming-of-age story for women but back a century, for those of you who might look to the past to prognosticate the future." April wondered whether he framed such thoughts previously or could conjure them in the moment.

Certain that Richie wanted to call her, April retreated. Her room was a safe place, and that was essential. She had her record player and a few albums, the radio from her bedside table back home that she had decided to take at the last moment, books, and a couple of legal pads. April was keeping a journal. Hudson had told her that she was a potentially talented writer. "April, without knowing so, you're able to mix your verbal paintings," he had said. "Your essays take off when you imagine within them." Maybe she knew what he meant.

The room allowed for her introspection and release of emotions. A window opened upon the countryside, and words came to her so she wrote and wrote more. April was relieved to lend a voice to her conflicting feelings. It was confusing—who she was, where she was headed—and each day challenged her. Her work at Silverbirch was a panacea: She got to teach first and then experience the joyful reward when little kids, the campers, had fun or even succeeded. Feeling emancipated to express herself, April would record random thoughts, well-developed yet unproven theories, and the magnetic pull she felt to not one or two of the men but all three. Later, she would place the yellow pages, her notes, back in her bureau drawer until next time. She was relieved to have an outlet to express her feelings and equally heartened that no one else would ever read her words. The pages were filling. At times, she thought she actually could move along from adolescence to adulthood. How, though, would she make a decision when it came to the three men? This assumed that the choice would be hers.

Chapter Twelve

April's Journal

Richie

YOU ARE MY BROTHER or my lover? Are you both, or can you flip from one to the other?

My first memory is of bicycles. Our parents bought identical ones from Sears, I later found out. We had probably moved into those houses just weeks before and were getting acquainted. We had the bikes out on the new sidewalks. I don't recall the details, but you rammed into me. I fell off, skinned a knee, and started crying. What I do remember is how you instantly ran to me and hugged me. I mean, we were six years old, Richie. The only way I can visualize what we looked like is through snapshots. My hair must have been fine because my parents always had it clipped to stay out of my eyes. Yours was even lighter and thick: short, sticky crew cut. You must have inherited grooming habits from your father. He has great hair, and it's always identically parted as if there's a permanent line on his head.

That must have been sometime during the spring in 1953 because they told me we moved after winter of that year. It probably was the following December or January that they strapped on our ice skates and took us to the pond. This time, I think, I crashed into you. Neither of us had any balance or control. I could have been grabbing at you just to stay vertical. I guess we tumbled together, but it was at the edge of the surface and I smashed you into a log. I can still see the red blotches, the blood on the ice and on both of us. My folks filled me in with the rest of the story. Evidently, I picked you up and gave you a kiss to make it better. Our first kiss!

Next thing I can see is your yellow bedroom with both a basketball and rainbow painted right onto the wall. Maybe this was a couple of years later. My room was all in pink, probably my one typical girly touch. Maybe my parents wanted a girly girl. I guess that didn't really work since—presto!—I'm a tomboy forever. I did have a unicorn hanging from the ceiling, along with a black-and-white picture of Bob Cousy for a balance. The first time I saw your room, I was so surprised. Guess I expected blue and, I don't know, baseball players?

For a long time, I was like an inch taller than you. It helped me to know that when we shot hoops in your driveway or had our one-on-one games at the school. I wonder if our parents talked and decided that one hoop at your house was enough. I always wanted my own, in my driveway, even though we just shot at home and saved the games for the school court. Remember when you ran into our street after a rolling ball and nearly got hit by a car? We were so competitive that I bet you thought you could get off a shot before I was guarding you. Remember the makeshift clock we had pushing us to shoot? The flip cards we devised to keep score? I cannot believe we sometimes carried all of these things to the school playground. Makes me laugh now.

It was years later when I fainted on the outdoor court and suddenly I was in your lap and you were stroking my hair. What were we? Maybe all of twelve? Temperature in the mid-nineties and really humid. We decided to play till thirty-five by ones. Like most of our games, it was a close one, and the humidity was draining even if neither of us would acknowledge that. When I came to and looked back at you, the first thing I asked was who was ahead. Really. We were the same for a long time. My shooting kept me competitive with you, Richie. I could not wait to play basketball with you. Afterwards, we would walk to Carvel, which we did even after the passing out episode. We got to the ice cream place by foot or bike. When we walked, we had a game: We took turns dribbling a basketball there, and then we did passing drills. This was on the edge of the road since the sidewalk wasn't big enough. If anybody muffed a pass, the other would have to buy the cones.

It was way cooler for you to be doing all of this. I always felt that people were staring and gawking at me. Like, "Why isn't she putting on makeup instead of sweating through her T-shirt?" This was the beginning of an awkward time when our bodies were changing, especially mine. Having breasts made it all different. We were playing one-on-one all the time, and how was I supposed to guard you, press up against you, when I had these? You didn't let on that anything had changed until the time when you caught me flush and I yelped. I don't know if you worried more that I was hurt or embarrassed. It was pretty early after I was developing, too, that I took off my sweatshirt one day and, well, accidentally flashed you. I did not mean for that to happen. I'm sure you got a good look because you turned away in an instant. Sorry!

It all just flew forward from there. Closer and closer we grew—until prom night and the ferry and the beach and I was sure we would get married the next day.

Plus Jonathan Hudson, the security guy at Point Lookout, gun in holster and all.

Jonathan

I would have been just fine knowing that you were my finest and most influential high school teacher. I could have savored that and even embellished your status years into the future. But, if I'm being honest,

I probably could have seen the attraction coming. Your interest in my writing, the encouragement. It was genuine. During the first part of senior year, beginning in September, you had us reading the multigenerational novels. Six months later, you told us to write about what we knew. I went for drama in relationships—not from my own experience, which at that point was zero, but based on things I had heard things about our extended family. Then, following your advice, I mixed in people I knew or just imagined out of my head. "April, not everyone is writing quality dialogue like this," you said. I was amazed at that nine-word note at the top of one of my papers. I cut off your comment and taped it to my bedroom wall.

Then one day, Richie and I went to the high school outdoor basketball court and there you were. You said you were shooting foul shots until you made twenty in a row. Eventually, you said, you wanted to increase that to thirty. Since I was never quite as good from that line as I should be, I asked for pointers. After you watched me, you told me to square not only my shoulders but my feet, too. You said there was a boy from the new high school in town who did that and shot more than eighty-five percent. When I tried, you came over and adjusted something about the way I was releasing the ball. "April, it's okay to have it on your palm if it rolls off your fingertips," you said. I never forgot any of this and use it even with the kids. Most are better off with one foot forward, but, like me, there's always an exception. I was surprised, too, that you touched me. Guess I will now confess that when someone accidentally bumped me in the hallway, I could react with some drama.

I knew you would be at Silverbirch, and it registered that having someone familiar would probably be really helpful. Until I saw you out on the dirt court, without your shirt on, practicing foul shots followed by bank shots Also, every time you speak with me, there's a reference to a novel or a play or a poem. I know this is just how you are, but I somehow think these references are especially tailored for me.

I mean, if I mentioned dirt to you, you would probably come up with some path a clergyman took in a Victorian novel, why it was the right or wrong choice, the road as a metaphor, and all of that. Okay, so I'm a sucker; I get taken in.

You know that I'm eighteen years old and in some manner attracted to you, a man in his mid-thirties, I imagine. This is ridiculous, isn't it? I must be in love with the literary Mr. Hudson—my teacher and maybe even my muse in terms of pushing me to write. That's very different from being together romantically. Sure, sitting at a table in the dining room or teaching kids not to look at the ground when they dribble basketballs is great to share with you. Still, I feel like a spell is cast when you talk about characters in novels. Maybe I want to write a book someday. So far, I have nothing to say. I was way more into sports than what is normal—for a girl, at least. Lately, my brain gets blown away with romantic thoughts, but I guess that's right, huh? You always talk about writing what you know. My stuff, so far, is too boring. But this summer hasn't exactly been dull: I lied to get this job, I spend my nights picking out which man to fantasize about, and I can't help but watch women and men seeking each other out.

Might as well play it out. Watch for me, Jonathan. I might come out of nowhere to shoot baskets with you very soon. I'm making notes about my experience here at Silverbirch, and these I will show you. My plans. What might seem a complete surprise to you has been percolating in my mind for quite a while.

What do you think about writing something together? That sounds innocent. It gives me a chance to find out more about you, not Mr. Hudson and not my fellow staff member; no, it's about you—this skinny, poetic jump shooter who could play Jesus in a fifteen-minute documentary. All you need is a scruffy beard.

Should I fall in love with you, maybe I would live in Greenwich Village. You started talking about *A Hard Day's Night*, which I guess you saw during the past year. I know you like The Beatles, and I do, too, since I started to pay attention. Finally, I'll admit I'm not only thinking about how to dribble behind my back, like Cousy, which I still haven't mastered. I'm also thinking about my footwork. Anyway, fancy footwork brings me to the least likely of my choices.

Lee

I associate you with sweat. The barn had your scent, and you smelled like some of the hay on the edges of the floor. I wondered if you ever slipped on it. That time you started twisting at Viv's, I thought you were about to climb right up on me in full view of everyone. That's probably the only part I would have taken back.

One night, I snuck into the barn and hid in the corner partially behind a support to watch you. You did not just appear out of nowhere with Elvis, Fats Domino, The Beatles. You were practicing steps to a lot of Motown, too—The Temptations and Smokey Robinson and The Supremes. It draws you right in. No, it draws *me* right in. I can't speak for anyone else.

How can—how dare—I even be considering this or you? I mean, the woman I trust most to under-stand me around here is Viv. And you two were married. Every so often, she drops a hint about what that was like. Taking a guess, with the two of you living in the city, you could not have stayed to yourself in a small apartment. That's just not you.

Out of the three, you are definitely the mystery man. An extroverted guy I really don't know. Just as well. Richie, I probably could tell you everything about his life. Hudson, what do I know? Small pieces but mostly gaps. You do get to sense teachers after a while, and I've watched his combination of fun and smarts with the kids. With me, he's always at ease and gracious. He tosses in a hint of comedy every so often.

You, Lee, are the exact opposite—a raise hell type. I mean, you just get my juices going. I acknowledge that I enjoy it. I suppose I should say that I want that. But how can I get it? I thought sitting next to you in the dining room would be a good, safe starting point. I tried out that theory last week, before Richie's visit. What I discovered, shockingly, was that you were quiet. I expected that person I'd watched to jump up and start dancing on the table.

You asked me if I loved high school, then told me that you did, especially a Shakespeare teacher. Again, this caught me off guard since you had talked of playing football previously. I was so busy playing basketball, being the girl jock, staying in my house, spinning my life around my parents and little worlds I invented. I kind of knew about people like you, but, until now, I had never met one.

You're a man who shows who you are and what you feel on your face: I can see it. Like every time I catch you around Viv, you totally light up. I don't know if you guys are officially divorced, but I would imagine you would for sure sprint back if she ever wanted that.

How can I possibly picture myself with you? All I know is when you dance with me, I feel like hitching to your legs and, well, it goes on.

I know you the least of the three, and that's probably why I daydream about you a lot. I'm able to come up with some elaborate stories—like living in a downtown brownstone with you. I would work as a waitress a little while in college and you would make your way around the music clubs. I think you do some teaching, but it would be great to get details. Is it a steady thing or the opposite, like substituting, or something in between? There wouldn't be any future in this relationship, I don't think, but I'm eighteen and why not pursue it?

Here's the obvious answer: You're still in love with Viv. You have history, you are both in your thirties, and I think you want back in. I don't know about her, but she's such a good person that I wouldn't want to ruin anything for her.

I can still be your friend, yeah. But what gets me about you is your body. I'm not supposed to say that because I was raised to be careful and all of that. Being up here has opened my eyes, the way these men visit their wives and kids at Silverbirch each weekend, then go back to Scarsdale or Westport or Great Neck and do what they want. The women aren't all that different. We have these boys who are counselors and staff here, and it's a field day for them. The women wear skimpy bikinis and tight tank tops and all.

I mean, if I had clothes like that and wore them, you would have me in bed in no time. The way I feel now, there's no way I would object. I'd better not go there. If the walls don't have ears around here, everyone else does. You even get kids spewing gossip during free time around the pool about one or the other of their parents when they don't even know the full story. There's one boy I teach diving to—he probably is eight years old, very young, and they push him to learn to dive. He told me that his mommy likes Kenny when we are at Silverbirch. The kid goes on to say this Kenny person comes to their bungalow every day. One time, he was there for breakfast.

I've noticed that you wear a bathing suit that almost looks like boxer shorts. You would think you would have a tight number for show. For all I know, you, this spinning hot-footed dancer guy is more shy than you let on.

Chapter Thirteen

Music Lesson

APRIL WONDERED IF THE three men would come together. It would have to be around food, like either the dining hall or Viv's. She began to play it out in her mind. If Richie came again soon, they would go to Viv's. It was so much fun the last time, why not do it again? She envisioned a day with a lot of clouds, all white and puffy. Viv would gently hug her and, seeing Richie, give him a bear-hug. April loved the scenario.

As she embarked upon a leisurely walk to Viv's on a Saturday morning, she thought about her situation and mused further about Richie and Jonathan and Lee. April was glad to be by herself: solo. The rolling countryside was deeply green: resplendent mid-summer in the Catskills.

April imagined Viv would be by herself. Upon her arrival, Viv, smiling, said, "I am so excited to see you, April. Jonathan's in the back room. He brought by an armful of records. My guesses were all predictable: folk and folk rock and not horrendously loud rock 'n' roll. I wanted variety, so I think he has symphonies and string quartets and piano solos. And Vivaldi, of course."

"Sounds just like him," April said. "Why isn't he out here?"

"He insisted that he get this set up perfectly on the old phonograph. You can stack five on it, and he wants one after another," she said with a shrug. "I wouldn't be so particular, but he was nice enough to come out here and share. So, fine."

Hudson, hearing the talk, appeared with the record player in his hands. "It's a matter of sequence," he said. "You want to ease in with something like 'Clair de Lune' and then go to maybe Vivaldi for some uplift. Then listen to a violin concerto, although this could come before *Four Seasons*. See, if it was up to me, and I guess this is my project, I would put on *Rhapsody in Blue*. Some people wouldn't consider this classical, and it is hybrid for sure. Then Aaron Copland's *Appalachian Spring*. If there is time, Beethoven's Ninth Symphony because it's rousing and because it has the chorus. I want to jolt people—raise the roof of this shop or the Silverbirch barn. What do you think?"

He was looking right at April, the same way he did in class when he came in with one of his lecturettes and thought she might be the only one getting some meaning or even listening.

"I have to trust you," April said, almost calling him Mr. Hudson. "In my house, classical music was mixed in with big bands and Sinatra. I always liked to listen but didn't often pay close attention. Both my parents whistle, but sometimes they clash when it comes to their taste in music, especially since my mother likes The Beatles and she will go to them while tending her flowers or cooking."

"Your parents modeled well for you, April. I mean, who they are and how they live. You are such a proficient person. They must have been just that for you. It's kind of an art, to take in instead of give out."

With that, he hit the changer on the record player and Debussy filled the air.

"Wish I had a long, flowing skirt to wear while that plays," said Viv. "It just makes you feel that, maybe, life is a dream. That's what it sounds like to me."

"They talked with me a lot," said April. "My parents, I mean. They were never, ever too busy. It was pretty great: Richie in the next house with just his parents and me, too, no brothers and sisters. Our parents were such major parts of our lives."

And then a car came flying around the bend. It was Lee, and he was wired. He parked in a swirl of dust, bounded out, and hugged April heartily.

"Hud, how are you?" Lee asked.

"What are you on?" Viv asked Lee with a trace or more of sarcasm in her voice.

"You know what I'm like, and I came out here to see you, Viv. These two are a welcome bonus."

"What's on your mind?" Viv asked.

"Would it be okay to give Viv and me a little private time?" Lee asked, gesturing to Jonathan and April.

"Sure," Hudson said. He quickly put down the LP he was holding, said good-bye to Viv, and opened the passenger door of his car for April.

"Nice seeing you, Lee," April said. "Barn dance tomorrow night?"

"You bet, sugar." He blew a kiss at her.

April asked Viv if it was really okay to show up at Bagel City unannounced.

"That would be wonderful. I will pick you up and drive you here soon, like tomorrow or the day after, whenever you have time."

• • • • • • • • • • • •

Jonathan Hudson started the car, put on a station that was playing Tony Bennett, and slowly began to drive April back to the reality awaiting her at Silverbirch. That evening the staff would be gathering to make plans for the coming week. Just her luck to hear "Embrace me, my sweet embraceable you." The lyrics served as a fantasy bridge for April to imagine sharing an apartment, maybe an hour from the high school, with Jonathan. Or perhaps they could live in Long Beach. Yes, it wasn't the greatest town, but it was right near the ocean and a half hour away from Columbia and college for her. If she wanted a room, he was probably the type who would be fine with it. He would ply her with novels, and they could take the train into the city. They would go to Lincoln Center or to the theater or to museums. Find a French restaurant somewhere and he would tell her more about the American expats—is that what they were called?—who came to Paris in the early part of the century. Later, she would try to wade through Hemingway, the man's man, or, more likely, Fitzgerald. But he wasn't part of that whole scene in France, was he? No matter. Fitzgerald's description of wealth on Long Island in *The Great Gatsby* got her thinking about who she was and what her life would be like if she had been born sixty years earlier. .Her father had the Sinatra album with "My Sweet Embraceable You" on it and this was the first time she was hearing the Tony Bennett version of the tune. Were these singers rivals or friends?

For that matter, were these three men in her life friends but rivals, too? Richie, she had always assumed, would be her best friend till the end of time. Now, though, he was her boyfriend. Jonathan and Lee were part of an equation. Jonathan and April saw each other every day, and one way or another, she kept bumping into Lee.

Before April knew it, they were back at Silverbirch. Jonathan drove right up to her door and then asked, "Could I come in for five minutes? I have the Saint-Saëns Piano Concerto record, and it's just so lyrical and flowing and dramatic that I wanted to play it for you, April. Possibly?"

They were in her room, and she was taking Diana Ross off her turntable as Jonathan removed his LP from its record jacket. The cover had a picture of Arthur Rubinstein with the Eiffel Tower and a bit of Paris behind him. April would have opted for more of the Parisian scene, but she loved the music, really adored it. She wished she could play the piano like that.

She had grown up with a family 1909 Steinway, a handsome furniture piece that occupied a full corner of the living room. The instrument surely minimized the depth of the room, but they all loved the piano. Her father, having lost interest in the drums, had taken lessons and, on occasion, would stroll by and play "Begin the Beguine" or "Night and Day." He could read music, and he knew schmaltz so it was pleasurable to listen. April's parents had encouraged her to take lessons, but after a brief try in elementary school, she told them she really would rather dribble. She added that woodwind instruments were more her type, too. That was it. Now, finally, a mild regret.

"Did you know that I once thought of pursuing music as a career?" Jonathan asked. Without waiting, he elaborated. "I double majored in English and music in college, but I wanted to become a pianist and thought of transferring to Eastman or even Julliard. It was going to be one of the two after starting at Williams College. I was good at it, but my college teacher was blunt. He always called me Jon. 'Jon, you will be a fine teacher and you might solo with a town group. That would be satisfying.' He didn't need to elaborate. So, I have an upright piano at home, with a great bass and good action. I play it all the time, but teaching English is a better fit."

April knew very little about Hudson's personal life and wanted to learn more. "So, why did you decide to teach high school and not college?" she asked. "Senior year, you treated us like we were university students."

"There are certain pivotal times in a person's life: age five or six, maybe twelve and thirteen, and either end of high school or beginning of college. I find it most fulfilling to catch young adults who are thinking ahead when they are seniors or even juniors and find a moment for them. You had basketball, and then I watched your creative self-flourishing. You're sweet and fluid on the court, and I wanted you to be able to find that through literature. If I can tap into someone's potential with a prose passage or a full book, that enriches my life."

"There's a piano under the staircase in the barn. Could you play something on it for me?" April asked. "Like a little Chopin, or is it unfair to ask?"

"I have some sheet music, including a waltz. I will practice and play if you will agree to dance with me when I play an LP."

"Touché," she said, uttering a word she believed she had never used before. April sighed. "Now, though, I need to rest."

"Good-bye, April. Sleep well tonight."

She nodded while wondering about this new reality. Or was she imagining?

Chapter Fourteen

Midpoint

R ICHIE ARRIVED ONCE AGAIN as the season turned to August, April anticipated another visit. She'd asked him to come back for the second ball of the summer. Dances were highlight occasions at the inn. You could dress up or not. April remembered Silverbirch balls from when she was around with her parents, years before, as special evenings. There was always a theme, and this time it was harvest. That word encouraged staff members to find appropriate wardrobe choices.

April wanted to be an apple. She would be looking outward from the core. People could see the skin and layers of fruit. She would peer out from under a cap. Her arms, maybe, could be slices of apple. As she envisioned this, it didn't occur to her that her creation might be impossible to make—even if she had some supplies, which she didn't. She needed fabric and the smarts to configure this into something more than an idea.

Even though Viv had urged April to call even on a blue day or when she just wanted to get away,

April had not taken Viv up on the offer. Now, she did. Viv was excited to hear of April's costume idea for the ball and immediately said she could help. Before April knew it, Viv said she could come by to get April the following night. They would go to Viv's house and devise a plan. April was thrilled.

Viv lived in a winterized summer cottage. To April, it looked like a gingerbread house, complete with light brown shutters, statuettes of a dog and cat in the front yard, and pale blue lights interspersed among bushes.

Before April opened her mouth, Viv said, "After living with Lee in a cramped, claustrophobic Manhattan apartment, I wanted a place where my imagination could run wild. It didn't look like this when I bought it. It had drab gray shingles that were curling up and peeling away."

"Your colors and creative touch amaze me. Like the bagel sign with a little guy sitting up there munching away."

"I was cat in one musical in high school and I was pretty good. It became apparent, though, that my talent level would never carry me anywhere. So I learned how to design—first sets for plays out of little models and then clothing using only my head. Yeah, whenever there's a chance for me to tap into that supply line, I jump on it. My sewing is in the bedroom."

Viv had a Monet poster, of the Seine, swinging on her door. She didn't want it to be stationary.

Viv, too, hated to be sedentary, swaying from side to side when she walked. April had mused about Viv with Lee, but her imagination now bequeathed a new image of the wistful grace Viv brought in contrast to Lee's red heat. April glanced at the ancient-looking sewing machine that dominated the corner of the bedroom; with thread turning on a spool, it appeared to still work.

"Meet Helga," said Viv.

"Why the name?" April asked.

"It combines Scandinavia with sacred. I like both," said Viv. "Just because it doesn't breathe doesn't mean Helga hasn't a soul. She does, and she and I have spent many hours together. We can make you an apple dress. Okay? Let's talk colors."

"Ruby red," said April. "I grew up idolizing Dorothy's shoes in *The Wizard of Oz*. One of my few girly indulgences."

"You sure? Let's go over the choices," Viv said. "Yellow—no, golden yellow—might be the sun for you, April. Green apples are often tart but distinctive. You're not quite prepared when you take a bite. Even the name, Granny Smith, is cool. There are many reds, whether they be solid or mixed with yellows. You can go sweet or not."

April quickly replied, "I don't want just one. How could we possibly represent them all?"

"Maybe with swatches sewn together?" Viv suggested. "You tell me your ideal, and I'll let you know what's possible."

April envisioned looking at people from the inside of the apple. Maybe the core of the fruit could become a sharp eye. Then, though, where would that be on the outfit? She started laughing about the possibilities.

Viv, reading April's mind, said, "We could do the back in green with yellow sleeves and the heart of the fruit, the front, in red delicious. We don't want it too sexual, so let's stay away from anything catchy on your upper half. Midsection, just below, is safer. Come with me." She led April through the kitchen, out a rear door, and to a shed. It had a sign hanging down that read "Sew You Later."

"I had a small shop in The Village, and this was the sign over the sales counter," Viv explained. "It's one of the small pieces from the city that made it to the country."

She opened the door to a kaleidoscope of bright color. There was fabric everywhere: on furniture, pinned to the walls, atop lamp shades. April laughed with joy.

"Funny, I'm used to this since I spend hours in here with Helga. I know it's unusual but she travels with me from room to room," said Viv. "Why are we doing this anyway, April? Is it for something—or somebody—special?"

"Richie is coming up tomorrow for the big ball."

"He knows how to pick his spots," said Viv. "He's cute."

"I don't know what to think, Viv," April said. "He would probably run away with me, far off or closer, so we could get married instantly. But it's too much too soon for me. Yes, he's always been a cutie, even back when the whole world revolved around shooting baskets at the playground.

"I invited him to the ball," April continued. "He will probably be wearing shorts and an alligator shirt. He thinks that's a dress-up outfit. As I told you, Richie and me, we're different now—obviously not kids. Dances come along, and we go. Not that we stay. Like when we left the prom. Going somewhere always starts something. I want my outfit to be special."

"I can promise you it will be," said Viv. "I need to measure you, April. Take off what you can, but remain comfortable."

April was not often at ease with her body. Viv's casual, colloquial approach, though, allayed her anxiety. "Sure," said April and took off layers down to her underwear.

"No wonder men want you," said Viv. "You must get the up-and-down all the time."

"I might not put it that way," April said.

Before she knew it, Viv had draped one fabric swatch and then another and so forth all over April's upper body, pinning keepers together as she proceeded. Rejected pieces piled up on the floor of the shed. Viv then gestured to April and mouthed, "Put on your pants and shirt." Viv was at the ready.

Within moments, it seemed to April, sections of cloth and brightly colored patches were attached to her.

"I think I know what to do," Viv said, smiling broadly. "I can get this done in two days."

"How can I be helpful?" April asked.

"Spell me at the cash register as you always do," said Viv. "I don't trust just anyone out there with the money. You couldn't take a nickel if I handed it to you."

A couple of days later, Viv appeared before supper at the dining hall and intercepted April before she entered. "All finished and hidden on the back seat of my car," she said. "I used my imagination. I hope you approve," she added.

The costume featured a hood with a visor that allowed April to peer through. Viv had glittered "apple of my eye" across the upper-most portion of the headpiece. She had also glued together red, yellow, and green lengths to simulate three apple types, and these extended from the head to just below the waist. She added golden tights. "We need to show you off, April," said Viv. "You are one girl who never touts or struts. You negotiate the Silverbirch den of promiscuity with such an easy confidence. How?"

"Jonathan—Mr. Hudson—spent a little time with us on acting, trying to show us that the best performers don't seem to be obviously at work all the time. I have his voice inside of me, and it calms me down when I see certain things. Like my hero,

Bob Cousy. He just glides down the court and then flips it behind his back. It doesn't look like he's been practicing all of his life to get this right. Ask him, though, and I'm sure Cousy would tell you of his Queens days and how hard it was to find a solid playground hoop with a rim that wasn't falling down. I know—it's hard to believe. I would do almost anything to meet this man."

"Let's see," said Viv. "We don't want anyone getting a preview. Can you change in my car?"

April quickly swapped clothing. She pointed to her breasts. "This is deliberate, I know," she said.

"It might be a bit much to say if you've got 'em, flaunt 'em but why conceal them, especially at a costume ball? For some occasions, a more modest look works. But a ball begs for flamboyance."

• • • • • • • • • •

When Richie arrived and April opened the door for him, he was wearing a new alligator shirt and striped shorts. In his deepest voice, he sang, "Zorro!" and waved his outfit at her. Once inside her room, he quickly changed into the getup,

They happily went to the ball as the sexy apple and equally enticing Zorro. By now, certain staff members knew Richie by name, but within this disguise, he stumped them. As always, Lee was running the show. He decided to lead off with several different versions of the classic "Summertime" which prompted Richie to hoist April high and she was quite aware that he was pressing her upon his head and face. She was certain that she was blushing, but no one could see. The Louis Armstrong/Ella Fitzgerald cut that followed was way more jazzy. Miles Davis's rendering was so mesmerizing that a number of people paused on the dance floor to listen more intently. When Lee asked for a final request, someone shouted out, "Another woman like Billie!" Eyebrows arched, Lee reached into his carton of LPs and plucked out Sarah Vaughn, who blessed her version of the *Porgy and Bess* soul stirrer with unrivaled spirit.

Already emotional, Richie predictably asked April if they could leave, saying, "Go for a walk and back in twenty minutes?"

She said, "Neither of us has a watch, and I don't believe you have any plan to come back." He shrugged. "We have these outfits on, Richie. We really can't. I don't want to take this off before a few more people see it. Viv's not even here yet."

"I haven't seen Hudson either," he said.

"I assume Jonathan will come as a writer, like Shakespeare. In fact, if I had thought of it, I would have told him to do something out of *Midsummer*."

"April, he probably tapped into that years earlier. Ten-minute walk?"

"Okay," she said. "We can each silently count the minutes to get it right. Let's go the long way up to the tennis court. You've never done that, and we can walk straight back."

Thus, the unlikely pair—the exotic apple and the masked Zorro—walked, with April leading the way, along the path toward the pond but then veered to the right, through a trail in the woods. Before they knew it, the tennis courts were in sight. One light barely illuminated the red clay, but it was enough to create a slight, muffled glow.

"Sit and lift your visor," said Richie.

He took off his mask, embraced her, and kissed her passionately.

"This makes it worthwhile. The stroll, I mean," said April. "Now we go down the hill."

They hugged each other tightly through the outfits, waist to waist.

When they arrived, there on a bench outside the barn sat Jonathan Hudson, recognizable even under his flat hat, silver shield, and spear-like staff. Only a horse was missing. April and Richie, having studied the masterpiece with him in class, knew who he was right away. From twenty-five yards away, they recognized the lanky figure, the character. Who else would try to save the world?

Before they could say anything, Hudson said, "I've been following the development of a new musical that might open in New York either later this year or early next year. It's going to be called *The Man of La Mancha*, and, from what I've read, it is about Don Quixote and his sidekick, Sancho Panza.

So, I thought I would try to be the knight who chases windmills and dreams. What do you think?"

"Mr. Hudson, you're the source—completely up to date on plays, on and off Broadway," said Richie. He then added, "Sorry. I will try, like you asked, to call you Jonathan."

"I go to plays in the city. I also have one friend who is an actor, and he tells me what he hears. Word is that this particular production is supposed to be a smash, although I am not sure where it begins, which theater," he said.

"Silver is perfect for you: It suits who you are," said April. "Gold would be too much."

"You guys probably also wonder why I'm just hanging out here and not inside. Well, it does seem an occasion for couples. I know that many in there are by themselves, but I just felt odd about going in solo."

"Come in with us," said April. "I see that you also have something to cover your face. We can be like a trio."

"Okay, let's go for it," said Hudson. "I'm sure Lee has an agenda ready."

The three of them walked into the barn and, as if awaiting them, Lee waved and yelled, "I have a special for you."

"Teacher's Pet" echoed just above the din. It was Doris Day singing the tune. April felt herself redden beneath her outfit, and Richie looked directly at her and said, "This must be you."

Jonathan Hudson, however, lifted his face gear, put his arms around his former students, and said, "Maybe you find it odd, but I'm touched." He smiled at Lee, who bowed just a bit at the waist.

April wondered if Lee and Jonathan had planned the whole thing. What would be the motive? These two men had met maybe a couple of years earlier at Silverbirch. Before April could give it any more thought, Lee, not surprisingly, asked her for a dance.

She didn't count on anything slow. Immediately, she realized she knew this one because the song, Baby I'm Yours," had come out a few months before.

It was played at the prom that spring, just before April and Richie left. Now, Lee? Richie wanted out. He asked April, who politely whispered to Lee that she needed to go. Lee shrugged and April eased away, as inconspicuous as one could be wearing a multicolor apple outfit. Richie was already at the back door. April followed but then remembered that Viv had yet to see the costume. She grabbed Richie and after she explained why she wanted to stay, he agreed to wait for another fifteen minutes or so, hoping Viv would show.

When Viv did arrive, she looked sexy in her striped snake outfit. Its distinguishing feature was a richly pink tongue that Viv flicked at various people. The tongue was a discoverer; it led around the body of the snake. April wondered how her friend had rigged the getup to encourage a free-flowing tongue that immediately drew attention.

When Viv spoke, it was with a lisp. "A snake like me is not quite like the rest of you humans. I cannot quite fit my tongue where it should go. So, my s sound is more like th. Thank you," she said.

"You're a genius," said Richie. "Some people just get creative genes."

"Someone just came in who can shake and swivel. She has an outfit no one else could have delivered. Come on," said Lee, "everybody in for a snake dance!"

April immediately placed her hands on Richie's waist, thinking this would head off a potentially awkward situation. She was also aware that somebody would now be grabbing her from behind as they lined up. Problem created. Who was behind her, the person with the tightening grip on her? She did not feel comfortable twisting around to make a discovery. April, instead, held fast to a delighted Richie as he smiled through his mask.

Viv-as-snake led the way. As she made a first curl, she saw the man behind April.

"Lee, eathy," Viv said, lisping her way forward.

"It's okay. I know," he said.

Viv knew better than to trust him fully. Sometimes he seemed to be a playful hustler who might have grown up playing, gambling, and even pilfering a few items if need be. Lee then became, in order, a charismatic boyfriend and husband. Lee was more than pleased to hang out with neighborhood toughs. If questioned, he would brush it off. "Just a few minutes with my element," Lee would say. He had charmed Viv ages ago, and now she was wary, susceptible. Viv worried that April, whose quiet beauty Lee found sweetly attractive, might be taken in. Viv also knew it wasn't her place to say anything. He could be telling the truth. His dance instructions were sound: "Put your hands around the waist of the one in front of you, be considerate, and do whatever he or she does." This seemed innocent and sincere. Viv watched, and she was certain that Lee had placed, with care and precision, his fingers around April's middle. Viv was lost in thought when she heard, "Snake Lady, step in behind me." Lee was never one to be discouraged.

Listening to the exchange, Richie suddenly spun around, took April's hand through her costume, and said, "Let's lead people around in pairs." April was delighted to lace her fingers through Richie's, and she felt herself smiling. No one could see her grin through the apple outfit. Lee chose to assume his P.T. Barnum role and went back to playing records for anyone continuing to snake around.

He chose, first, Del Shannon's "Do You Want to Dance?" As the number played, the lead couple began shimmying together, interlocking their arms around one another's waists, looking lovely as they improvised. Others followed their lead. April did glance around for Jonathan Hudson, who seemed to have vanished. Lee, though, was at home at the turntable. That was his place, and a neat fit it was.

After shaking and snaking and sensing that April was ready to leave, Richie led her out of the barn. She wanted to walk and signaled for him to follow her. They climbed uphill toward the tennis courts and then walked a bit downward before veering off near the pool. Hearing classical music emanating from the shed, April realized Hudson was there—reading, writing, or contemplating, as he oftentimes said, "the fate of the world." She had an impulse to engage him in conversation but quickly thought better of that notion. Instead, April steered Richie toward her room.

Richie, mostly silent, spoke as soon as he closed the door behind them. "Let's go to bed, April." Before she could respond, he continued, "What if we took some time together before the whole college thing?"

"I have a job, Richie, and that runs until the 24th. I don't know. Can we talk in the morning?" April asked as she began to unfasten and disassemble her apple contraption.

Positioned beside one another in a slightly-larger-than-twin-sized bed, April and Richie fell deeply asleep. He placed his arm upon her shoulder, and it seemed to him that she was smiling.

Chapter Fifteen

April in August

A S A CHILD, APRIL had loved those final weeks of summer at Silverbirch. Camp would conclude with a flourish: the banquet dinner, complete with awards for all; the ripening McIntosh apples; a few tree leaves turning slightly golden.

Now, April knew that she needed to find her way through her confusion about three men and into her own future, one without definition. Her parents—her mother, specifically—began to call at least twice per week to urge April to ready herself for September, for college. She tried to maintain a measure of calm through her job: on the dirt basketball court, teach the kids how to follow through; at the pool, how to dive backward by initially bending their knees and straightening them after springing off the board. She pretended to be at ease with both Jonathan and Lee. When Richie called, she said yes to his request that they spend one more night together. She did not know exactly what this meant, but April knew she couldn't constantly push him away. Besides, she thought she might be in love with him. The problem, she acknowledged, was that she did not know what it felt like to be in love.

Viv invited April for Sunday breakfast. "I'll pick you up at 7:30 and we will have at least an hour, probably more, before anyone gets to my place," she said.

It was a cool morning, a harbinger of fall to come. Yes, she loved the July heat of the Catskills, but now she was ready for a change. Aside from Jonathan, those on staff assumed she would be returning to college. The truth was that she would be a freshman at NYU—unless Richie pulled even harder on her. April could not say, however, whether she wished for more of the enticing familiar or a departure. It was unknown. Always, she had assumed she would go to college. Lately, she wondered what it might be like to become a professional student. The ceramics staffer told her about spending eight years on advanced degree work combined with fellowships. But was that right for April?

"A million years ago, I would glance in my mirror and see what I now see upon your sweet face, April," said Viv. "I want to fold my arms around your shoulders, around all of you, and protect you—from love affairs gone south; from loud, boastful boys. I don't mean Richie."

April wondered if Viv was taking a shot at Lee. She stayed quiet, watching as birds were making a later appearance than usual on this day of rest.

Viv went into the back room and came out with blueberry muffins and a thermos of coffee.

"For you, impressionable one. You've already made my summer a special one," Viv said.

"Me? I did?"

"You aren't corrupted. The world of experience robs us of innocence," said Viv. "You help me to remember who I was once upon a time."

"I could run off with Richie or maybe next semester transfer to where he is. That's not so radical. He wants me with him," said April.

Viv walked behind April and kneaded the younger woman's neck and shoulders. "That's what I would have done. I married Lee before I was ready, before he was ready. At first, it was dazzling. He is still such a rush of fire. I really didn't know him, and we were together and living in the city," she said. "He had an in with Columbia records, and he did work there for a while." Viv's voiced trailed off as she stopped the massage and, sitting opposite April, smiled ruefully and gently shook her head from side to side. "Lee is a good person. I'm not certain that, during those days at least, he looked beyond the next day. You see what he's like—completely, joyously in the moment."

April turned and clinched Viv, who hugged her hard. "I just don't want you hurt," said Viv. April realized she wasn't used to embracing anyone except for Richie. Her mom always half hugged, and, ever since April had matured, her father would either smooth her hair as if to brush away emotional distress or hover while barely touching her.

"Spend a year by yourself or, at the very least, six months. You told me how you jumped from high school to here without a break, April. Richie is head over heels about you, sweetie. He will not touch anyone else, I assure you," she said.

"What do you think of Hudson?" April asked. "He is just so smart, polite, and, well, quiet."

"Jonathan's like a brother to me," said Viv. "I've always truly cherished our Silverbirch friendship. He is gentle, I agree." She stopped speaking, but April wasn't certain the story was quite so brief. "We're a variation of the brother/sister friendship," Viv continued. "After Lee and I split, Jonathan consoled me. We went to dinner. It never felt, to me, that I was dating him. He saw it differently."

"He's like your best friend when I've seen him here. He was my favorite teacher," said April. "The first day of orientation—I mean, at Silverbirch—he swooped around me to be sure I was comfortable with the place. Especially during the first week."

"That's him," said Viv. "His role. Hudson knows so much that he is taken off guard when he is not the resident scholar."

"I can see what you mean. But I've never been in a scene with him where he was unsure or lacking. Do you know what I mean?"

Viv nodded and said, "He will go to that shed by the pool. It's his hideaway, his sacred study. Did you know he writes?" Viv didn't wait for an answer. "He has an outline for a piece pasted onto the walls. Swimming, floating, meditating. The second section is about conducting a symphony. That was the part I asked him about. He lets me come to the shed. He showed me sketches of musicians floating on water. They are all dressed in white and sitting on lily pads and playing Debussy. Jonathan sings and sketches, too. His ideal is Ancient Greece—the arts and sciences. We began to have dinners because he loved the way I decorated my little cottage."

April really wanted to return to Viv's house—back to that special place where Viv created her costume. She didn't want to push and overstep. April sensed people might begin pouring into Bagel City within an hour or so. She asked Viv if they could go to the house.

"It will be busy here till 2:00 or 2:30. Stay around and help me, then I will drive you to Genie."

"From *Aladdin*, you mean, Viv?"

Viv began to laugh. "Yes, April, you will discover just why."

April had never seen so many bagel lovers congregate, during an hour or so, at Bagel City. Many hoped to eat on-site and were pleased to sit entangled within stray grass, backs pressed up to the building. Couples, families, and even new-to-driving teenagers made up the populace. So intense that Viv worried she might run out of bagels, the run lasted until 1:30 or so and then dramatically dropped off to almost nothing. Viv held up a couple of fingers, and April understood that she would begin to close at 2:00. People wished to sit outside at tables, which meant a few more moments. Finally, Viv wished her customers well, assured them there was no rush, and asked them to please leave necessary utensils around back.

She eased April into the car, and neither of them looked back.

April was enchanted by the glorious, extensive farmland, realizing she had not been far off Silverbirch grounds the past six or seven weeks. "I never saw so many horses," said April.

"I learned to ride at summer camp. For a while, I just wanted to be around horses, only horses. I know this is sometimes a thing for adolescent girls. For me, I find them comforting. People my parents' age tend to worry about horses' size, but that is exactly what I like. Most of the horses I know understand how much bigger they are and so do not exploit it. I feel totally safe in the saddle, like I'm hovering above the earth beneath me. Can you understand any of this?" Viv asked.

"Completely," said April, "even though horses make me seem tiny."

"That's just it. You are small and I'm not even as tall as you, but I feel protected. They are actually majestic and not scary. It's only when you tell them that you're afraid that they freak out a bit, April. If you watch a group of horses running together, it's almost like a symphony: multiple parts but with a madness to their romps. I learned that much from Hudson," said Viv.

"Tell me about Jonathan. He always gets in the conversation," said April.

"This part won't surprise you. I was at the Silverbirch pool—they are nice enough to let me swim there during off-hours—and I heard classical music coming from the shed. I dried off a bit and knocked, and there was Hud in only those off-white shorts, no shirt, listening to the music. He told me it was Mahler, and I honestly did not know who that was. He stopped the record and put on something that was so different and even more contemporary. It was Aaron Copland's 'Billy the Kid,' and I was hoping and believing it was about pioneers in the West. Again, what do I know? Before I could say a word, Hudson has this old slide projector out and he has pictures of beautiful stallions on the small white wall. I sat there totally transfixed, April. They were this combination of grace and energy. It is such a different spirit from mine," she said. "I tend to fall in love with these animals again and again, which is probably part of the reason I am here," Viv said as she slowed her car in front of the small, eclectic house that looked like it might be sporting colorful play Velcro fabric little kids love.

Viv took her around to the back portion of the home which April hadn't seen first time there. April saw that Viv had strategically situated the shingles in a scheme so that when anyone stepped back, the name GENIE became more evident. April knew if she tried something like this, it would not have worked. She wondered how Viv could possibly have devised such an eye-catcher around the entire exterior. Viv always had a nifty touch; it never fell flat.

"Tell me you used a book or a model or something," said April.

"No, just old-fashioned trial and error. I'm much better with colors than placement. I keep having to switch things around before getting anywhere," she said.

Walking up to the house, April saw that Viv had painted tiny animal figures on many of the slabs. Viv favored dogs, and April noticed that most were painted in shades of red, orange, violet, blue, and even green. She looked quizzically at Viv.

"No one said they all had to be brown or tan or black or white," she said. "I just imagine what I think the dogs might like if they were not color-blind. I take who they are and move on. Mixing dog and art worlds. Come inside," said Viv, pushing open the front door.

Many mobiles hung from the ceiling. There were Christmas ornaments (even in summer); baubles; iridescent and some translucent kittens; dogs galore: Saint Bernards, golden retrievers, labs, beagles, and Dalmatians; stallions: black, brown, and blazing white; a perpetually swiveling Beatles four;

apples: green, dark red, yellow; cherry tomatoes; small, bright yellow birds; and three blue jays all peering out upon the objects in the room.

April was stunned. "Genie. What's the connection, Viv?"

"I could not have possibly done this all by myself. The genie popped out of the lamp"—she gestured toward a corner near a working fireplace—"and magic!" she said. "You told me that Hud taught you about Aladdin rubbing the lamp and the appearance of the magical genie? It's one of Jonathan's go-to stories out of, what, the Middle Ages or so."

"He did," said April, "and I don't totally recall but all about Aladdin and the sorcerer and how when the lamp is rubbed, out pops the genie. In the end, Aladdin is okay, right?"

"You have the main idea," said Viv. "When I found this place, it was nothing more than a shack. I looked for signs of life, something that revealed humans were here even once upon a time. The only object I found, partially buried under a log in the fireplace, was the lamp. It was grimy and dirty, pretty much blackened with soot. Naturally, I wanted to clean it up. I know you won't believe this next part. I rubbed it, no cleanser or anything, with a dry cloth."

"You're going to tell me a genie popped out, and I can't quite believe it," said April

Viv spun around and bowed to the fireplace, then the lamp, and finally toward April. "Smoke came out and then a voice from somewhere. Don't worry—it wasn't a person," Viv said. "It only happened once. Later, I would rub and rub, then put the lamp back where I found it. Nothing. That first time a soft, low, and mellow voice thanked me for releasing her, and I swear she was singing about nighttime. I thought if I kept the lamp out of the sun, maybe it would speak again, but no."

April looked around and noticed moon-themed mobiles hanging in the four corners of the room, glowing dimly. Viv said, "It fits with my personality in here, the way it's more serene." Viv began singing "Moonlight in Vermont." "As you know, I'm not that way in the shop."

"You are all sunshine there. Everything's bright. Bagel City is out in the open, and it oozes warmth, even heat," said April.

"One of my selves is the person you know there: welcoming to everyone, including even those I do not like or trust. Men come along when I'm at the counter by myself, give me the head-to-toe, and order a bagel with cream cheese. Yeah, I think about motive. After all, I studied acting and it's all about what moves a particular character."

"Hudson had us do some scenes just to see what performing was like," April said. "I always thought I was too shy. I saw people do things like *Oklahoma!* and could not imagine it could be me. Until he pushed me to do some Shakespeare, like Ophelia. Jonathan insisted I could handle the mad scene."

"What happened?" Viv asked.

"Well, I loved it. Maybe it's because she is way out there. I've always been the good girl, under control. Not that I objected to growing up that way. It was safe. I don't know who Ophelia is, exactly, but she doesn't play it safe."

Viv laughed. "I can barely remember when I was not only curious but wanting to experiment." She sighed. "Now I have Genie, and my imagination is freed. The only thing is hardly anyone ever gets to see this part. I'm so excited you're here, April."

"I feel special," April said. "This is like a fairy tale."

"When I go away, I would trust you to be at my place. I mean, with Richie," said Viv. "How much can you find out in a six-by-ten-foot room like yours? Or, even when I'm around, you guys can have the sofa bed right here in the living room. It's kind of private and there's this cozy bathroom just off the kitchen."

April allowed herself to consider. "I would love that—of course, assuming he would also agree. A big part of him is still a boy. He wants to marry me, yes; at least, that's what he says. But he doesn't really know much about living. I mean, I don't either, but at least I can admit to being in between, which is what both of us are: part kid, part grown-up. I can fall for his incredibly seductive pull. If he says boat ride, I'm there. He wants to hold my hand, like The Beatles sang a couple of years ago? Yes. But I don't want to be a wife, whatever that is."

"That was my mistake," said Viv. "I had a white gown and veil, flower girls, church . . . all of that. Not that either of us was religious. No way then and same now."

"People in their thirties must know something," said April.

"We are old enough to have failed," said Viv. "I don't totally get it. You try and then it doesn't work. Some people come back for more, and others never again. Single life has its strong points," she said. "I'm sure you have the end-of-summer banquet starred. Jonathan asked me to that dinner, and I sort of want to go. But given how burned I've been, I'm not sure. Hey, how weird would it be if you and Richie sat with us? This assumes he would want to be there."

"Yes, I will be at the banquet and Richie already said he's coming. Can we separate Hudson, English teacher god, from Jonathan, the guy who hangs out in a rickety pool shed and listens to classical music? I'm willing to try, Viv."

Viv hugged April and spun the younger woman a couple of times. April was reminded of Lee.

Chapter Sixteen

Final Banquet

Richie drove up wearing black-and-white–striped shorts and a white shirt with an olive-green alligator on the front. He opened the car door and when he got out, April, watching from her window, noticed his moccasins.

"Where did you get those?" April, pointing at his feet, asked.

Richie invited himself into her room "My mother wanted me to look good seeing you," he said. "She gave me these, so I put them on. I have my old sneakers in the car and totally meant to change. These things aren't that cool, huh?"

She hugged Richie, his familiarity warm and welcome. She knew his physical contours by memory: all the body parts and, increasingly, how they fit with hers. She was not facing new-boyfriend anxiety. "My father is the master of cliché. He would be saying 'cool as a cucumber.' Hey, are cucumbers in any way cool? I always think of you as sweet, Richie. Cool I don't know," said a smiling April.

"You didn't tell me what to bring for the banquet, April," said Richie. "Is this like a formal event tonight?"

"These are rituals. The dinner will start late. When I was little, I got invited one time to get some special girls basketball award, and it turned out to be a feather. I don't know where that came from. I will at least put on some clean clothing. I remember some people were wearing really nice eat-out-at-a-fancy-restaurant stuff, but I also remember one kid who had on a red Silverbirch Inn T-shirt. I suppose I was in between. What do you have?"

"A white shirt and a bow tie," he said.

April and Richie began to laugh. April was laughing so hard Richie had to hold her so she wouldn't tumble to the floor. "What else?" she finally asked. "Do you have long pants?"

"Yeah, but I haven't tried them on lately. So, you might see my ankles or my socks."

Which set the two of them off once again.

"Might as well make them into pedal pushers," said April.

"Thanks," said Richie. "I did save some of the prom outfit and could've brought that. But that may be a bit much."

"My gown is probably still drying out from Point Lookout," said April.

"The smell of saltwater is one of our things," said Richie.

"What else did you bring?" April asked.

"Chinos, madras shirt. My usual wardrobe."

"Just wear that, okay?"

"We're starting to sound like a married couple," said Richie.

April, a bit taken aback, replied, "No. I mean, we're still teenagers. I just want to get through the next couple of weeks."

"April, the words just slipped out. I didn't mean to suggest anything."

"I'm just sensitive these days, Richie. Transitions all over. I want it to be simple, like dribbling to the park and easy one-on-one."

"I know," he said. "Me, too. Can we do something for a little while? Just fun. Transistors all over the place? Sounds like me listening to the World Series with a midget radio hidden in my high school World History book. Anyway, what are you going to wear?"

"Something I almost wore to the prom—a kind of snug-fitting dark green dress. Luckily, my mother told me that it wasn't exactly a match. So, it's only been on me in a fitting room or in our house. It's time."

"Do I get a preview?" Richie asked.

"You'll have to wait until tonight. It's only, like, three-plus hours until the banquet. Before I wiggle into that thing, let's do something else, okay?"

"I'm yours. What did you have in mind?"

"Let's go swimming. I don't care where. Pool or pond."

"I don't have a bathing suit, but maybe boxers will do? The pond is probably more private. For all we know, Hudson's in the shack listening to Chopin or something. Just now, let's not go there."

They changed, and April led the way along a secondary, hidden route to the pond. As they approached, Richie immediately began to strip down further. He had on nothing but thin, off-white boxer shorts when April said, "Richie, I can see everything."

"White is white, Ap," he replied. "No one here anyway."

Hearing the frogs calling, April mimicked them, puffing out her cheeks loudly to burp a few sounds.

"Do they have their own language?" Richie asked.

"Are you Jonathan Hudson or what?" April said.

"He did sort of cast a spell, but not once by screaming or yelling."

"I watch him with the kids here. Same thing," said April. "He explains, coaxes, makes suggestions—and everyone listens and tries. Whatever he does, it's with grace: shooting foul shots on a dirt court, sitting back on a frayed beach chair in a seedy shed and listening to Bach, or even teaching us some George Eliot or Arthur Miller."

"Except what about the gun he had when we saw him at Point Lookout after midnight the night of the prom? We were shocked out of our minds."

"Yeah, I know," said April. "It doesn't fit. I think it's just extra money for him. What can he make?"

"I don't know anything about teachers' salaries. Can't be much," said Richie. "Sometimes, though, I think about what it's like to be him. Taking kids like us and lighting candles, watching us respond to even one novel, a short story, maybe a couple of lines from a play."

"I've had some of it here," said April. "When a kid catches on to, say, how to dive headfirst into the pool, I experience that sort of joy. It comes right back to you as the teacher. I saw that with Jonathan, so I try for the same. I know you can't manufacture it."

Richie took April's hand and led her to the edge of the pond, whereupon a frog bellowed brashly, loud enough to cause April to hop.

"That your imitation of a frog?" Richie asked.

Suddenly, April took off the shirt and shorts she had on. She did not cover up.

"Whoa," said Richie. "You must be going into your second year of college," he added.

"One thing I've almost learned is how to play the game," April said. "My parents and I know yours well enough. Your face tells me when you're stressed, but you never hold back the truth if I ask. People around here, women by themselves, are lying right and left. It's all around. When it comes to people staying at Silverbirch, I don't know who is real and who is fake. I have eyes, and these women don't want to go back. I mean, to their homes. People on staff . . ." she did not complete her thought.

"Did you . . . do you have a crush on Hudson?" Richie asked.

April's face turned deep red. "Yes," she said before adding, "But it's not like I'm comparing him to you."

"So when was it? Was it when we were his students or now?" Richie asked.

"He's watched out for me here, especially that first week or so. Like an older brother, maybe, showing me how to be, kidding around. You know how he is," she said.

"It's sort of okay, April, because I like the guy, too. I just want you to love me more," said Richie.

"I'm not about to go off with him, Richie," she said. "Let's do a quick swim 'cause we have to get back and be ready for the big dinner." She walked directly into the water, windmilling her arms to get him to follow. He did.

Fully soaked, they kissed and he hugged her hard.

"Okay, this makes me feel better," said Richie. "Let's go back and change."

"I would rather stay here," said April, "but I can't very well skip the banquet."

They took the shortcut back to her room, not really caring if anyone saw them sopping wet, towels draped over their shoulders.

April quickly dried, put on the green dress, and modeled it for Richie.

"Holy moly or something like that," said Richie. "What am I going to wear?"

"Just the chinos and, wait, you left a pink shirt here one time. Let me get it." She quickly snatched it out of the closet and smoothed out the wrinkles with her hands as best she could. "Put that on and you are the picture of a private school kid."

Richie did look the part of a rich prep school senior.

"Perfect," said April. "I love you." She kissed him.

"I hope so."

Off they went to the dining commons. They didn't expect to walk in and find Lee impersonating Bobby Vinton and playing "Blue Velvet."

"This is too much," said April.

"I just love you," was Richie's response.

"We could run off, but after dinner," said April. "Let's eat here and then go to the barn for a dance," she suggested as Vinton sang, "Lonely, I'm Mr. Lonely."

"That could be me in a month," said Richie. "We need to at least stay together."

"A semester apart?" April asked. "Let's go outside for one more minute. We have to talk." Without waiting for an answer, she pulled him out the door with her.

"We've been together so much of the time till this summer, Richie. I, well, I've been watching the people here—the men going away after spending maybe Saturday evening and Sunday morning here. What happens that the relationships become like that? I need more time to figure some things out. I don't mean you. This is me."

"So you want to go out with other people?"

"It's more that I want to know that I can. Just that it's not officially off limits. Otherwise, I could feel stuck or trapped," she said.

"You're so logical, April," said Richie. "You're right, but I have one focus—being in the same room with you. On this night. You didn't plan out the Bobby Vinton with Lee?" He lowered his voice to a whisper, "It's all I can do to keep my hands off you in that dress."

She smiled. "I did plan out this part, but not the music. You're a man, after all."

"And what about me, in my wrinkled, pink pretty-boy shirt?"

"I find it very seductive," said April.

Jonathan Hudson wore a summer off-white three-piece suit. Seeing April and Richie, he quickly walked to them, stood between the two with his arms draped over their shoulders, and said, "I first met both of you when you were fifteen, and even then I was thinking of the balcony scene from *Romeo and Juliet*. Now is a likely time for it."

"I wouldn't know the first thing about it, what to do," said Richie, taking him seriously.

"You are familiar with the play. I remember in your essay you talked about just how young they were, Richie. That tells me a lot. I've seen productions where the actors are thirty or even older, and that's wrong. Romeo and Juliet were kids."

"Like teenagers going steady, right?" April asked.

"If you mean adolescents who cannot keep their hands off each other, yes," said Jonathan Hudson.

"You were the one who assigned us novels with sex scenes," said April.

"Part of life, part of literature. It doesn't make any sense to pretend that people haven't any interest," said Hudson. "Can I sit with you, or does that make you feel like kids with their teacher?"

"Sure," Richie said before April was able to even think about it.

Lee, at this point, shifted his selection to what he called, "Frank, then Ella and Satchmo." Several older staff members clapped hands, snapped fingers. One of them asked for "Summertime." Lee nodded, indicating that it was coming.

After a short while, the meal was served. Usually, there was a buffet. This time, kitchen help brought platters of food to each table as a partial wait service.

"What, no lobster?" Richie asked.

"That is the difference between here, the Catskills, and where we grew up on the Island," April said.

"One of the perks when I work at the beach is proximity to seafood places," Jonathan said. "That time you saw me, in the middle of the night after your prom, I much earlier had enjoyed the best dinner. An hour later, I'm walking around with a gun strapped to my waist."

"So you like novels and plays, lobster, and classical music. What else?" Richie asked.

"You forgot the reason I'm here and part of why I know you, Richie," said Hudson.

"Basketball," said April. "Take us to your pool shed and play us a symphony," she added.

"Now?" Hudson asked.

April looked at Richie. "Wouldn't you rather be in that little house instead of here?" she asked.

Richie nodded. "Beethoven?"

"Perfectly willing," said Hudson. "We could listen to a movement and be back for dessert and awards. Let's go."

A few minutes later, Hudson unlocked the shed, took out his LP of Beethoven's Sixth Symphony, and, just before spinning it, said, "It's very much like here, at Silverbirch—the nature part. Someone is in love with country settings, and the strings immediately say this. Now, soak this in."

April and Richie immediately recognized the beginning of the piece.

"You've played that before," April said.

"For homeroom, but neither of you were in mine. Then, yes, when we discussed Thomas Hardy, maybe *The Mayor of Casterbridge*. Do you remember the story? The Henchard family is in the countryside, arrives at a small village. We did read it."

"I did," said Richie. "You were even more into George Eliot, though. You gave some of us the choice of either *Silas Marner* or *The Mill on the Floss* in addition to your favorite."

"I can see why he loves *Middlemarch*," said April. "He always speaks up for girls and women, both here and in high school. Dorothea Brooke from *Middlemarch* is such a great person, but her marriage didn't work out."

"For all I know, you two could just run out of Silverbirch together," said Hudson.

April and Richie looked at each other before Richie spoke. "Not now," he said. "We have to figure out who we are first. I'm parroting what wise old heads tell us."

April smiled. "Not yet," she said. She looked at Richie and added, "Richie either believes it or he knows what to say."

"He's an essay writer already and potentially a trial lawyer," said Hudson.

"What do you mean?" Richie asked.

"You naturally persuade people," said Hudson. "Besides, you know when to up the ante and when to back off. Symphonies have a number of movements, and you gauge yours accordingly. I could see this as the work you gave me became better and better."

"Well, I will never be pre-law," said April.

"No, but you have both the sweet disposition and the silver-sharp smarts to run, maybe, a school.

You've shown everyone this summer what a gracious and wonderful teacher you are. You would save lives during precarious years—like ninth grade or freshman year of college, either at the front office or in the classroom."

April said, "If what you say about us is half-true, Jonathan, you need to get some of the credit. We were under your spell each day for years. And I had your guidance at Silverbirch, too."

Richie added, "I watched you a lot. It wasn't necessarily what you said, even if I hung on each word. Just the way you comforted someone or got the best out of him—with a sideways glance or by raising your eyebrows."

"Comforted?" Jonathan asked.

"If anyone even thought he had an answer, you encouraged. It mattered whether the answer was right or wrong, but you also acknowledged that it's brave to raise your hand and give a public response," said Richie. "It's at least as valuable as getting it right."

"Well said, Richie," Jonathan answered. "I hope I did that."

April added, "Your classes were not only about the literature. Sure, it mattered and you spent time deciphering characters, pushing us in that direction. But it was also often a strong nod to having the chutzpah, as my dad would say, to put yourself out there. I've been able to use that here, too. I haven't always been a hundred percent sure of myself, especially with the swimming. You go far with logic, smarts, and what you always give me, which is confidence."

"I'm glad that I was able to do these things for you—both of you. I'm sometimes not as sure of myself as it looks. That's probably why my original goal was to act on stage. I'm better as somebody else."

"That makes me wonder whether I know the real Jonathan Hudson. Is he the guy from school who wears those soft, classy sports jackets or the one here with the loose, white shorts? Or maybe he is someone else," said April.

"What does it matter if we're feeling inspired by him?" Richie asked.

By now, the Beethoven was nearing its rousing conclusion.

"He was deaf and he wrote that?" April asked.

"At some point, but I'm not sure when," said Hudson. He shook his head. "Imagine shooting foul shots if you couldn't see the basket. How many out of ten would you make?"

"If someone lined me up and I got one," said Richie, "that would be great. After that, maybe I could sink another. Getting started is the hardest part."

"So I wonder how Beethoven, just sitting there and losing his hearing, could possibly write," said Hudson. He slowly shook his head back and forth. "I am thinking that he cannot hear, yet he composes symphonies and sonatas that will last . . . Well, they have immortality. I studied piano until I did not get accepted at a major music program for university study. Had I gotten in, I never would have taken the Romantic Novels in Literature class that fueled what I teach. I thought I might be a music educator but, when I was younger, never a writer. I can listen and hear but am not really able to translate onto a manuscript page. I don't know why," he concluded.

"Mr. Hudson? Jonathan?" said April. "Remember how you constructively criticized my papers, my essays, with your green pen? I read those notes over and over again. It was like you were responding with poetry to my basic attempts. I am really lucky."

"Me, too," said Richie. "I will only tell you now I was embarrassed that I loved reading F. Scott Fitzgerald for its high-handed kind of prettiness. It was easier with Faulkner because you told us that he was depicting the South with his own paintbrush. Isn't that how you put it?"

Hudson nodded. "Music and literature and much of theater are all about palette," he said. "I should say, too, that character is fuel for drama."

"So, those Chagalls you showed us could be part of a set design. You can see the images," April said.

"Perfect and true," said Jonathan. "If you are lucky enough to come close to one of the actual paintings in a museum, its texture will jump out at you. That should be experienced."

"This Beethoven has it, too," Richie said. "Part of it felt like a pond without ripples and other parts like flowing ocean waves." He paused. "Maybe you can adopt us?"

Hudson laughed. "During the months you're apart or, if the stars are aligned, when you are together again."

"It's just better, calmer, being here with you and Beethoven than trying to navigate the world outside," said April.

"I love Lee, too," said Jonathan, "and we are of the sometimes-great-friends variety. We especially like going to a truck stop near the bridge and eating cheeseburgers in the middle of the night," he said.

"That doesn't fit," said April.

"I was raised on that type of thing," he said.

"Let's go get some instead of heading back to the banquet," Richie said.

"Okay by me," said Hudson.

"I love it," April said.

Hudson shut down the record player, closed the shed, and led the way to his car, an early 1960s pale blue Mercedes sedan, parked beyond his main lodge suite. As a senior staff member, Hudson was given a place far more expansive than a sparse room.

"I am not exactly the type to drive this, but I didn't buy it new and it is a dreamy ride," he explained and began the ten-minute excursion to Marty and Mary's. They arrived at a shack, a building supported by wooden beams that appeared to have suffered through a siege of animal and insect invasion. Still, the truck stop beckoned. Dressed as they were, April and Richie felt out of place—until Hudson introduced them. "Mary, meet two of my brightest and sweetest students ever," he said.

She yelled behind her, "Marty, out here! JH brought some friends!"

Marty, smiling broadly, his apron stained with grease and food droppings, greeted them with "Hudson, are these beauties your kids?"

"In a sense, they are," said Jonathan. "I taught them both, and April has been on Silverbirch staff this summer. I wanted you two to meet these two."

Marty smiled widely, showing a gleaming set of teeth. Mary extended her hand to shake Richie's and then hugged him, saying, "You don't think someone who looks like me is going to give a queen's dainty little shake, do you?"

"I've only seen that on TV," said April. "I'm already glad Jonathan took us here. It gets us out of the banquet dinner."

"Banquet here every night," said Marty. "What you want? Three with cheese? More?"

"Cheeseburgers for these two. For me? Every so often, you have fried chicken," said Jonathan.

"Oh, boy, there he goes again, spilling our secrets," said Mary. "Marty, get some out of the fridge and start dipping."

Marty gave her the high sign and retreated.

"April, do you need to go back to the dining hall? Will you get in trouble if you're not there?"

"You're always too sweet to be true, Richie. Maybe in an hour and a half, for dessert. I expect Jonathan will cover which will explain why I or we were away," she said. "I want a cheeseburger."

"Inside or out?" Mary asked.

April wasn't aware of any tables outside, though there were a half dozen and the counter inside.

As if reading April's mind, Mary added, "We have two picnic benches behind us."

"Could we just sit here?" Richie asked. "I want the full thing."

"Wise choice," said Jonathan. "Could we have some Dean Martin?"

"You got it," said Mary.

Marty was now busy with the only other customer, who had ordered two cheeseburgers "with the works." Marty alternated between cooking burgers and prepping chicken to be breaded, dipped, and fried. "Everybody Loves Somebody" sounded forth from the record player.

Marty blurted, "That's me, Martin," as April blushed and Richie gladly clasped one of her hands.

"See? I told you this place is special," said Hudson.

Marty, in a flash, produced the burgers and a large cardboard, cone-shaped container of fries, then slid the food down the counter, where Hudson intercepted the dishes.

"I know this drill," he said. "Blink at the wrong moment and it all lands on the floor."

A few minutes later, Hudson received his chicken, a portion sufficient for two people. He began eating immediately while waving to Mary, who produced take-out bags adorned with pronounced splotches of grease from the food.

"We need to go back," Jonathan said. "They'll be expecting April and, even more so, me to be there.

Within twenty minutes, the threesome was back at Silverbirch as most were finishing the main meal. Hudson explained that Richie had asked to see the pool shed and they'd lost track of the hour.

Lee marked their return by announcing, "Let's welcome Mr. Hudson and also his proteges. You know how talented April is, and Richie's with her. We've seen him around quite a bit these past two months, so he can't be all that bad."

The evening continued with the awards ceremony as cups of coffee and hot chocolate were distributed.

"The Silverbirches wanted me to thank you for being here, for your time well spent as workers or guests these past weeks. I have to say that, for me, this has been one of the best of my many summers on this scene. More fun and no conflict. It must be the presence of the younger generation," Lee said, winking at April.

Several people clapped, and then everyone caught the spirit. Lee placed both his palms downward to quell the applause.

"As some of you know," he continued, "this is the time of the evening when we recognize, well, ourselves for having made this a memorably sweet summer deep in this Catskill valley. Our owners could not be among us tonight, but they've asked that I make special mention of a certain individual before we distribute everything else. I think I should read their words, which speak for themselves: 'To Jonathan Hudson, who personifies Silverbirch. A gentle person, he has graced our presence for decades. First as a guest, then as a weekend instructor, and for years as a permanent staff member, Jonathan has reached hundreds of individuals through his expertise, style, and, most of all, personal touch. He is a gifted teacher, and we, too, have been nurtured through his being. We share our lodge with him and wish his sun to be forever shining.'"

Turning to Hudson and beckoning him forward, Lee took out an LP of Miles Davis's: *Quiet Nights*. A muted trumpet began to play as Jonathan gracefully ambled forward. Lee greeted him with a handshake, then placed his arm around Hudson's shoulders and handed him the microphone.

"I'm absolutely stunned," said Hudson, "I hadn't the slightest inkling, and I am a bit embarrassed. We all know that Silverbirch summers equal the sum of all the parts. It isn't any one man or woman who makes this place caring and wondrous and, really, more special than any other spot I know."

April was first up to applaud, and she lifted Richie with her. Together, they raised their arms as Hudson softly bowed at the waist and smiled broadly at his former students. "Sometimes, those you teach bring out the best in you. If that is true, in my case it is so because April has been here. Come up here—and you, too, Richie," he continued.

April held steady, but Richie pushed her forward. Hudson stepped between them and said, "When you have students who are both smart and intuitive, it's natural to reach and teach to and for them, which probably accounts for a better experience for all. This mitigates boredom and rote procedure. Sometimes less motivated students do not notice. They're after grades rather than knowledge. I met both April and Richie back a few years or so. They live in houses separated by a back lawn, as I understand it. Best friends with abundant futures before them. They inspire me. This summer, April and I became colleagues and all of a sudden, it seemed, our relationship shifted to another plateau. She already is a blazingly effective instructor. Her future is filled with promise." Hudson stopped for a moment. "Sorry to go on, but that's why I'm standing up here.

"I hope you'll indulge me for just a few more minutes. I can imagine Richie someday saying this to April: 'But soft! What light through yonder window breaks? It is the east, and Juliet is the sun. Arise, fair sun, and kill the envious moon, who is already sick and pale with grief, that thou, her maid, art far more fair than she.'" He looked around and, finding few who seemed restless, said, "Just the final three lines: 'See how she leans her cheek upon her hand! O, that I were a glove upon that hand, that I might touch that cheek!'"

No one in the hall moved, no one clapped; it was as if Hudson had hypnotized his audience. April and Richie, holding hands, looked at one another and smiled.

It was Richie who finally broke the silence. "I only hope I can find someone like you who works with me and advises me in college," he said.

April hoped nobody would ask why Richie was beginning college when she'd told everyone at Silverbirch that she was soon to be a sophomore. She tried to lighten the mood by saying, "We are all still long car trips away—not even a plane flight. Meanwhile, we need Lee to move along with the most fun part of this event. So, go for it."

Lee bounced up immediately and took the mic as Jonathan, April, and Richie stepped aside and then behind him. It was April who signaled and more or less pulled them to their seats. They listened and watched as most of the people in the room received awards. Finally, staff members distributed feathers to anyone who did not receive special recognition.

The evening was, thereafter, subdued. Lee was unusually quiet. April associated Lee with noise, music, hubbub, and even celebration. April barely recognized the man who gently drew the proceedings to a close. She saw that he was handsome, with high cheekbones and dark hair slicked back instead of typically flopping forward, as it did whenever he danced.

Jonathan Hudson stood, and April realized this was a departure signal. She had often watched, during class, as he drew a period to its end by standing straight and tall, his eyebrows arched, before uttering a word. This time, however, he faced April and Richie and said, "See you in the morning, April, and see you soon, too, I'm sure, Rich." The name sounded alien to April, who had always referred to her best friend as Richie, not Rich.

"Thank you for including me. You've always done that," said Richie.

"It's all about journey. That's where I am with each of you. Good night for now," said Hudson.

April and Richie walked, in silence, back to her room.

As they were about to go in, April said, "Let's just sit in those chairs and take in the stars first."

As they settled into the well-worn seats, Richie said, "They don't look anything like what we saw from the ferry or Point Lookout."

"These big hills submerge at night, and you can really see the sky and the shadows just beneath," she said.

"Next week at this time, where will you be? Back in the house?"

"Yes," said April. "Not for long, though. We need to figure out what's going to happen in a couple of weeks."

Richie, considering, looked at her, but April felt his eyes peering through right to her core. He was atypically subdued before finally saying, "For the first time, we really don't know, do we, April? Until the past year or so, we could always find the common window in the houses or play some basketball. For me, the best dream—the prom and all—has led to the unknown."

"It's just so hard to figure," April said. "I love you. At least, I think I do. But I'm eighteen."

Richie pulled her out of her chair. "Let's go inside and not obsess and worry."

He fell asleep as she began to speak about needing space. April laughed because she knew he wasn't about to awaken: Richie could sleep anywhere—on the beach, on a couch in front of the TV, and, finally, in bed. She so adored this all-or-nothing, charge-forward-or-full-slumber guy but wanted a few months. Viv had advised her to "make room" for herself. April needed more time with Viv at the bagel place or the gingerbread house or anywhere. Thoughts came upon her: Richie,

Jonathan, Lee, even her compassionate, resonant father. They were all men, but each was so different from the others.

She smiled at Richie as he slept. April understood they could not address the situation before Richie left early the following morning. April hugged him and kissed him on the lips. Then she said, "I will be home in five more days. We will get it right."

He softly nodded in agreement and mumbled, "Promise me two days?"

"Yes," said April.

The following morning, they got up early, ate some breakfast at the dining hall, and Richie soon drove away.

• • • • •• • • • • • ••

With Richie temporarily out of the picture, April called Viv, who invited her for dinner. Viv would come to get her.

"I'm not really saying good-bye, April," said Viv, after driving them both to her home and then opening the front door. "You're like the little sister I never had," she said. April could not have possibly anticipated such a sweet going-away event. Viv had decorated the entire house with crepe paper, and April could not suppress a wide grin.

"And for me, Viv, you're the big sister I've missed," April answered. "Wow. Now tell me, Viv, how you get inspired to create these things."

"For you and very few others," said Viv.

"What is that song?" April asked, hearing some classical contemporary music emanating from the rear of the house. "It sounds like something Jonathan would bring."

"Not quite but, I suppose, accurate, sweetie," said Viv. "Mussorgsky was a Russian composer who was close friends with an artist named Hartmann. When that man died before he was forty, Mussorgsky composed this piece about his work, like a tribute. Guess the year," said Viv.

April figured she was thinking too recently, so she said, "1920."

"It was the mid-1870s," said Viv. "I also thought twentieth century when Jonathan asked me that question. He gave me the inside scoop about these guys."

"Hudson is like a music, um, interpreter. I'm not that surprised."

"He likes to look after people, and we've known each other during, well, not the easiest periods of life. So, yes, he calms me with music even when the music isn't particularly gentle. A good read on his part," Viv continued.

"It sounds a lot like how he was as a teacher. He would always instill confidence when we said anything that was even halfway intelligent. I can only speak for myself but, for sure, I felt better about trying out something even when I was far from sold on my answer. I know I keep repeating this, but I still feel like an insecure kid. I wonder when that stops."

"Yeah, Jonathan is maybe the most reassuring man I've ever met," said Viv.

April wondered if Viv was speaking in code. Reassuring—what did that mean? April's education, in terms of men and boys, was specific but not extensive. Her mother was the foremost adviser. She harped on April to be certain no one took advantage of her. No man would sweet-talk his way to and through sex. Above all: never be submissive.

On the other hand, if you weren't open, how could you figure out your feelings? April hated to admit it to herself, but she wanted to show her vulnerability and see how someone reacted. Richie coddled her, but, well, he was Richie. April realized the music had stopped.

Viv continued, "He—Jonathan—is so able to intuit. He is the master in that regard and knows how to respond. We'll be talking outside the shop and then he's gone. After dinner at Silverbirch, he will drive out here, maybe bring a record—the Mussorgsky or Bach or even soft jazz ballads . . ." She looked toward her bedroom and shook her head.

"You love him?" April asked.

"Sometimes I do. Now, what that means gets complicated when you're past thirty."

"Maybe. Right now, I'm trying to figure out whether the person I'm closest to is, at age eighteen, possibly Mr. Right," said April.

"You probably need to spend more time together, not less," said Viv.

"What? You're taking his position while I tell him I need time to find out who I am?" April said.

"Someday people won't take a flying leap into marriage like I did. I mean, sure, Lee and I hung out, carried on, went to clubs, drank, and a lot more than that. Look at him now and multiply that by three. He was nonstop, so dynamic and charismatic. I was totally smitten, you know?"

"I'm so many years younger, and there have been times this summer when I could not wait to see him," said April.

"I know," said Viv. "It's always an experience. Lee does that thing where he takes your hand, gently prods you, guides you around the waist. I know the whole deal. Lee had me right away. Doesn't mean we should have run off to a justice of the peace."

"You're so smart, so settled," said April. "I just don't get it."

"Which is why I'm saying you can't do either the stargazing or star-idolizing thing. Go to your college, sure, and then find time to spend just with Richie. He cares so deeply for you, and he really is a cool boy. Whether or not you two could ever think about growing old together, well, that's probably like fifty-fifty. You would have a much better chance of making a good guess if you were together all the time for more than a couple of days."

"How should I react to his hand around me, like, investigating?" April asked.

"What do you mean, sweet?"

"Richie presses in and, I mean, maybe I've lost a couple of the pounds I gained right away. At the beginning of the summer, there was more flesh like this to press around my waist. One time, I think he was, like, testing it or something."

"He must not like skinny women," said Viv. "So, an extra pound or three was probably a turn-on for him. You're so innocent," she added. "Look at me. When Lee and I were married, I was a good dozen pounds up from this. He wanted that. I was getting fat and couldn't take it off because my husband didn't like fondling bones."

"There isn't enough time to make a decision. Silverbirch is about over. Then I'm home for a week and off to school. Richie wants a weekend together. Well, he would rather a lot more than that."

"He is incredibly nice, and I mean it," said Viv. "Yes, you don't want to cast your net exclusively as a single, but you also don't want him released to the world. Take it from me. Be yourself but be smart. Let's eat and get you back to your room," she said.

Within moments, Viv produced a large tray filled with fresh vegetables as well as a number of mini-bagels. April laughed and said, "Pleasure mixed with business. You're perfect."

Viv lifted a glass of red wine, handed it to April, and poured one for herself.

"To my little sister," Viv said and clinked with April.

Viv, turning toward the kitchen, looked back and said, "Sit. We'll eat in here. I'll be right back."

Moments later, she brought in a large tray including both pasta and bagel that complemented the two glasses of red wine. "I like mixing colors and delicacies," she said, edging beside April on the couch while she placed the food and drink on the coffee table before them. "I love the kitchen because the light flows through at the end of the day from behind. But it's way more comfortable out here. Besides, we can have music. I assume something Jonathan gave me will suit us both," she said.

With that, Viv rose and placed *Rhapsody in Blue* on the turntable. "Classical but sporty, too," she said. "If he were here, we would be listening to something like Mahler or even deadly Wagner, ugh," she added.

"He plays more melodic classical for Richie and me," said April.

"He cherishes you both," Viv said.

"Which brings me back to men and the reason I wanted to see you," said April.

"To me, it seems like you and Richie match like hand-in-fitted-glove. The old adage about absence makes the heart grow fonder? You will know in a month or two," said Viv. "For now, though, let's enjoy. Look out the side window. You can see the reflection of the sun as it goes down. Imagine the first star and then the moon. Sweetheart, when you think about this dilemma with men, remember that so many of us envy you. You have three different kinds of partners in the mix, even if you and I both know Richie is the one. Each of those men has what I have to say is a distinctive cool."

"You're saying I'm lucky to be caught in this position?"

"It becomes more of a scramble as you get older. Take it from me," Viv said, shaking her head. "I do know that I sound like a wise old aunt or something." She hesitated for a moment before adding, "I wasn't as smart as you, but I was just as trusting."

"One part of me wants to play it safe," said April. "Then the other April wants to do just what Richie wants." She took a piece of pizza, nibbled at it, and then washed it down with wine. "This is hard."

"Don't borrow trouble. That was another of my problems. Even now, I think, 'What if my bagel place doesn't score in summer? Can I survive winter?' Gotta go back to Alfred E. Neuman and say, 'What, me worry?'"

"The editor of *Mad* magazine, Al Feldstein, lived a few towns over from mine. We knew all about his front lawn, with good and bad jokes scattered around," said April. "One time I drove over there with my dad, and we were amazed to find Feldstein building a horseshoe enclosure around signs saying 'ha ha' and 'no ha ha.' I know: what?"

"He has to be a genius to put out so many issues of *Mad*. I would have trouble being funny for two pages," said Viv.

"But you could be an illustrator for him, Viv," said April. "You are much more talented than many cartoonists and have way better taste." She paused. "So you think I should shack up with Richie for a while, huh?"

"He's worth far more than anything out there. If it doesn't work, you have a long life ahead of you. Why not try?"

April was more or less convinced—but still nervous. She also didn't know how to negotiate the next few weeks, one at home, then off to school.

"Okay," she said, "but only if I can come running back to you if it doesn't work. I have tonight here and my last day at Silverbirch tomorrow. My parents said it was okay if Richie drives me."

"Drink up," said Viv. They finished the pizza and the bottle of wine. Viv brought out coffee, cognac, and apple pie. They shared dessert silently, each staring out the rear window as the skies lit up the Catskill evening. Viv didn't think her glass of wine would prevent her from driving April back to her room. Off they went. "April," said Viv, "I'm not leaving. And I will never leave you. You're stuck with me and my bagels for as long as the oven works."

Laughing, April said, "See you, Sis. I will call." Viv, then, was gone. Before going inside, April walked to the barn and peered in a side window. Lee was there, by himself, holding onto the standing mic, spinning a record and gyrating as if he were the lead show on a weekend at the Copa. She couldn't hear the music and allowed herself to imagine Elvis. April walked away. She slept soundly and without interruption until the sunlight blasted through a window whose shade she had forgotten to draw. Upon awakening for what could be her final day ever at Silverbirch, April thought she heard a soft-voiced, sweet man singing "Love Me Tender." She poked her head out the front door of her room and was certain it was not her imagination.

The last day of the session was subdued and clichéd—filled with requisite tears and good-byes, some of which were more genuine than others. Richie would appear after lunch, and the lie about her age would be history.

• • • • ● ● ● ● • • •

Except that he came early, way before lunch. Many people knew him by now, and he felt at home when at Silverbirch. He wanted to thank Jonathan Hudson, who typically was sitting sidesaddle on the wooden swing situated just outside the dining hall.

"It doesn't seem right that I won't be sitting in your classroom in a couple of weeks," he said. April stood by Richie's side.

"You are always welcome," said Jonathan, "and I will long for each of you more than you will miss me."

Chapter Seventeen

Toronto

Brief—Beyond

T HERE WERE TEN DAYS before school started, and April and Richie agreed to spend five of them together. This was the kind of runaway April read about in books. There was a rumor that her older beatnik cousin living in Greenwich Village, whom she barely knew, flew off to Paris with her much older portrait-painting boyfriend. Everyone was hush-hush about it. She asked Richie if they would be grounded forever, and he correctly answered that they were two weeks away from temporary grounding territory.

Richie suggested Niagara Falls, and April said she didn't think getting rained on with him would be fun for more than, at most, several minutes. She knew the Beatles had just played in Toronto, and she thought she might like that city. Besides, it was close to the Falls, which pleased Richie. It would take large portions of two days to drive there and back. Not worth it.

Their impulses and minds matching, the two of them, utilizing some of April's summer wages and

Richie's savings, were able to travel. Flying was the only option, and Richie, his voice sounding that much older, made the arrangements. Their parents, had they been consulted, would have had problems with the decision. Only wild kids would try such a stunt. No one, though, had the opportunity to speak out against the trip. This excursion would happen.

The plane reservations booked, Richie excitedly planned the getaway. He snagged a room in The Omni King Edward Hotel. He wanted old, and this one was built early in the 1900s. He told April that Yorkville was supposedly way beyond convention-al. Why not stay in a traditional place and hang out elsewhere? Best of everything, he reasoned.

They took off for the Canadian city late on a Friday, found their way to the hotel, and slept in the next day. April was up first. After sitting in bed for quite some time watching and listening to Richie, she jostled the sheets and then the bed. Richie awakened as if he were up all morning with an immediate transition from out cold to full tilt in twenty seconds.

"We have to go to The Mynah Bird," Richie told April. "It's all about music and art."

Her head swam, but she remembered Viv's ad-vice. She smiled, gave a thumbs-up and said, "Okay, but that is a strange name. Why that one?"

"I actually called ahead and found out about this place and others. The Penny Farthing was another I was interested in. The Mynah Bird, by a little bit, has the coolest name. Someone named Neil Young plays there with his band, and he's supposed to have a high and haunting voice. This whole area is, I think, kind of like The Village."

"Okay, sure, that's good," said April, still trying to make sense of her life: end of high school, subsequent summer at Silverbirch, Richie, more men, college . . .

They arrived at 6:00, in time for an early dinner. April liked the cozy feel of the place and in about an hour, a warm-up band was on stage to tune instruments. They began cranking thirty minutes later by running through a repertoire of melodic rock tunes, including popular Beatles and Stones songs.

April, though, began to wonder if this was the main act for the evening. Finally, a husky black man with abundant curls came to the stage with a band. As they were setting up, shaggy-haired Neil Young joined them. April knew the name Neil Young, but it was Richie who had actually listened to some of his sweet rock through more folksy music. The musicians were all playing electric instruments—a lot of guitar and piano. The leader, the front man, introduced himself as Rick James. "I played military, but now I'm on my own. Going to form my own sound. Assembled some wonderful players," he said. "Thank you very much for being here and listening. We are on late, but we will also stay late." They then launched into something James described as "Chantilly Lace." Some in the audience applauded. "I can do The Big Bopper," he continued.

April loved the song and the performance, but, as Richie clapped hard, she wondered if the words were a bit insulting. "I like the music Richie, but when I have a ponytail, am I that much sexier?"

He squeezed her waist. She had thought it was getting smaller at last, but at the moment she wasn't so sure. Another something to worry about. She had heard that college freshmen, especially girls, put on ten or fifteen pounds in a flash. Perhaps she would change something else, like her hair: cut it shorter and ditch the ponytail—not even use a headband.

James and his group played on and, as they had months earlier at the Copa, April and Richie departed early. They spent the night at the opulent old hotel and enjoyed the breakfast bar the next morning. It was Richie who said, "Let's get out. Fly home."

April brightened and said, "One more night, please. We haven't done The Falls. I want to do that with you."

Richie grinned, and April realized this was different. She knew his kid smiles, goofy mannerisms, the close-lipped embarrassed look he manufactured when he couldn't figure anything else. This current expression, though, was slightly wiser and older, not that of the naive teenager. She could almost imagine furrows in his forehead and laugh lines. Never, though, would his hair thin.

"Okay, Apie, you're on," said Richie.

The childhood friends didn't want to bother with a rental car and instead caught a bus to the Canadian side of The Falls. They were greeted with torrential sprays of water, which exceeded all expectations.

"Look at that boat, Richie," said April. "My folks used to tell me stories of sideways rain here but, wow, this is a stretch, huh?"

"Here you go, Ap, this little sign says, 'Scow stuck since 1918.' What's a scow?" asked Richie.

"I don't know. The only person who might would be Hudson. We will positively see him again," she said.

"Probably sooner than we think. Do you think we'll get married, April?" Richie asked.

She shushed him and managed to compose herself quickly as rounds of water doused them while they stood at the railing overlooking the waterfalls. April said, "It has entered my mind, but it's just too much right now. Anyway, Hudson told us about the Maid of the Mist ride. Let's do that. Let's enjoy this moment, just have fun, and forget about what happens years from now, okay?"

"Sure, April, sorry. It's just how crazy I am about you; that's why I say these things. I still do wonder what music Hudson would have in mind for this—one of those Beethoven symphonies, I bet, or something like that."

April hugged Richie for yielding ground while not really giving in. She was glad he didn't push further. She might have backed away. In a flash, they were in the boat, getting soaked, laughing, hugging, playing—just as they had since they were little kids.

Richie wanted closure, and April wished for time. Then the boat closed in upon The Falls, reminding April of Point Lookout and the evening of prom.

"Hudson with a gun?" asked April.

"It was such a huge weapon," said Richie, "dangling from his belt, almost weighing him down. He's built like a weeping willow, carrying this thing that looks like a small torpedo."

"What?" April asked.

"Wistful weeping willow, that's our teacher. His music."

"Baggy shorts, always, even when they fit," she added. "But he's so up and positive with his words."

Just then, they were deluged—as if a hidden force lowered and dumped a barrel full of water directly upon their heads for an absolute drenching.

Dripping, April shook herself free, wanting to talk on. "Hudson was a rock for me at Silverbirch. And Viv. The last few weeks, I was at her place a lot. Three categories of men. She helped me sort out my feelings about all of you."

"I thought you were the one doing this moment and not overthinking," said Richie.

"It's impossible for me not to wonder if those two, Viv and Lee, will ever be together again," April said.

"They sure don't look like a match," said Richie, wringing out the bottom of his shirt. "He has to be more than a foot taller." A direct hit splashed them again. This time, April lifted her top and shook her stomach at the Falls. "Take that," she said, laughing. "If we have a dog, let's name it Scow."

"This isn't the shy girl I dribbled basketballs with to the park almost every day, is it?"

She winked. "The water's spitting at my eyes. Hudson reminded us that water is one of the four primary elements. Just my way of communicating, big guy," she said.

"You've never called me that before," said Richie.

"Yeah. I'm not a little girl, and you are certainly not a little boy," she said, adding, "Lover."

Richie grinned, jumped, and grabbed April. He caressed the girl—the woman—and she laughed till her sides hurt. She raised a hand to signal him so that he might catch her vibe and ease off. The Falls of Niagara rained huge drops directly upon their heads and through their clothing.

"Lover?" Richie asked and led her in a cozy, enveloping slow dance. They moved together, completely in sync and with delectable recall. Their limbs entwined as they stood and dared the water to rain on them yet again. April took Richie's hand, and they lifted their arms: kids again celebrating a winning hoop.

"Well?" Richie wondered.

"Boy, it's like that old song: "I Only Have Eyes For You.""

• • • ● ● • ● • • •

Acknowledgements

Two men, each of whom is a good friend, proved formative as I have evolved as a novelist. It was Tom Hallock, a dozen years ago, who urged me to complete MENDEL AND MORRIS. Tom, whose work life often centered around publishing, spoke of my writing attributes and gently coaxed the fiction. Mike Moran, a librarian and man of books, reads my characters as I write them. He has seen early drafts of my work and, with enthusiasm and support, provides me with further incentive to continue.

Erin Binney is a masterful and versatile editor. She is precise with particulars for certain. Erin, now familiar with my work and voices I seek to find, offers commentary and notes which are more than welcome. It is my luck to have her aboard my team.

Lisa Sprague, as an excellent early reader, offered support and engaging notes which helped me develop character. Additionally, Lisa, with care and precision, proofread the manuscript.

Linda Cardillo, novelist and woman of multiple talents, has been my guide as I am now transitioning to my new imprint, Anatevka Press.

I thank skillful Christine Richardson for formatting this book.

Personal Words

My family is my reservoir. Betsy, my wife, has been by my side as I've grown as a fiction writer. I am fortunate to have sons, daughters-in-law and grandchildren who are precious and who keep me from taking myself too seriously. The New Jersey contingent includes Scott Sokol, Ashley Sobel and their daughters, Allison and Summer. Situated north of Boston are Jason Sokol, Nina Morrison and their son, Arlo. We all have one another.

Finally

As a community college and college theater leader, I spent days, months and years coaching students who were the same age (18) or slightly older than April of SILVERBIRCH SUMMER. Thank you.

About the Author

Fred Sokol currently writes novels and, less frequently, plays. He was Director of Theater Arts at American International College and Bay Path University. Fred was also for three decades, the theater department at Asnuntuck Community College. In all, he has directed and produced 45 shows. He is Professor Emeritus at Asnuntuck Community College. He has taught theater, film, literature....

Additionally, he wrote theater commentary for The Springfield Republican for twenty-plus years. These days he reviews professional theater, covering Connecticut and the Berkshires, for www.tal kinbroadway.com. He enjoys teaching small acting workshops during his semi-retirement.

Sokol is co-author of the book MUSES IN AR-
CADIA: CULTURAL LIFE IN THE BERKSHIRES.
His plays include THE FOREVER BOYS and THE
LEWIS SISTERS.

As an arts journalist, he reviewed more than 2500
plays and has interviewed such artists as Idina Men-
zel, Christopher Reeve, William Styron, Joanne
Woodward, Bernadette Peters, Mandy Patinkin,
Dizzy Gillespie, Olympia Dukakis, Vanessa Red-
grave, August Wilson, Ethan Hawke, Suzanne Vega,
Savion Glover, Martha Reeves, and Susan Saran-
don.

He was the founding editor of The Connecti-
cut Quarterly, and published, in 2011, his novel
MENDEL AND MORRIS. A follow-up novel, DES-
TINY, appeared in 2020.

Follow or get in touch with Fred via his website,
fredsokol.com.